The cup slipped from her hands when the shape of his eyes changed. Gage sat there looking at her with the most gorgeous cat eyes she'd ever seen. She had never felt her heart beat so fast. As her thoughts registered, she jumped up from the chair and backed away until her back hit the door. Turning, she opened it and ran inside the house.

She couldn't focus on any one thought as she stumbled toward the stairs. She made it up three steps before a strong arm wrapped around her waist and lifted her, only to set her at the bottom step again. Struggling against Gage's grip, she tried to take his arm off her.

"Kelsey, honey, it's okay." His tone was a whisper. He held her tight against his chest, so tight she could feel the vibrations as his spoke. "I'm sorry I had to do it that way. I didn't know…"

She stopped fighting his hold. "Let me go." Taking a shaky breath, she relaxed as much as she could. "Now, Gage." He slowly released her.

Turning around, she looked up at his face, relieved to see Gage's normal blue eyes looking down at her.

"I'm sorry, honey."

Kelsey swallowed the lump in her throat. "Your eyes…"

He nodded. "Yes."

"So," she sidestepped feeling trapped where she was standing, "So, what are you?" Glancing over her shoulder, she was thankful her hadn't followed her across the room.

"A shifter. I take the form of a cat. A tiger."

She nodded not even knowing why she was. "Tiger."

"Yes."

"And … and you're saying there are more like you?" She froze. "Your parents? Gage, do they know?"

His eyes widened slightly. "I hope so, I got it from them."

ANIMAL SENSES
1 *Heart*
2 *Scent*
3 *Passion*

MAGIC SEASONS ROMANCE
1 *Beltane Magic*
2 *Solstice Heat*
3 *Harvest Dreams*
4 *Autumn Dance*
5 *Winter Mist*

Dreams
Three steamy stories that started with a dream

Curses
Two tales of curses.

After the Silence
Volume 1 Bree

SINGLE TITLES
Solitary Witchling
Salvation
Café Serenity

Writing As: J. Risk

THE ALTEREALM SERIES
1 *The Huntress*
2 *The Seer*
3 *The Empath*
4 *The Witch*
5 *The Chronos*
6 *The Warrior*
7 *The Telepath*
8 *The Healer*
9 *The Kinetic* (coming soon)

SCENT

Animal Senses Book 2

Jacqueline Paige

Published by FRP
Copyright © 2019 Roxane Kerr
Edited by Gaele L. Hince
Cover art by: Off the Wall Creations

Previously published in 2014
Updated 2020

Excerpts from *Passion* Animal Senses Book 3 by Jacqueline Paige and The Huntress Book 1 in the Alterealm Series by J. Risk copyright ©2015, 2019 by Roxane Kerr

ISBN (paperback): 978-1-7774387-1-5
ISBN (digital): 978-1-7774387-0-8

Author's note:

When *Heart* was first published I had a trilogy in mind. After writing the second book, I knew there were too many wonderful, intriguing characters to stop at three stories.

The trilogy has been reworked to become the *Animal Senses Series*.

Find a comfortable corner and hang on... this is going to be quite the ride. I hope you enjoy reading it as much as I do writing it!

Jacqueline

Chapter One

Gage watched the eyes of the man he passed to climb into his truck. His expression was hollow, his eyes were void. He had to be close to his own six foot five, but this man held himself close, small and inward.

Turning, he glanced at Jesse. "What the hell happened Jesse? He looks like he's been broken like a god damned horse."

Jesse sighed and rubbed his jaw, the exhaustion clear on his face. "The sad thing is, he's in better shape than the others." Flicking his eyes back to the passenger in the truck, he met Gage's stare. "Devin said it would do him good to be around other shifters of his kind," he shook his head, "I don't know if he'll ever fully recover though."

"What about the others?"

A haunted look flashed in Jesse's pale eyes. "They're at the camp. I doubt any of them will ever be able to integrate back into society."

"What the hell did Tomas do to them?" Gage struggled to keep his anger from showing.

Slamming the door on the car, Jesse spun around shaking his head. "The two women we managed to get out were used as breeders, as near as we can figure. They shrink away from any male like they've..." He stopped, clearly not wanting to continue.

Gage fought the bile that rose in his stomach, swallowing it down with an audible sound.

"The three men, including him," he motioned to the other vehicle, "were used worse than slaves. They're not very forthcoming with details." Shoving his hands in his pockets, he looked up and Gage's muscles tensed when he saw the depth of the anger in the otherwise mild-mannered man. "They've been beaten into complacency and carry the scars to prove it."

"Aren't they all pure bloods?"

"Yeah."

Something in Jesse's tone made Gage's cat want to growl. "Then why are they scarred? Shifting heals fresh..."

"Not if they're prevented from shifting until after the wounds have healed."

"Holy hell." Shuddering at the thought of the torture the man now hunched in his truck had survived, Gage took a deep breath and nodded to Jesse. "I'll see what I can do for him."

Jesse stepped back toward his car. "Devin said to give him a call."

"Will do." Gage watched him get in his car and then slowly walked around to the driver's side of his truck. He had hundreds of questions but didn't want to bombard the damaged man with them.

Forcing an easy smile, he looked at the man beside him. "I suppose Jesse should have introduced us." He held out his hand, "I'm Gage Lockman. You'll be staying with some of my clan."

With hesitation, the man extended his hand and grasped his briefly. "Noah Reyes."

"They're getting in touch with your family, Noah. If later on you decide to go be with them, then we'll get you there." He watched as emotions flickered through Noah's amber tinted eyes.

"No," his voice was heartrending, "I-I don't want to go there." Apprehensively his eyes met Gage's again. "I'll stay with your clan, if that's all right?"

Nodding, Gage put the key in the ignition and tried to appear relaxed, even though he wasn't. "That's fine by me, we can always use a hand at the shop."

"Shop?"

Starting the truck, he put it into gear and pulled out of the empty parking lot. Watching the dust kick up behind them in his mirror, he kept his eyes from going back to the injured soul beside him. "Yeah, my family owns a heavy equipment business. We lease all the big rigs and do the repairs and upkeep ourselves."

"I don't know anything about shop work."

Ignoring the fear in his voice, Gage shrugged. "We'll find something for you to do that leans to your strengths."

"I doubt it."

Glancing at the empty man beside him, he gave him an easy smile. "Why's that?"

Noah turned and looked out the window. "I've only been a guard."

"Like a bodyguard?"

The silence was tense as he waited for an answer.

"No. Like a guard that keeps others against their will."

Shit. "Well, we'll find a place for you." Every muscle in Gage's body was taut, he had to strain to keep his animal under control. He breathed it away for a few seconds. "I don't want to pry, and for the most part I won't, but I'm bringing you into my family and need to know some of the facts." He paused for objections then continued when none were voiced. "How long did Tomas have you?"

"Fifteen years."

It was said with venom that Gage was almost happy to hear, that brief expression of hatred meant there was some fight left in the younger man. He was going to ask more when Noah's tortured voice silenced him.

"Since I was six. They got my sister and I."

3

He glanced at Noah for a moment to let him know he was listening.

"I don't know what happened to her. I tried to find out when I got older, but..." His voice cracked, "I wouldn't even know her now."

Swallowing, Gage kept his eyes on the road. "Your cat would know family. If she ever crosses your path, you'll know."

"I didn't know that." Noah sighed softly. "I don't know a lot about what I am, or how to function in a group. The things I do know are only from what others that worked..." he cleared his throat, "were held by Tomas told me."

Gage glanced at him and tried to give him a look of encouragement. "We'll work it out, Noah." He took a moment to look at him. Biologically this man was only twenty-one, but he appeared much older, and Gage suspected was aged beyond anything he would ever understand.

"So, are you the clan alpha?"

Gage grinned. "No. The second. My father's the alpha, but he's away right now."

Noah nodded and then sat there for a moment, Gage could see the questions going through his mind.

"Do you have a mate?"

Snorting, Gage nodded, "Yeah, only she doesn't know she is." He grinned, not even knowing how to explain his own personal torment. "I'm sure the boys will love filling in the details for you."

"I found mine...at least that's what the others told me."

The silence that followed his admission stabbed pain right through Gage. "And?"

"When," Noah closed his eyes and inhaled deep for a moment, "when I recovered enough to remember, she was gone."

Holy hell. Is Devin aware of any of this? What the hell do I say to that? "You may still find her someday. Fate is a tricky bitch."

"Yeah."

The word meant he agreed, but the heavy overlay of emotion inside the cab told Gage the man beside him didn't believe it would happen. He tried to keep his tone from revealing anything that could be considered close to sympathy. "You'll be bunking in with four others while you're here. Jake, Gary and Blair are close to your age. Then there's old Cooper, no one can even guess his age, but he's fairly easy to be around." He continued to ramble out the stories of things the men closest to him did in hopes to give Noah a sense of what he could expect. Not once did he offer comment or ask for more.

Dropping him off at the large house his men lived in just off the shop site, Gage backed out, heading for his own home just along the roughly paved road. He needed to talk to Devin and find out just what he was supposed to do to help Noah.

He didn't even get both boots on the ground when his phone started vibrating in his shirt pocket. Glancing at the screen, he shook his head and answered it.

"I just dropped him off."

Devin's whispered on the other end. "I figured you'd be there by now. Jesse called when he left you."

"Why are you whispering?" Slamming the door, he walked up the path and stomped up the porch. Deciding he needed the air, he dropped into one of his mother's favorite white wicker chairs and swung his boots up to rest on the railing.

"Rayne is exhausted and just went to try and rest."

He heard a door close quietly.

"She's been helping the two women that were brought back and is emotionally fragile, to say the least."

Gage's shoulders tensed. "Jesse mentioned a bit." Running a hand through his hair, he sighed. "Don't tell me any details right now; I'm still digesting the shit I learned from Noah on our trip back."

"Then you probably know more than I do. I'm sorry I had to send him your way, but the women were terrified of him."

Gage closed his eyes, feeling the pain he'd heard in Noah's voice. "With good reason, he was probably forced to be the guard used to make them stay put."

"Listen, if he gets out of hand…"

"My instincts say he won't." He kicked his feet back to the porch and leaned forward on his knee. "The boys will keep an eye on him." Rubbing a hand over the back of his neck, he sat up again. "Where the hell is the Alliance in bringing that bastard Tomas down for good?"

"They've gotten a lot of the captives out. We have close to a dozen here at the camp, healing as much as they'll be able to. Some were born into Tomas's organization, Gage, I don't know if we'll be able to get through to them, they've never been associated with their own kind, or understand the dynamics of a clan and family."

"Yeah, Noah said something to that effect."

He could hear the exhaustion in Devin's tone.

"Look, Gage, I really didn't want to send Noah there, not with everything you have going on." He heard another door close and could then make out the sounds of nature at the camp as Devin must have gone outside. "Is Kelsey back?"

Not able to sit any longer, Gage got up and paced to the other end of the large porch. "She was supposed to be back this week, but decided to stop and see my folks on the way home."

"I thought your parents left so you'd have some alone time with Kelsey."

"They did. I'm one hair from going insane, Dev."

He heard the soft chuckle on the other end. "I don't know how you've held out this long, my friend. I didn't last a day when I was near Rayne."

Jamming his hand into his pocket, he leaned back against the wall of the house. "Well, she was only sixteen when I realized what she was to me. That worked like fucking ice water in my pants for a few years. Then she bailed and took off to school, and you know that's been three years of hell for me." Pushing away from the wall, he stepped over to the railing and looked out into the thick trees surrounding the house. "I can't hold on much longer." He closed his eyes and swallowed. "I just hope..."

"You'll do the right thing, Gage, the animal inside you won't let you do anything but."

"I hope you're right because it will kill me to wait this long and then screw it up."

Devin chuckled again. "I can relate."

"Speaking of...how is our Queen now?"

"Surprisingly forgiving. Thank God for that."

Not wanting to dwell on his mate, Gage opened his eyes and stared out into the bush again. "Calum reach you before he left?"

"Yeah. He said he knew the region where his missing clan members had been seen last. He's supposed to contact you if I'm out of touch once he knows more."

"I'll be here if he needs me. Is the Alliance up to speed?" Turning, he went inside to see if there were any messages on the house phone.

"For the most part, they have their hands full right now trying to bring Aiden Tomas down."

"They don't think the clan members Calum is tracking down are part of Tomas's ring?"

The silence stretched out for a few moments before Devin answered. "It's nowhere near the regions he operates in, but who knows?"

Gage could hear voices in the background and knew Devin would be ending the call soon.

"Listen, Gage, keep Kelsey close to home. We've been calling all the clans and warning them. Tomas isn't going to take all of this without striking back."

"Will do."

"Good luck with your mate, my friend, you're going to need it."

Gage sighed loudly and grinned at the phone. "Yeah, thanks for the vote of confidence."

"Oh, I have every faith in you, but I also know the fucking hell you're walking into when nothing you know is as it was."

Gage's stomach tightened. "Something to look forward to."

"I'll talk to you later."

"Will do." He hung up the phone and stared at it for a moment. *Good news all round today.* Glancing at the phone as he walked into the office, he stopped when there were no messages. The tension in his neck was multiplying as it had been for the past month. *Kelsey, whatever games you're playing, you better end them soon.* He felt like a time bomb just waiting to go off.

The cat inside him moved over his skin, wanting out. He'd spent more time in animal form the last seven years as he waited for his mate to be old enough to claim. Of course, there was no law stating the age, but his own morals wouldn't allow him to do anything until she was old enough to understand.

Snorting out loud, he turned on his heal and headed for the door. Kelsey knew nothing of her own heritage. She didn't know what her parents had been before they were killed, or that her family were part of the clan and not just good friends they'd known for years. Many times, after she had come to live with his parents he'd wanted to tell her. She was only fifteen at the time and completely devastated her parents were gone. His jaw clenched knowing it had been Aiden Tomas's father that was responsible for their death. After that, the more time that passed the harder it got to tell her she was part of a world she didn't even know existed.

Gage didn't know why his folks hadn't told her when she got older, and as the son of the Alpha, it wasn't his place to overstep his position and fill her in. In hindsight, he wished he'd disobeyed and told her. Maybe then he wouldn't be walking out his back door stripping off his clothes so he could go run off his frustration.

By the time he reached the bottom step he was in his animal form. Large paws padded across the grass, as he scented the air to choose a direction. Jumping across the creek in one motion, he landed his eight foot, four-hundred-pound body with fluid grace and then turned to look at his reflection. A pale, almost white, Bengal tiger stared at him through his deep blue eyes.

The scent of prey filled his nostrils as he lifted his head. With a low sound from the back of his throat he turned to start the chase.

Come home soon, Kelsey.

Chapter Two

Pulling out onto the highway, Kelsey gripped the steering wheel tight. She'd procrastinated three days longer than planned, avoiding heading home and going to face Gage.

In the three years since she'd gone away to school, she'd only seen him twice and both meetings had been brief, polite, and cordial.

Now she was going back for good. School was finished and instead of going in the other direction to begin her life she was driving to the place that called to her. No matter the arguments she had with herself, she just *had* to go back there. She really didn't know why. It wasn't as if the location was appealing, unless you liked rocks, lakes, and trees which she did, up to a point, but it wasn't the draw. At least she didn't think it was. Another thing that drove her crazy was with everything else she was determined, had tunnel vision and didn't give in, everything except home, where she felt conflicted and confused all the time.

Turning the radio on, she tried to end the silence that made her twitchy. Surely things had changed between her and Gage. They weren't awkward kids anymore. They were both adults and the cause of the discontent would be long gone by now.

Things hadn't always been odd with them. She remembered visiting his family a few times as a young girl with her parents. He'd just been a boy that she mostly ignored at that point.

When her parents were killed, she'd only been fifteen and went to live with Ed and Beth Lockman, Gage's parents. They'd been warm and loving. Without them she never would have made it through that horrific time.

Gage was six years older and had been like a big brother. She knew he resented the gangly girl trailing around after him, but never once did he make her feel uncomfortable. He'd take her to the shop and show her things, even let her help. Without him she may have gotten lost in her own grief.

Something changed after she turned sixteen and in hindsight, she only had herself to blame. Instead of a brother she began to see him differently, began to feel things toward him that weren't sisterly in any way. It was her own fault he'd made himself scarce, and she couldn't blame him for avoiding a giggly teenage girl that threw herself into his path at every opportunity.

It broke her heart each time she saw him with other girls, ones that were his own age. The string was endless, as if he set out to date as many as he possibly could. Unable to watch him a moment longer, she packed up the day after she graduated high school and went to a college that was the furthest away she could find, without leaving the province.

With each kilometer she drove, her stomach knotted tighter and tighter. She'd be lucky if she wasn't crippled when she finally got there. Stopping and seeing Ed and Beth on her way back was something she had to do. She had kept in constant touch with them, but they never let the weekly phone calls reveal a word about Gage or what was going on in his life. For all she knew he was lost in love with someone and living his happily-ever-after.

Sighing, she flicked off the radio that was nothing more than an annoying buzz in the background. *So, what if he's with someone else. These feelings you're having are leftovers from silly teenage fantasies, you probably won't feel a damn thing when you see him.* Nodding her head, she grimaced. *I'm not a child anymore, someday I'll find a man that makes Gage Lockman fade into the background.* She sighed, close to a groan. *Keep telling yourself that Kel, maybe eventually you'll believe it.*

In the three years she'd been away, she'd dated. Nothing serious, but she was focusing on her classes, concentrating on being the best. Her roommate once told her she had the absolute worst taste in men and seemed to find all the guys that were damaged beyond salvation. After the fourth wreck of attempting yet another relationship, Kelsey swore off males and went back to being the above average student in all her classes...classes that wouldn't do her one bit of good where she was going now.

The plan when she'd fled her home had been to have a career in business consulting, something that would thrive in a major metropolis. Something that would keep her in the city and forever distracted from the beautiful, desolate area she'd grown up. For the first two years, she was sure the plan was working, the constant buzz of the city and school distracted her better then she could have imagined. It wasn't until the last year that the hustle and non-existent silence began to get to her.

Quite often she'd hole up in her room and block the noise outside her window with headphones streaming nature sounds. Her roommate thought she was completely crazy by shutting herself up for such long periods of time. She'd even tried going on short trips to remote areas to find her balance, but something was always lacking.

The longer she stayed away the worse it got. She was restless, sometimes not sleeping for days. Her grades dropped more times then she could count, and that would snap her out of it long enough to pull them back up, but it never seemed to stay that way. She debated going to talk to a counselor or some other professional but didn't know how to define what her problem was. She couldn't very well go in and tell them she felt like something was missing, and about the long periods of time feeling bereft. That would have just earned her a psych leave from school. The only thing that seemed to make her feel better during those times was being outside, so she'd worn out a lot of shoes jogging through the large parks and conservation areas.

She thought she'd managed to hide her problems and feelings from Beth, but even over the phone the woman she adored had sensed Kelsey's anxiety, and it wasn't until she convinced her she needed to go home and sort through it that the feelings began to ease up. The closer graduation got, the more her apprehension about being near Gage grew. Kelsey hadn't even stayed for the ceremony. She'd packed and told them to mail her diploma.

The last few days had been relaxing, she'd missed being around Beth while she was away. She still didn't understand why they weren't at home, something about new contract dealings, but the love she received from her guardians filled her heart with warmth. Ed had seemed more distant than he used to be, which Kelsey wrote off to him focusing on the new contracts and deals.

Beth had taken her to a day spa where they'd spent the entire day being pampered and it had been so wonderful, Kelsey decided it was something she'd have to be sure to do from time to time. She had a new haircut, which was so much lighter than her long heavy hair, and it gave her a new confidence. Hopefully it gave her enough to handle being back home.

What was she going to feel when she saw Gage? She could only hope it was nothing alarming. The amount of time that had passed should have been enough to erase those notions she used to have. The ones that made her body hum whenever he was near. Maybe, she'd told herself over the last few years, it was just his looks that appealed to her so much. She didn't have any comparisons to go by though, because she'd never met another male that seemed to have the particular gorgeous gene that Gage did.

She wasn't short at five foot seven, but he still dwarfed her by almost a foot. Of course, he had the build to go with his height; broad shoulders that tapered to a slim waist and powerful legs. The first time she'd seen him without a shirt on, she'd almost swallowed her tongue. He had an eight pack, not six, not just toned but an *eight pack* of abdominal muscles. If she was lucky he will have gotten pudgy with age. How old was he now? Close to thirty, so it was possible.

Gage's eyes were the feature she liked the most, even more than his build. His eyes were such a deep blue, she had thought he had to wear contacts to have eyes that blue. He had a way of looking at you that saw into your soul and held you captive at the same time.

She almost hoped his hair would have some grey by now. She'd always envied him his hair color. It wasn't red or a strawberry blond, but somewhere between brown and rust and all the shades in between. He had so many natural highlights and waves, if he was a woman it would be heavenly. Compared to her strawberry blonde straight as a needle hair, anyone's was nicer.

Glancing at the clock, she realized she was only a half hour away as her stomach tightened again. Would he be at the house or the shop? Maybe he wouldn't be at either, that would give her time to settle in before she had to face him.

Chapter Three

Securing the safety chains, Gage flipped the power switch for the overhead pulley. Working around equipment that weighed fifty tons or more was second nature to him. Most men would be wary standing beside a machine with tires as tall as these, but to him it was no different than leaning against a regular pickup.

Satisfied that the winch hanging from the ceiling was supporting the weight of the bin, he hit another switch to lock it in that position.

"Need a hand, Boss?"

Glancing over his shoulder at Jake as he sauntered across the floor, he shook his head. "No, I got it."

"Hydraulics go?"

Shaking his head, Gage walked over to the wall of tools, he grabbed one of the rolling carts filled with tools. "No, the cylinder won't retract." He motioned to the side of the truck. "Looks like it got dinged by the loader's bucket, probably just a bent cylinder bracket."

Jake nodded and stopped. "Give me a shout if you need a hand. I'm in limbo waiting on parts that are three hours late."

"See if Gary needs a hand with that wheel dozer. They need it back on the site by tomorrow night."

"No problem." Turning on his heel he walked out of the bay whistling softly under his breath.

Gage stopped and watched him leave. Sighing, he dropped his chin and stared at the floor. The last few weeks he'd preferred to work alone. Grinding his teeth, he inhaled deeply and tried to let some of his tension ease. Kelsey's delay in coming home was really starting to put him in a place he wasn't comfortable with. Shaking his head, he laughed softly and picked up the pry bar. Who was he kidding? He'd been in an uncomfortable place for seven years.

He hadn't slept at all last night. Just as he'd been about to drift off, a stupid thought had crossed his mind. What if Kelsey had found a boyfriend while she was away? More than once he'd struggled with this, almost going to find out a few times, but he knew that he would have ended up marking her as his. The very idea of another male touching her filled him with thoughts of violence. An emotion his cat clung to tighter each day.

Exhaling loudly, he looked down at the bar he was white-knuckling in his hand. Clenching his teeth, he moved back over to the truck and studied the bracket on the cylinder. He just had to keep busy, she'd be home soon.

Then what? Well, he had his own delusions about that too, and could only hope some sort of miracle happened and she walked in wanting him just half as much as he wanted her. With a snarl, he brushed the thoughts aside and began prying on the arm of the bracket.

Widening his stance, he put a little more muscle into it; he only had to get it freed up enough that he could get the bracket off. The damn thing wouldn't budge one way or the other. With a curse under his breath, he reached deep inside and tapped into some of his animal vigor, if that didn't do it he'd have to get the torch to get it off.

Yanking hard, he felt it move a hair. With a low growl, he reefed on it once more and it let loose, smashing his knuckles into the sharp metal on the edge of the frame. Cursing, he heaved the tool across the floor and looked down at the flesh ripped off the back of his hand. Blood ran across his knuckles and dripped onto his boot.

"That's not quite the welcome I expected."

Spinning, Gage looked over to see Kelsey standing there with her hands on her hips, brows furrowed and the pry bar he'd tossed just a few feet from her boots. Shit, he'd almost hit her with it.

The expression on her face changed when she spotted his bloodied hand. Grabbing a handful of paper towels from the dispenser on the wall, she started walking toward him. He could only stand there, unable to move. "I didn't know you were there." How hadn't he sensed she was there? "Sorry." God, she was lovely. A chill moved up his spine when she was only a foot from him and he caught her scent. It was Kelsey's unique scent, only more potent than it had ever been before. There would be no holding his animal in check now.

She stopped in front of him and placed the paper towel over his bloody hand. "Let's rinse this off and see how bad it is." Taking his wrist, she tugged on it and walked in the direction of the sink.

He followed her like a cub on a leash. If he'd been in his right state of mind, he would have objected, but all he could do was breathe her in and let her scent soak into every pore of his body. Later he'd admit he was in deep shit here, but for now he just wanted to take pleasure in knowing she was finally here. She was home.

She grabbed his hand and put it under the water, only to pull it out a few seconds later and start dabbing at it with a dry cloth. He knew it hurt like a bitch, but the pain wasn't really registering in his brain. He couldn't take his eyes off her, she was breathtaking. Gone was that pretty girl that had gone away. She was now a beautiful woman. Her light auburn locks were much shorter than the last time he'd seen her, now falling to frame her pale freckle-dusted face. He wanted to reach out and touch her hair to see if was as soft as he thought it would be.

"You're staring," she said softly still bent over his hand.

"I haven't seen you in over a year. You've changed."

She smirked as she examined the gash. "Not really."

"You're beautiful, Kel," he admitted in a whisper.

Color flooded to her cheeks as she glanced up at him. "Are you all right?"

He blinked to break the hold her enthralling amber eyes had on him. "I'm fine."

She raised both eyebrows at him. "You just paid me a compliment and didn't growl it out."

Gage knew she thought he'd been indifferent to her for years, but he hadn't thought he'd behaved *that* badly. "I've always thought you were beautiful, Kel, just didn't voice it for fear you'd smack me over the head with a wrench."

Her hand froze holding the cloth on his; slowly she lifted her head, her eyes searching his face. A confused expression filled them. "Who are you and *what* have you done with Gage?"

He smirked, even though it wasn't the emotion he was feeling deep inside. He'd been an ass to her on purpose, to keep her from getting too close to him and apparently, he'd done a good job of it. This wasn't going to be as simple as letting nature take its course. He was going to have to convince her of his sincerity first. Why did he fear that was going to be harder than the rest? "I killed him and took over his body."

She smiled and shook her head. Lowering her head again she checked his hand. "It's not bad. You heal quickly, so I'll just clean it up a bit."

All he'd have to do is shift and it would be healed when he took his two-legged form again, but he couldn't tell her that. "How are the folks?"

She was quiet for a minute while she held his hand over the sink again and poured some peroxide over it. "Good. Your dad seems really distracted with the new contracts though." Glancing up at him, she gave him a concerned look. "Business is good, right?"

He nodded and tried to keep his expression easy. He knew the reason his father was keeping his distance. Kelsey was close to her body announcing what she really was and it played havoc with any male cat in range. The fact that his cat was clawing inside him only confirmed what he thought. "Business is great. We're having a hard time keeping up most of the time."

"Summer is peak time."

She had always been aware of everything going on at the shop, even when she was in school and wasn't able to be here other than weekends. "Keeps us out of trouble."

Grinning, she gently placed a large strip of tape over the gauze on his hand. "I'm sure you guys still find time for trouble."

She finished covering the cut but continued to hold his hand.

Before he could reply, Jake came wandering back in. "I thought I heard a sweet voice." He smirked at Gage. "Either that, or boss man was getting in touch with his feminine side."

Kelsey laughed and released Gage's hand. "I mention trouble and you walk in."

Jake came over quickly and pulled Kelsey into an easy hug. When his eyes connected with Gage's he knew the other man sensed her change being close. Subtly stepping away from her, Jake looked down at Gage's hand. "Truck try to take a bite?"

Gage studied his eyes for a second more, his pupils were huge, and for the easy-going Jake that was rare. "Just a little bite." He glanced back to Kelsey. "Did you get your stuff in the house?"

She shrugged, "I'll bring the rest in later." Her smile was directed at Jake. "I had to come and see if you guys were staying out of trouble first."

Jake jammed his hands in his pockets. Gage could see how tense the muscles in his arms and neck were. "Speaking of trouble, I better go make a few calls and see where the hell my parts are before they're all over my ass when their digger is not finished on time." He sent her a brief look. "It's great to have you home, Kels."

"Did he get bigger or am I getting shorter?" She asked, as she watched Jake walk out.

Gage wanted to growl knowing that she'd even looked at the other man. "He may have filled out a bit more. You were gone quite a while."

"Yeah." Tucking her hands into her back pockets, she looked around the shop. "You guys expanded this bay too. Its great things are going so well."

It took all he had to lean back against the sink and try to look unaffected by her being there. "Are you staying?"

"At the shop?" She gave him an odd look.

Shaking his head, he crossed his arms over his chest. "No, home." He watched her inhale deeply, trying not to react when it pushed her breasts up under the t-shirt that she more than filled out.

"Yeah, I think I am. I need some time to find a direction."

"I thought you found it with all those classes you took." *That kept you out of my reach for years.*

Moving over to the wall of tools, she walked along, hands still in her back pockets and looked over them slowly. "I thought I had too, but now it just feels…" she shrugged, "lacking."

Torn between wanting to reach out to her after hearing that desolate tone in her voice and doing a dance on the spot, just knowing she was starting to feel what he'd been going through for seven long years. There would be no waiting this time. Before she knew it, her body was going to make all the decisions for her. Her cat would know what he was to her, even if she tried to flee again. "Maybe you can put some of it to use here. Mom's behind in the office and Dad is so busy with contracts lately and all the politics that go with it, that he doesn't have time for the business end much."

"I'll see what I can do to help."

She wandered over to the truck he'd been working on and then turned to look back at him. So many emotions were going through her eyes, he cringed inside. At least he knew why he was a complete mess, she didn't have a clue.

"Gage?"

The hesitant way she said his name made his heart stutter. Not trusting his voice, he just held her eyes with his, safely keeping the ten feet between them.

"Can I ask you something?" She crossed her arms over her chest in a protective manner and he nodded.

"I know here is where my family is, I get that, always have, but…"

"And Kitty-Kat has finally come home." Cooper walked into the bay, striding quickly in her direction.

Kelsey smiled wide and rushed in his direction.

Gage stood there fighting every instinct he had when the older man enclosed her in a tight hug.

"Hey, Coop." She said, genuine emotion in her voice.

The older man leaned back while holding her shoulders and looked her up and down. Gage shouldn't feel envious for their close relationship. It had been Cooper that had brought her to them after her parents died. He'd left the alliance then too, and made here his home as well as hers. Gage often wondered if Cooper felt responsible for her parents dying, responsible for her.

"You're home for good, right? It sure as hell has been a dreary place without your sunshine around here."

She laughed. "I'm home for now, at least. I have no definite plans."

Cooper's eyes met Gage's over her head. It didn't take a genius to figure out the man was telling him to get it done and keep Kelsey where she belonged. For the most part he'd always gotten along with the man, except when Gage had let her go off to school without telling her the truth. Even thought it hadn't been up to Gage, he still took the brunt of everyone being pissed about it.

"Are you going to show me around?"

Gage realized she'd still been talking when he got lost in the past. Cooper was nodding, a smile on his old scarred face.

"Absolutely. We have some new toys you're going to want to check out as well."

Kelsey paused and looked over at Gage, the hesitant look flashing in her eyes for a split second. "I'll talk to you later, okay?"

Nodding, he continued to lean where he was. "Sure thing."

Cooper led her toward the outer door, sending Gage a brief scowl.

Blowing out a breath, Gage turned around and grasped the edge of the sink. Dropping his head down to his chest, he stood there trying to let go of the tension that was riding him hard. Why had he thought it was going to be easier now that she was older? Clearly, he didn't have a handle on rational thought right now.

Out of the corner of his eye he saw Jake and Noah come in.

"Cooper wrangle Kelsey out of breathing distance for a few minutes?"

Gage inhaled deep and let it out slowly. "Yeah."

Jake came over to lean against the counter beside him. "How the hell are you still standing there?"

Pushing away from the sink, Gage turned and crossed his arms over his chest and stared at the concrete floor. "I've had practice controlling my baser instincts."

"Practice or not, I don't know how you're going to survive it." Jake whistled a low drawn out sound. "I almost lost it and I was only with her for a few minutes." He gave Gage a wide-eyed look. "You have to live in the same house with her."

Gage blew out a loud breath. "I know."

"You lost me," Noah said quietly. "She'll know soon that she's your mate, so what's the problem?"

Jake snorted out a loud noise. "She doesn't *know*."

Gage looked up to see the confusion on Noah's face. "She doesn't know *what* she is." He glanced at the door Cooper had taken her through, making sure they weren't heading back this way. Noah shook his head. "She doesn't know her own heritage."

Noah's mouth dropped open. Staring at Gage then turning to Jake, he finally closed it and swallowed. "Oh." Standing to his full height, he eyed both of them again. "I can help keep things under control."

"How?" Jake leaned back against the counter and crossed his arms over his chest. "You know a secret way to prevent mating?"

Gage eyed him, noting he rarely stood at his full height. A cold look filled Noah's eyes as he looked back toward the door.

"No, but I can ignore the draw of being around females during their cycle."

There was a pain in his voice that made the hair on the back of Gage's neck stand out. He didn't have to ask how he managed to ignore being around females ready for mating, he knew it would have involved beating and pain.

Jake made a strangled noise in the back of this throat. "Man, you should sell that gift. I know a lot of clans that would make you rich to teach them that."

Noah's jaw tightened. "I doubt anyone wants to learn the way I did," he said in a low tone with his teeth clenched together.

"Oh, shit." Jake straightened up, "I'm sorry, Noah." He gave him an exasperated look. "Sometimes my fuckin' mouth spews before my brain catches up."

"No harm done," Noah said quietly.

Gage took another deep breath. "I appreciate you putting yourself out there, Noah, I really do…" He rubbed the back of his neck taking a minute to think it through. "I don't know how I'll deal with you being near her."

Noah nodded. "I'll just step in if needed."

23

"We'll all run interference," Jake grimaced, "if we can stand to be in scenting distance."

"Fuck," Gage said under his breath. "You can't avoid her completely, she'll know something's up."

"Then tell her."

They turned to see Blair standing in the open side door. His almost white hair was as always standing straight on end like he'd run his hands through it every few seconds. He always looked out of control until he moved. With a long, easy gait, he came toward them.

"She's family to all of us, Gage, and we've been playing this cat and mouse game far too long. You wanted to wait until she's old enough. Respect that she is and tell her the truth." He stopped and stood beside Noah.

Gage looked from one to the other. "I don't have a choice."

Jake reached out and grabbed his shoulder in a tight grip. "Are you going to be all right with her at the house?" His eyes were deadly serious. All of them respected him, but they loved Kelsey and would protect her, even from him.

Looking around at the concerned expressions on the three men's faces, he exhaled and ran a hand down the back of his neck again. "Honestly? I'll have to get back to you on that." He shrugged. "I'd like to say it was just bad today because it's been a while..." Hearing voices, he turned back to the open bay door.

Cooper and Gary were walking in, with Kelsey between them chatting a hundred words a minute. The glare Gary shot him from those twenty feet away was clear enough for Gage to see with his enhanced vision. He had no choice; he had to tell her tonight.

"Tour over?" he looked at Kelsey to see her grinning.

"Yes, I'm returning them so they can get back to work." She paused when she saw Blair grinning at her. With a squeal, she was across the floor and practically throwing herself into his arms.

Gage's teeth clacked shut tightly. He felt a hand at his back and knew Jake was bracing to stop him if he did something extra-special stupid, like toss Blair across the garage for being close to her. Then he noticed the expression on Blair's face as he held her. He looked like he was in pain, but it wasn't the same thing as when Jake had hugged her.

Swallowing down the envy of seeing her in his friend's arms, he had no one to blame but himself. All the years he pushed Kelsey away it was Blair that stepped in the most to stop him from doing something he'd regret.

"When you're done mauling our playboy, I'd like to introduce you to the newest member of our team." Cooper said while sending Gage a warning look.

"Oh." Kelsey released Blair and turned around. She paused and looked Noah up and down. "I was hoping you'd be normal sized."

Jake snorted. "This is normal around here, Kels."

She gave a dramatic sigh and pouted. "I can always hope."

Gary winked at her. "You can probably still out maneuver the rest of us in the rigs, so as far as I'm concerned, size doesn't mean a damn thing."

Kelsey laughed. "If you advertised that view men would hate you and you'd have a line of women three miles long."

"One can hope," Gary drawled softly.

Straightening, Kelsey stepped over and stopped in front of Noah. She smiled sweetly at him and held out her hand. "Kelsey Jennings."

Noah's spine stiffened as he looked down at her hand. Gage was sure he was picking up on the scent that he'd just assured them he was immune to. It wasn't until he saw the surprise in the other man's eyes he realized it was because she was willing to touch him.

"Noah Reyes." He grasped her hand briefly and then his shoulders relaxed a bit. "Do I want to know what this is about, you being better in the rigs?"

Kelsey's smile was beaming, she shrugged. "Most girls played with dolls and their hair, I played with big rigs."

Noah smiled. Gage's eyebrows rose as he glanced at Jake, no one had seen him smile since he'd come here.

"Good, maybe you can teach me."

Eyes widening, Kelsey looked at Gage. "I, uh, sure." She looked around at all of them and then her eyes settled back to Gage. "I guess I'll go get settled in and let you guys get back to work." The glow in her eyes faded. "I'll see you at the house."

Nodding, Gage jammed his hands into his pockets to keep from reaching out to her. Every other male here had held or touched her, except him. "Yeah, I'll be done here by five."

With a smile to all of them, she nodded and then turned and headed toward the door. Not one of them moved until she was out the door, then they all turned to look at him. Taking in the hard looks on all their faces, he exhaled loudly. "I know. I'll try to tell her tonight."

"*Hell* of a homecoming," Gary muttered as he spun on his heel and walked toward the truck.

Gage stood there as they all turned to head in different directions. Every nerve in his body was strung so tightly, he was sure he should be paralyzed. Shaking his head, he closed his eyes and took a deep breath. It was going to be a long night.

Chapter Four

Putting the empty suitcase beside the door, Kelsey turned around and surveyed her efforts. It looked like her room again. When she'd walked in and seen it so barren, it had struck her harder than she thought. Beth had said she was thinking of redoing it, but Kelsey didn't think that meant all her stuff would be boxed up. Having gone through the boxes and pulling out a few things made her feel better.

Happy, she turned and headed down the stairs. It was almost five and her stomach was reminding her that she hadn't eaten anything but a bag of chips when she was driving. Biting her lip, she wondered if Gage would be home for dinner. She hadn't thought to ask if he had plans or not.

Opening the fridge while she bit down on the unexpected jealousy that flooded her at the thought of Gage going out on her first night home, she sighed and shut the door, leaning back against it. The feelings she had convinced herself were leftovers from a teen crush were not gone. If anything, they were worse.

Closing her eyes, she groaned. When she'd walked into the shop and stood just watching him, lightening had flashed through her veins. He'd been totally focused on what he was doing and hadn't known she was there. Just seeing him had been a shock to her system, but when he'd gone all he-man on the truck he'd been working on, she thought she was going to swoon. She rolled her eyes toward the ceiling. Who the hell uses a word like *swoon* nowadays?

Shaking her head, she moved to look in the freezer. The lack of food was making her angst worse. If she were a smart woman, she'd get back in her car and leave while she could. She'd been so close to asking if he thought of her as a sister. At least she'd know if there were obstacles. Gage thinking of her as a little sister would put a kibosh on her pursuing these feelings any further. Did she really want to pursue them? Not entirely. The emotions that swamped her from just seeing him scared the hell out of her. It was unnatural to be *that* drawn to a man.

Finding several containers stacked in the freezer, she dug through and found one that was her favorite stew Beth had made. It wouldn't take her long to whip up biscuits to go with it. It might not be a gourmet meal, but it would work well enough to fill the void in her stomach. This way, if she was eating alone, it wouldn't be a waste and she could just put the leftovers in the fridge for lunch. She couldn't believe her fear of seeing Gage made her forget about eating.

Moving around the kitchen as she gathered what she needed, she felt better than she had in a long time. It was familiar and comforting. That was another thing she noticed when she moved away, no matter where she was it had never felt like home.

Without warning, heat flashed through her and all the hair on her arms tingled. She heard the porch door close softly. Turning, she watched Gage walk into the kitchen. He stopped in the door and stood there looking at her. She felt her cheeks flush and couldn't remember ever having this feeling.

"I was making biscuits to go with the stew I found in the freezer."

He gave her an easy smile. "Sounds good." Moving further into the room, she couldn't help feeling like he was an animal stalking her, the controlled power in his stillness. "I'll go get cleaned up."

She nodded, probably a little too enthusiastically, not knowing what else to do. Suddenly, the air was too heavy to breathe.

With a brief smile, he walked through the room with a grace that no man that large should have. When he was gone, her shoulders drooped and she let out a shaky breath. *This is crazy*, she scolded herself, *and it's completely insane the way I feel when he's near.* Frowning, she turned back to the counter and finished mixing the biscuits. *Whatever it is, I need to back off. He is so far out of my league that I'm delusional, thinking he could ever see me as more than his sister.*

These thoughts continued while she got everything ready. Her constant brain chatter kept her occupied and no closer to any sort of decision. By the time he walked in, she had everything ready and on the table.

Pausing at the end of the table, she went around to sit in the chair she always had. Gage sat across from her as he had for years, whenever she was home. She remembered how defeated she always felt when she looked over at an empty chair at the table.

"Thanks for making this. The last few weeks have been fend-for-myself, and most nights I'm too tired to care what I put in my stomach."

She picked up a hot biscuit and broke it open butter it. "Your folks go away a lot now?"

He grabbed a couple of the biscuits and set them beside his plate. "Not too much."

Kelsey may have been gone a few years, but she could still tell there was something he wasn't saying, not to mention that she could see the tension in him. "At least you have more help at the shop with your dad away."

Gage hesitated for a second before he took a bite. "Yeah. Noah's been here a few weeks now, I guess."

"Did he come here to train?" She blew on a spoonful of the stew.

Shaking his head, he took a drink of his water, studying her over the rim of the glass. "No. He's been through hell and needed somewhere isolated and quiet to heal."

"Oh." She looked down at her food, not sure what she should say or if she should ask. "Well, here should be isolated enough."

Gage chuckled softly, making her spine tingle. "I would think so."

Chancing a glance, she found he was sitting there with his spoon poised over the dish watching her. She felt her cheeks flush and wanted to groan, embarrassed that it kept happening.

"It's good that you're home, Kelsey."

The sincerity in his voice gave her goosebumps. Focusing on his dark eyes, she offered a simple smile. "It's actually good to be here." She shrugged. "I feel a little out of place, but it still feels like this is where I need to be."

"We never really talked when you came home to visit. What did you do all summer when school was out?" He paused, waiting for her to answer.

"I worked. Mostly waitressing, sometimes helping out in the kitchen."

He gave her a strange look. "I don't see you waitressing,"

Grinning, she picked up her glass. "Well, there weren't any equipment shops in the neighborhood, so I had to take what I could find."

"You could have come home for the summer." He took a few bites, glancing at her between them.

"It was too hard to find a decent place to live, so my roommate and I decided rather than lose it and find a new place each year, we'd stay through the summers." She couldn't tell him she didn't come home because of her broken heart. When she'd realized he was avoiding her, after throwing herself at him at seventeen.

"What thoughts are you lost in, Kel?"

Startled, she looked over, his deep blue eyes were searching her face. "Nothing important."

Setting his spoon down, he sat back and gave her a teasing grin. "You're lying."

Raising her eyebrows, she smirked. "Maybe saying nothing important was my way of letting you know it wasn't anything I planned on sharing, with *you*."

"Is that so?" His eyes were sparkling back at her.

"It is." She took a bite to avoid having to continue looking at him.

A few minutes passed with neither of them speaking. She knew he was watching her, but she refused to look up. Finishing, she got up and took her dishes over to the sink.

"What did you want to talk about when you were at the shop today?"

Surprised, she met his eyes. "I can't remember."

He chuckled. "You're lying, again."

Reaching across the table, she picked up his bowl and turned away quickly. "Then I guess you'll have to wait until I feel like talking about it again." What was wrong with her? Setting his dish in the sink, she quickly poured the tea into the cups turned and yelped, he was right behind her. "Gage, don't sneak up on me like that." Taking a deep breath, she stopped short and held her breath. *Holy, what kind of soap did the man use to smell that good?*

"Sorry, honey." He placed a warm hand on her shoulder. "I thought you heard me get up."

Shaking her head, she went to turn around when he placed his hand under her chin and tipped her head up so she had no choice but to look at him.

"I have to talk to you about something."

His tone was low and serious. Holding the cup out to him, she waited until he took it. "What is it?"

Taking a deep breath, he held it for a few seconds before exhaling. "I don't even know where to begin." Motioning with his chin toward the door, he gave her an earnest look.

"Let's go sit on the porch and I'll try to figure out how to say this."

Frowning, she picked up her cup and went to the door. What could possibly be this serious? She didn't even make it to the chair on the deck before she had to know. "What's going on, Gage? Is something wrong?" Her heart picked up. "Your parents, oh my god, tell me they're both okay."

"Kelsey. They're fine. Nothing is wrong."

"Promise." She had always made him promise when she'd been younger whenever it was something important.

He gave her a gentle look. "Promise." Looking at the cup in his hand, he set it down and leaned on his knees. "I need to talk to you about your parents, your family."

"I don't have any relatives, Gage. You know that." Sipping the tea, she watched several emotions go through his eyes.

"I know, honey. I'm not talking about blood relatives, I'm talking about family. Your type, my type…" he blew out a breath and sat back, looking out into the yard. "I am screwing this up so badly, I have no idea how to do this."

"Your kind of freaking me out a bit." Holding the warm cup between both hands, she focused on the comforting warmth. She had never seen Gage like this. "Just say it."

He studied her for a few breaths, silently. "What would you say if I told you there were species that you would never have imagined?"

"Species? I-I don't understand."

Leaning forward on his knees again, he kept looking at her eyes as he spoke. "People that could change into other creatures."

In the seven years she had known him, she never would have guessed he was one of those conspiracy-slash-alien believers.

"I can almost hear your thoughts, Kelsey, I'm not crazy."

He had to be joking, this was some kind of weird joke.

"Kels, look at my eyes. Keep watching."

She did as he asked and stared at his deep blue eyes, waiting for the punch line. There had to be a punch line. When he blinked, she figured he was just about to fess up, and then she focused on his eyes as they lightened, no, actually the pupils began to expand and the rings around the blue thickened.

The cup slipped from her hands when the shape of his eyes changed. Gage sat there looking at her with the most gorgeous cat eyes she'd ever seen. She had never felt her heart beat so fast. As her thoughts registered, she jumped up from the chair and backed away until her back hit the door. Turning, she opened it and ran inside the house.

She couldn't focus on any one thought as she stumbled toward the stairs. She made it up three steps before a strong arm wrapped around her waist and lifted her, only to set her at the bottom step again. Struggling against Gage's grip, she tried to take his arm off her.

"Kelsey, honey, it's okay." His tone was a whisper. He held her tight against his chest, so tight she could feel the vibrations as his spoke. "I'm sorry I had to do it that way. I didn't know..."

She stopped fighting his hold. "Let me go." Taking a shaky breath, she relaxed as much as she could. "Now, Gage." He slowly released her.

Turning around, she looked up at his face, relieved to see Gage's normal blue eyes looking down at her.

"I'm sorry, honey."

Kelsey swallowed the lump in her throat. "Your eyes..."

He nodded. "Yes."

"So," she sidestepped feeling trapped where she was standing, "So, what are you?" Glancing over her shoulder, she was thankful her hadn't followed her across the room.

"A shifter. I take the form of a cat. A tiger."

She nodded not even knowing why she was. "Tiger."

"Yes."

"And ... and you're saying there are more like you?" She froze. "Your parents? Gage, do they know?"

His eyes widened slightly. "I hope so, I got it from them."

Stepping back like he'd hit her, she dropped down onto the couch clutching her head. "Your whole body changes?" She closed her eyes.

"Yes, my whole-body shifts."

Opening them, she studied him. This man she thought she knew. "Who else is like you?"

Moving with slow steps, he crossed the room and sat on the edge of the chair across from her.

"Everyone with the company, and many of other people you've met."

Leaning back, she clutched the sides of her head again. "S-so Jake and Blair and…"

"All of them. We're all the same clan, or species, to put it roughly."

He looked so calm, so patient sitting there yet she wanted to scream. Her whole body was quivering. "Who else that I know?" Dropping her hands into her lap, she squeezed them together and tried to stop the shaking.

"Devin, Calum…"

"They're cats too?" Her voice cracked. She began to feel nauseous.

"Devin's actually a wolf and Calum…"

"There are wolves too?" Jumping up, she paced quickly across the room only to stop and stare at the floor because everything seemed to be moving. Tigers and wolves walking around in bodies that looked like normal human beings. A chill moved up her spine. "Why are you telling me this now? I mean, shouldn't I have been told a long time ago? I should have known what I was living with."

"I know."

His voice wasn't across the room. Spinning, she found him a few feet from her. He stood there, rigid and straight, his hands held loosely beside his body. He looked like a predator waiting to pounce.

"I tried to get the folks to tell you. It wasn't right to keep it from you." He tensed. "Not for this long."

"So why *are* you telling me now?" Her legs began to shake.

Taking a deep breath, she watched his chest rise slowly. "Because your parents were from my clan…"

"My parents," she whispered as her chest began to ache. "My parents were tigers?"

He nodded and continued to stand there looking at her.

Her legs gave out completely and she found herself sitting in the middle of the floor. Gage dropped down in front of her, close enough she could smell him. "I…" She fought to take a deep breath, but her chest was so tight she couldn't. "I can't…"

He slid closer, his knees brushing against her legs. With a gentle touch he grasped her shoulders and leaned down so his face was level with hers. "Take a deep breath, honey. It's going to be okay."

"Okay?" She struggled to inhale. "How is any of this okay?" Her world wasn't what she thought it was. Her friends, her parents, they were people that changed into animals. Her parents were *tigers* for god's sake. She took a shaky breath. Tigers. It made sense in some small corner of her mind; they were always rubbing against each other. She'd always thought it was cute that they were so affectionate. "Can I …" she finally lifted her eyes and looked at him. "Will I…" she couldn't say it.

"Probably. You're a pure blood, and most female pure bloods shift to a certain extent if not completely. You're not from a diluted line."

This couldn't be real, she had to be dreaming. "Diluted?"

"When only one parent shifts fully. Both of yours could shift."

"Completely?" She swallowed and kept looking at his eyes. Even though she'd seen them change, she still felt a comfort staring into them. "My m-mother turned into a tiger?"

He nodded and took a deep breath. "You may not shift completely, but you'll develop speed, better sight, scents will…"

She held up a hand. "No. Don't tell me any more right now." Closing her eyes, she blew out a long slow breath before looking at him again. "Lately I've felt so weird, restless, like something was missing." She huffed out a breath. "I thought I was going insane, for real."

"You're close to the change, honey, not crazy."

She nodded and blinked at him as tears began rolling down her cheeks. "I should be happy about that but…"

Cupping her face in his palms, he gently wiped the tears away with his thumbs. "Just give it some time. It's not a bad thing." He leaned down so his face was only inches from hers. "I'm so sorry no one told you sooner. You should have known before the changes started."

She bobbed her head up and down as much as she could with his large hands holding it. "For the last few years I felt so out of place, everywhere. It was hard to stay away from here." She swallowed. "Is this why I had to come back? Why I only feel peace when I'm here?"

"For the most part. You'll always feel the need to be around others from your clan. Cats function better as a group." He smirked, "except maybe Calum, he's a bit of a loner."

"Calum's a tiger too?"

Slowly releasing her face, he dropped down to sit completely on the floor. "No, he's a big moody panther."

"I've always gotten strange vibes around him, like he's dangerous, but safe."

Gage nodded. "That description would please him, far too much."

Wiping at her damp face, she hid behind her hands for a moment and tried to process all the new information. Dropping her hands, she pulled her knees up, wrapping her arms around them. "Is there more I need to know, like right this minute?" She leaned her chin down on top of her knees. "Because, to be honest, I don't think I can handle any more. So unless I'm going to start running around eating people, just save the rest," she searched his face. "Please."

"There's more," he paused, "stuff, but nothing that can't wait."

Nodding, she continued to sit there looking at him. It was like the first time she'd really seen him. The watchful presence he had, the lethal grace, it all made sense to her now. "I feel so lost but somehow b-better."

"I know, honey, and after it all sinks in you'll see it's not a bad thing." His voice was soft, soothing.

"I can't believe no one told me before now."

He chuckled softly. "Well, Cooper and I were in a constant battle with Dad about it." He shrugged. "We didn't at first, because losing your parents was almost more than you could handle at that time. Then Mom, she was so attached to you the way you were. The daughter she always wanted, she wanted you to be happy…"

"But I wasn't, Gage. I was lost and empty."

He lowered his eyes to the floor. "I know. I sensed it all the time from you, so did the boys, but Mom wanted what she thought was best for you."

She sniffled and then sighed. "Well, thank you for telling me." She inhaled a ragged breath trying to keep the tears from starting again.

"Gage!"

The porch door slammed and Gary came running into the room. Gage was on his feet in one swift movement.

"It's Noah," Gary panted, "we finally persuaded him to try shifting and he's freaking out." Doubling over, he huffed out a few more breaths. "I don't think he can shift back. He's going berserk, Gage. We can't stop him."

"Shit," Gage hissed out. Looking down at her, he gave her a quick nod. "Stay here, I have to go deal with this."

Kelsey struggled to her feet. "I want to come."

Gary looked at her, as if he just realized she was there. "I'm, uh …"

"It's okay," Gage assured him, "She knows."

"Oh fuck, thank God."

She turned to go through the door and Gage stepped in front of her. "You should stay here."

Placing a shaking hand on his chest, she shook her head. "Sink or swim. If this is what I am, you're not leaving me here like a helpless woman."

Gary cleared his throat. "No time to argue, Gage, I've never seen it this bad before."

Clenching his jaw, Gage nodded, his eyes not leaving hers. "Take the four-wheeler across the trail." He took two steps toward the door then stopped. "And stay out of the way when you get there."

Kelsey nodded. "Go." She didn't know anything about this, but the tension and panic coming off Gary was almost crippling. Taking a deep breath, she watched them run out the door and move faster than she ever remembered seeing before.

Chapter Five

Gage cleared the trees, not pausing to see what was going on around him. Moving faster, he headed to the fenced in yard, clearing the six-foot chain link barrier without touching it. Landing on the other side, he straightened to his full height and moved slowly toward Noah.

Cooper was there, talking in a low voice, hunched forward, he had his arms out beside him and was moving slowly toward the three cats in the corner. Both Blair and Jake were in cat form, low to the ground, poised in wait to spring if needed. Noah was backed into the corner, his sides heaving. Gage paused; Noah was a huge animal with vibrant orange markings that shone brightly, even in the fading light.

With cautious steps, he moved closer. "Noah, you need to calm down." He kept his voice steady, but with enough authority in it to be heard.

Noah emitted a low yowling cry. He was in touch with his human and listening, but too panicked to do anything.

Gage cursed silently to himself. A panicked or trapped tiger was more dangerous than one on the hunt. "Noah," he moved closer, keeping his stance with arms out to the side in case he needed to move quickly. "Enough." He rarely used the harsh tone that came with his position, but a calming tone wasn't going to get Noah's attention.

Blair's large white body was pulsing as his muscles contracted, ready to pounce. He emitted a low warning hiss to Noah, only making the orange animal focus on him, ears flattened back against his head.

Carefully, Gage's hands went to his belt and undid it; if he needed to change in a hurry he didn't want anything in the way. "Noah, we're trying to help you."

Cooper moved closer, his shirt already off. "I should have brought the tranq gun."

"You didn't know." Gage pulled his shirt free from his jeans as he unzipped them. Without moving too quickly he pulled the shirt off and dropped it on the ground. "Noah." He tried again to inflect enough dominant tone to grab the man's attention.

Jake chirruped, trying another approach to get the frightened man's attention. Noah didn't even pay him any heed; he was too focused on the white cat, his tail twitching with impatience.

Before Gage even sensed her, Kelsey pushed between Cooper and him and came to a sudden stop.

"Can't you see you're all scaring him and making it worse?" She shoved Gage against the shoulder and took a step closer to the three coiled animals. "Back up."

Gage chanced a quick glance at Cooper, who had the same gobsmacked look on his face that he was feeling. "Kelsey," he said trying to keep his tone non-threatening, "back up, slowly." He noticed that Noah had his full attention on her as he moved closer to the ground. Jake and Blair had inched back a few feet, putting themselves between her and the man they that was a danger to her.

"No. All of you back up and give him some space." Her voice shook but left no doubt that she wasn't going to listen. She inhaled a startled noise and looked at the animals in front of her. "Blair..." her voice was filled with awe, "Jacob, leave him alone."

Later, when his heart wasn't paralyzed with fear, he'd ask how she knew who they were, but for now he had to get her out of harm's way. He took one step and then Cooper grabbed his arm. Looking at him, his eyes wide as if asking *what the fuck?* Cooper only shook his head. He was insane if he thought he was going to back away and leave his mate open like that.

"Let her try," Cooper said no louder than a whisper.

Cursing under his breath, Gage gritted his teeth. "Jake, Blair give him space."

Even in his cat form, Gage was able to make out what Jake was thinking and it wasn't far from his own thoughts of *are you insane?* "Do it."

Blair backed away from Noah until his side was touching Kelsey. He was listening to Gage, but made it clear he wasn't going to just let her walk up to a panicking cat.

"Blair," she said on a breath as she reached down and ran her hand along his hip. Kelsey took a soft breath in, like she was reaching for the courage to continue. Cooper's grip on his arm tightened as Gage fought every natural instinct in his body to protect his mate.

She held her hands in front of her and began to inch toward him. "Noah," her voice crooned a softness that Gage had never heard from her before. "I know you're scared." She moved closer and held out her hand. Noah was completely focused on her, scenting the air swiftly with every breath. "I am too," she admitted in a tiny voice, "I need you to calm down, this can't be good for you."

Noah pranced on his front paws, muscles quivering beneath the lush fur covering his body.

"No one is going to hurt you," she moved toward him an inch at a time, her hand stretched out in front of her, "I won't let them."

Gage swallowed, his heart was beating in his throat. Never in his entire life had he felt fear like he did right now. If anything happened to her, he wouldn't be able to control himself, or what would follow.

"Easy," she whispered so softly only an animal would hear her, "it's going to be all right." She was only a foot in front of him now, with slow movements she lowered until she was squatting in front of him.

One move from Noah and he'd have her in his teeth, or one swipe of his large paw and she'd be sliced wide open. Gage's muscles began to shake as he fought to stay where he was. He hadn't realized it, but Gary now held his other arm, pinning him in place.

Noah stretched out of his hunched position until his nose was an inch from Kelsey's held out hand. "That's it," she breathed, "no one is going to hurt you." He jerked his head until his nose touched her fingertips. His sides weren't heaving as fast now, he slowly straightened his large body so his belly was off the ground. "You're beautiful, Noah," she reached out and touched the side of his jaw, "so soft..."

Gage had to bite back a growl seeing her touch another man in his animal form. Cooper's hand squeezed to the point he knew he'd have a bruise there tomorrow. It was his job to protect any member of his clan, whether born into it or adopted, but his mate's well-being took precedence over everything else.

Kelsey was on her knees now, both hands stroking the orange coat of the male cat, now standing perfectly still and scenting everything around him. There was no doubt he would pick up on the adrenalin rushing through Gage's body as he watched her hands move over his body.

"That's it, just relax," she continued. Blair and Jake were both standing at full height again, looking on from a few feet away.

Jake looked over at Gage and made a soft chirruping noise. Blair turned and looked at him and then with slow easy steps moved toward Kelsey and Noah. Rubbing his large head against her side, he gently pushed his way between the cat and woman's body. Jake was on the other side of Noah nudging him in the chest. Noah backed up a few steps, rubbing along Blair's body as he did.

Gage let out a soft breath and jerked out of the hands holding him. "Kelsey, come here." His voice was shaking with pent up emotion. He didn't want to make any sudden movements and alarm Noah again.

Watching the three animals in front of her, she got to her feet and backed toward him. Gage reached out as soon as she was close enough. "He'll be fine now." He pulled her back against his chest, wrapping an arm around her and turning his body slowly so his back was to the cats.

"I…"

"They're going to be naked when they shift, honey."

She tensed in his hold. "Oh," she squeaked in a startled voice, "I hadn't thought about that."

Cooper looked at her and then grinned at Gage. "We've got it from here, if you want to head back."

Gage nodded, slowly moving Kelsey back toward the gate. Gary held out his shirt, taking it from him he glanced over to see Jake lying on the ground staring up at the sky. "Make sure Noah gets some rest."

Jake turned his head and looked at him. Exhaling loudly, he propped himself up on his elbow. "Kelsey too, the vibes coming off her are making me nauseous."

Kelsey tensed in his arms, but she didn't try to look around him. Gage tightened his hold. "We'll see all of you tomorrow." He watched as Noah's form began to phase back and then practically picked Kelsey up, moving to the four-wheeler with long strides.

She was shaking in his arms as he straddled the machine and pulled her into his lap. The adrenalin was gone and shock was now starting to hit her. "That was the both the bravest and stupidest thing I've ever witnessed."

Her quivering body leaned into his bare chest, her head resting in the cradle of his shoulder as he started the engine. "He was scared, I was scared…"

Nuzzling the top of her head, he glanced over at the men as they began to move to the other side of the yard, propping up an exhausted Noah between them. "He'll be all right now."

"Does that happen often?"

Knowing she'd already had more than enough to digest for one night, he shook his head, twisting the accelerator and turning back toward the trail. "No, it's rare."

"Good. It's frightening." She snuggled in closer to his him and relaxed against his body.

Gage wanted to let go of the handlebar and wrap his arms around her. Since she'd come back he hadn't touched her and it was driving him crazy, but he needed to get her back to the house. At some point, all of this was going to sink in and he preferred not to be in the middle of the bush when it did. Tonight was not the introduction to their world he had planned.

He heard the door open but wasn't going to release the sleeping woman in his arms to go see who it was. Inhaling deeply, he scented Cooper just as the man appeared in the doorway. Standing carefully, Gage cradled Kelsey into his chest and moved over to the stairs.

He didn't want to put her into bed alone but knew Cooper wouldn't have come if it wasn't important.

Tucking the blanket around her, he backed up as she turned to her side and placed her hand under her cheek. His heart ached looking at her. Running a hand through his hair, he went back out before he changed his mind.

Cooper was on the porch leaning against the rail staring off into the darkness. "How's she doing?"

Gage slouched into one of the chairs. "As well as can be expected." He rubbed his forehead trying to ease the throbbing, "I can't believe she dove right in the mix of three of us when everything was so fucking volatile."

Cooper grinned at him. "I can." He crossed his arms over his chest and studied him for a moment. "I've been telling you for years that dealing with her was going to be like taking the proverbial cat by the tail and trying to hold on."

"Yeah, I know, but one minute she was sitting on the floor crying—one step from a complete meltdown, and the next..."

"The fear pouring from her was suffocating, but she barreled right through it and helped another clan member in need." Cooper shook his head, "She's so much like her mother it's haunting."

Gage watched him for a minute. "You loved her." In all the years he'd known the man he had never been able to put the pieces together.

Cooper gave him a sad smile. "I did, but she chose Phillip, so I had to respect that."

"Were they mates?"

Cooper shook his head. "No. As far as I know she never found hers." He nodded toward the door. "Kelsey is one of those rare births in an unmated pair."

Gage blew out a breath realizing the seriousness. "It happens sometimes."

Cooper moved over and sat in the chair across from him. "Not often enough. Our numbers are dwindling." Taking his cap off, he rubbed a hand over his short hair and then put it back on and sat back. "Sometimes I wish we were like the clans that don't need a mate to have children."

Gage ran his fingers across an aching temple. "That could get messy with the way the women are when it's their cycle."

Cooper grinned. "Yeah, family trees would be taken to a whole new level."

"And then some." Lifting his chin, Gage absorbed the silence of the night; he leaned back and let the cooling air move over him. "How's Noah doing?"

"He's passed out." Cooper made a soft exasperated sound. "Tonight was the first time he'd shifted in *two years*, Gage." He paused and stared at him. "He was beaten, even more brutally if he shifted while Tomas had him."

Gage shook his head slowly. "I suspected as much."

"The boy has more scars on his body than a road map has lines."

Gage's easy feeling was gone. "I don't understand why Tomas has them if he's not using their full potential."

"I don't know really," Cooper sighed, "even in two leg form, we're stronger and faster than regular humans."

"Yeah." Sitting up, Gage gave him a serious look. "Do you think Noah's going to be okay? Is he going to make it through the emotional scarring?"

Cooper sat there and looked at him for several minutes, taking his time before answering. "I think he will be. He's sorry as hell about tonight, which, in all honesty, wasn't his fault. He said if it hadn't been for Kitty-Kat he doesn't know if he would have been able to calm down enough to shift back."

Gage exhaled in a steady stream. "I'm pretty sure no female he's ever been around would openly come near him."

"Well, he's grateful for her help, and for you not killing him on the spot for it happening."

Groaning, Gage stood up. "It wasn't his fault." Leaning on the rail he stared out into the bush, inhaling all the scents around him.

"Does she know everything, Gage?"

He'd known Cooper would eventually get back to that. Dropping his head down, he closed his eyes. "No. Gary came screeching in before I could tell her everything."

"So, she doesn't know you're mates?"

Shaking his head, he opened his eyes and pushed away from the rail. Straightening, he crossed his arms over his chest and took a deep breath. "No. I didn't even get as far as telling her she was changing and driving every male in scenting range insane."

"You more than the rest of us."

"Still, she was wrecked that no one had told her before now."

"Do you blame her?" Cooper stood up beside him. "I don't even understand how her parents hid it from her."

"I don't know either. Then again, I was raised knowing, but my father is an Alpha, so I didn't have a choice in the matter."

"You have to tell her soon, for your sake and hers. She's going to start pining for things she can't even understand. Not to mention the changes in her body are going to be more noticeable soon."

Taking a deep breath, Gage held it in for a few seconds before exhaling loudly. "I know. After tonight's events, I thought I'd let her get some rest and come to terms with some of it." Looking over at the door, he tried to ignore the draw to go back inside with her. "Can you hang out here for a bit longer, Coop?"

"Need to go for a run?"

"Yeah, just a short one. I don't want to be gone too long in case she wakes up."

Copper moved over and sat back down. "You do what you have to, I'll be here."

"Thanks, Coop." Not giving him a chance to change his mind, Gage went down the steps and walked to the tree line, stripping without missing a step.

Chapter Six

Kelsey lay there looking at the ceiling. She'd been awake for a while now, a bit confused about where she was. It had been a long time since she'd opened her eyes to find herself in this room. It was a good feeling until she'd remembered the night before. It was an odd moment to think, *oh yeah, I'm a big cat.*

Sitting up, she looked down at her legs, still in her jeans, wondering if she'd notice anything different after learning what she was. Shaking her head, she got up and went over to the window. It was so nice to see the trees with no towering buildings blocking the green space. This is home.

Sighing, she turned to get changed and ready to face Gage, which had a totally different meaning than it had before last night. As much as she tried to accept what he'd told her, she still needed to know more. So many things he said last night were flagged for further discussion. So many questions after finding out something she should have known her entire life, she sure as hell was going to get the answers today.

When she stepped into the kitchen, Gage was at the table looking through a folder. He looked up at her, his dark eyes appraising every inch of her.

"Hey, honey. Did you get some rest?"

She poured herself a cup of coffee and added a touch of sugar before turning to face him. "I actually slept like a rock. I don't think I moved at all."

He closed the folder and sat back. "That's not surprising, last night took its toll."

Sitting down, she traced the handle on the cup. "I have questions."

"I'll answer what I can, and if I don't know the answer I'll find someone who does."

His tone was soft and gentle, as if he was afraid of upsetting her again. Sipping the coffee, she looked over the rim of her cup. The only serious conversations she had planned to have with him was whether he thought of her as a sister, now, that was the furthest thing from her mind as she held his concerned gaze. Lowering the cup, she smiled a weak and helpless smile. "I don't even know where to start."

Nodding, he leaned forward on his elbows and clasped his large hands together on the table. "Pick one and we'll go from there."

"Okay." She took a quick breath. "You said I was close to the change. What exactly does that mean? How do you know I am? And why now?" She realized her one question bled into three, but he didn't seem to notice.

"Other shifters, especially from the same clan can sense, or smell it."

"I smell?" She cringed.

He grinned. "Not a bad odor smell. This is just a particular scent." He sat back and cupped his hands behind his head. "It's a scent that will only be noticed by your family."

"So, normal people wouldn't be able to smell me?"

He shook his head and dropped his hands back to the table. "No, honey, to them you don't have a scent."

"Okay." Turning the cup in a circle, she tried to stay calm enough to continue. "What's happening to me?"

"Your body is going through the natural changes…" he rolled his eyes when she glared at him, "Natural for us.

49

Women go through it later than the males," he shrugged, "ages vary. I'm thinking you're a little later than most, because you were away and not around other shifters." He pushed the folder to the middle of the table and clasped his hands again. "You're not going to suddenly turn into a large feline on a moment's notice if that's what you're worried about."

"I don't know what to expect."

"Most of the changes at first are going to be on a..." he let out a slow breath, "I really don't know quite how to explain it all. It's different for males, we just feel the change and want to shift, everything else falls into place after that."

"And for women?" She watched him bite at the side of his lip as he thought about it. "I'm not going to like it am I?"

He gave her a hesitant look. "You've heard the expression 'a cat in heat' right?"

Kelsey's eyes widened as her jaw dropped. Blinking, she closed her mouth as a shudder went through her body. "I'm going to..." shoving the hair back from her face, she looked everywhere around the room but right at him.

"Kelsey." Her eyes flicked to him at the tone he used. "It's not as bad as you're thinking."

"I'm thinking I'm going to be like a cat in heat, acting all needy and slutty."

His lips quirked, but he didn't smile. Points for him there. "You won't be slutty. This is natural with our kind and nothing to be ashamed of. It's not something you can stop or turn off."

"Wonderful," she muttered. Her mind was going faster with the adrenaline pumping through her veins. "So, when you said I was close to the change, that's what you meant?"

"Among other things, yes. The chances of you changing are high too, so your body is going to start wanting that."

Rubbing a hand over her face, she looked down at the coffee in her cup. "I need some time with that information before I can take in any more." Her heart jerked in her chest.

"Is there anything I need to know about it? Like *need* to know?"

Gage picked up his cup and took a drink. She watched his Adam's apple bob as he swallowed it. When he set the cup down, he looked uncomfortable. "Males can sense it."

"Sense it?" She jerked in her chair. "You mean they can smell I'm coming into …" she grimaced, "into heat or whatever it's called?" Shaking her head, she looked at him. "So, they know that I'm going to want to…" She couldn't even say it out loud to him.

He nodded but didn't offer anything further.

"Jake, Blair, they all know…" she couldn't even say it.

"Yeah." He gave her a sympathetic look. "Kel, we're used to it. None of us are kids; this is something that's normal for us."

Fanning her face with her hand, she knew her cheeks would be bright red. "Well, it's not normal for me." She covered her face with both hands and leaned on the table. "God, can I just hide in my room until it goes away?" Jerking upright again she sent him a panicked look. "It does *go away* doesn't it?"

He grinned. "Yes. The first time is going to be the worst, and then it will only be a few times a year. It varies, maybe lasts a week at a time."

"Oh good." She felt her face flush again. "I've never really been into …" she waved her hand around. "Stuff like that."

Gage looked down at his hands and seemed to be studying them instead of looking at her. "Everyone is different."

Unable to sit a second longer, she paced over to the window and looked out into the yard. "Is it still okay if I come to the shop? I mean, I was going to hang out there for a bit until I find my groove here again."

"You're always welcome there, honey, that will never change."

"Okay." She nodded and took a deep breath. "I think that's enough talk about *that* part for now." Turning, she leaned back against the counter and gripped it lightly to keep her steady. Her knees were a little shaky. "Can I ask about Noah?"

Gage gave her a puzzled look. "What about Noah?"

"Gary said they'd finally persuaded him to shift. Why did they have to persuade him? Does it have something to do with him needing to come here to heal?"

Blowing out a breath, he got up and picked up his cup. With slow steps, he came over to the sink and placed the cup in it. "You don't forget a word anyone says, do you?"

She smirked and shook her head. "I didn't hear a thing at the time, but it all came back to me in pieces this morning."

"There's so much I want to tell you, but it's like trying to teach you an entirely different language in a day." He tucked his hands into his pockets and looked down at her. "There's an organization, a criminal one, that seems to have a penchant for keeping shifters from any clan, in servitude."

Her heart thudded heavy in her chest as she waited for him to finish.

"Noah was forced to stay there for fifteen years. We don't know the full extent of what he went through, but we do know he wasn't allowed to shift..."

"Wouldn't that be hard to do? I mean, if it's a natural thing."

He nodded. "Yeah, and just how he managed it, I'm not even sure. We can control it but there are times you just have to shift or it becomes painful."

"So, he shifted last night and then freaked out."

"Pretty much."

Inhaling deeply, she looked up at him. His eyes were filled with pain and compassion. "I'm glad he's here now." Reaching out, she placed a hand on his chest near his heart. "You'll help him get through it." She left her hand there, feeling calm that she hadn't experienced in a long time from touching him. It was, she realized, the first time she'd ever just touched him for no reason. She wasn't sure what it meant, but in the chaotic emotions swirling through her, she'd take it for now.

Gage closed one of his hands over hers and smiled down at her. "You amaze me," he said in a whisper, "the way you're handling all of this." He squeezed her hand. "Thank you for what you did last night for Noah."

"I think, in hindsight, I probably should have run the other way."

He grinned. "But you didn't." Stopping, his look changed. Releasing her hand, he reached into his pocket and pulled out his phone. "I better take this." He answered it with a deep tone and then held it against his chest and looked at her. "Make sure you eat. That's a necessity now, regular food intake."

She nodded.

"Come to the shop whenever you're ready."

With that he turned, scooped up the folder and went out the door. Staring at the door for several minutes, she shook her head and turned around to look out the window. "Well, as homecomings go, this one had been quite special."

As she made eggs, she realized there were still so many questions she didn't have answers for. Then again, if the answers were anything like turning into a needy wanton cat woman, she wasn't sure if she wanted the answers at all. There was just so much information; she couldn't process it all at once.

She wasn't just a regular girl. She was a shifter, a tiger. It was just too much to take in. What was she supposed to do now? In any other crisis moment, she had always called Beth, but knowing that she had kept all of this from her, it just didn't feel right. She needed some time to deal with that, too. The people she held in the highest regard in her world had done everything possible to make her live a lie for her entire life. Her parents, Gage's parents even Cooper. Cooper who had been like her favorite uncle since as far back as she could remember. He'd been the one to come to her and tell her when her parents had been killed. He'd been the one that held her while she fell apart, and he'd been the one that had brought her here.

The only one who cared enough to end the lie was Gage, and he'd only done it because apparently things were happening now and he didn't have a choice. She sighed as she finished the last bite. She couldn't be mad at him, though, if it weren't for him she'd still think she was losing her mind.

Placing the plate in the sink, she turned back and looked at the door. She needed to do something to take her mind off all of this. It wasn't going to go away, but that didn't mean she had to sit here and mope all day. The idea of the guys at the shop being able to smell that she was going through some sort of animal thing made her cheeks flush, but it was also something she wasn't going to be able to avoid... according to Gage.

Maybe it made her a coward, she didn't care at this point. The guys were all giving each other strange looks every time she walked past them. When Cooper suggested she give herself a quick refresher on some of the bigger equipment, she practically ran outside, anything to stay out of smelling distance, or whatever it was referred to.

After the first few minutes in the knuckle boom loader she was happy to be alone with no one watching. She was more than a little rusty maneuvering it. She'd almost tipped over when she'd forgotten to put the stabilizer legs down. The guys never would have let her forget that, ever.

Glancing up from the joystick, she saw Noah walking in her direction. Turning the engine off, she opened the door and looked down at him. "Hey." The hesitant look on his face made her heart ache for him. "Come on up, I'll give you a crash course."

His amber eyes lit up with surprise, as he nodded and climbed into the cab. He hunched in the door until she moved over to perch on the box in the corner of the cab.

"Sit." She grinned. "It might be a real crash course. I'm a little out of practice."

Noah angled his large body until he was in the seat but turned enough to look at her. "You still know more than I do. All I have done since I got here is fetch tools and hold things. I feel like a nurse in an operating room."

She laughed. "There's an image."

He smiled, it was tense and a little awkward, but it was a start.

"I'm a bit embarrassed about last night." He cleared his throat. "Thank you for what you did. It couldn't have been easy to do." He gave her an anxious look. "I think it was your fear that snapped me out of it." He shrugged, "it was worse than my own."

Rolling her eyes, she turned so she could see him better. "Hey, I'm always happy to be scared witless to help someone out." She studied his eyes for a few seconds. "Gage told me a bit of what caused it." She touched his shoulder. "I'm glad you're here now. I think it will help."

He looked at her hand on his shoulder, then back to her face. "I hope it does." His chest rose with a deep breath. "I've done a lot of things I regret, but maybe I can still find a bit of peace."

Lifting her hand away from him, she clasped it with her other one in her lap.

"So, are you really out here to practice or are the guys getting on your nerves?" He asked it quietly, as if he was afraid of crossing lines with her.

She grinned. "I couldn't handle the looks they were giving each other behind my back. It's a bit embarrassing."

"Ah," he sighed, "Gage explained some things."

"Yeah. Why aren't you doing everything possible to get away from me?"

Gripping the levers, he looked out the front window guard. "Part of what I…" he clenched his jaw for a second before continuing, "I'm used to being around females while they're cycling."

She flushed at the mention of it. "You've built an immunity to this scent or whatever?"

Noah grimaced and gave her a coy look. "I wouldn't say I'm immune, I just have better control." He gave her a genuine smile that disarmed her embarrassment almost completely. "Truth be told, you smell really appealing to the cat in me, but as you saw last night, I'm more than a little apprehensive giving in to anything to do with *that* part of me."

She knew her cheeks were heated and he was only making fun of his situation to put her at ease, but it still tugged at her heart knowing he would do that. "Thanks for controlling yourself." She looked out at the shop. "I wished the guys would get a handle on it."

"They will." He tapped the joystick with his fingers. "So, show me your magic with this beast so I feel like I know something."

Laughing, she leaned over and started it again. "At least we're far enough away from everything that we won't drop the grapple assembly on anyone or crush anything." Disengaging the stabilizer legs, she motioned to the levers and foot pedals. "These are to move the whole unit."

He hesitantly touched one then the other to get a feel of how it moved. "That's some encouraging words; things get crushed often around here?"

Pulling the lever, she moved the loader back in so they wouldn't tip until she showed him how to engage the legs. "Not too much. I put a nice dent in the side of an off-road truck when I was learning." Grinning, she motioned to the shed at the other end of the lot. "That used to have an awning built on it. Jake took out two of the supporting pillars when he was first starting."

Noah laughed, his eyes shining. "I'll have to ask him about that sometime."

Forty-five minutes later, Kelsey turned off the engine in the second rig they'd used. "I think you've found your niche here, Noah." She patted his shoulder and grinned at him. "You did great. Just practice whenever the guys aren't working on them." She shrugged. "You may be able to go on some of the calls when they only need a piece of equipment for a day and don't have a qualified operator."

Turning in the seat, he grinned at her. "I feel better, more than I have in a long time. Thanks." Clearing his throat, he turned and looked out the window in the door. "I better get out of here; I don't need Gage wigging out because I'm alone with you."

Kelsey motioned for him to climb out. "Why would Gage care?"

Noah stopped half way down the ladder and gave her a wide-eyed look. "Uh…" he looked down at the ground, "I guess I thought you two had a thing going on."

She watched him climb down. "Not that I'm aware of." Turning, she climbed down two steps, getting out of these things always made her feel small.

Her boot caught the side of the bar and before she could grab onto anything, she dropped butt first toward the ground. Right when she thought she was going to hit the dirt, Noah caught her. She lost her breath when she hit his chest and grabbed onto his neck. Catching her breath, she exhaled loudly. "Nice catch," she made a noise close to a giggle, something she didn't really do, "Thanks."

He was smiling again as he set her on her feet. "Anytime." He sobered. "But hopefully not."

Placing a hand on his arm, she took a deep breath to steady her heart rate, and then she heard a low menacing growl.

Turning, she looked over and saw Gage and Blair standing a few feet away. Blair looked worried, which was odd for him, and Gage looked pissed off.

Noah stiffened and stepped back from her. "Thanks again," he said quietly.

She nodded, giving him a bewildered look before turning back to give Gage a narrow-eyed stare.

Blair motioned to Noah. "Come on, you can come with me to drop the wheel dozer off."

Noah nodded and then headed toward the gate, giving Gage a wide berth as he went.

With her hands on her hips, she stood there staring at the man she wanted to kick. What the hell was wrong with him? The expression on his face was cold. Spinning on his heels, he stormed off in the other direction without a word.

That ended her good mood. Looking around, she saw Cooper leaning against the fence a few feet away.

"Let's go talk, Kelsey."

Huffing out a breath, she threw up her hands and followed him out of the yard. Cooper rarely used her name, so that told her right then that she wasn't going to like their talk.

Chapter Seven

Was it a bad thing when you didn't like being right?

Kelsey sat on the boulder staring off at the rocks and trees. "Why didn't anyone tell me all of this, Coop?" She batted at the tears on her face with her knuckles.

Cooper was squatted down beside her, also focused on the view of the trees. "We planned to, wanted to. The more time that passed, the harder it got."

"I'd like a do-over," she whispered.

"A what?"

"I'd like to do the last two days over again. All of this..." she lifted her hands and then dropped them back into her lap. "All of this is just too much to process."

He was silent. Turning, she watched him study the patch of grass sticking out of the rocks beside his boots.

"There's still more isn't there?"

Lifting his eyes, he met hers. She felt like she could see right into his soul, the look he gave her answered the question.

Taking a deep breath, she looked away. "I just need a minute to process, Coop. It's—it's a lot to swallow in such a short time." She took a shaky breath and closed her eyes, trying to keep the tears from starting again.

"I'll just go give Gage a call and let him know where we wandered to. He'll be worried by now."

Nodding in agreement, even though what he'd said didn't really register. After he left, she shifted on the rock, her shoulders drooped down. It felt like an enormous weight sat on them. Picking at the moss on the surface of the stone, she tried to sort through all the information that had been dumped on her.

She hadn't meant to bombard Cooper with questions, but as they'd walked away she'd been so agitated with Gage's behavior she'd lost it and asked why the hell her parents, Gage's parents or even he hadn't told her, long before now, what she was.

One question led to another, and the answers got longer and bled into things she wouldn't ever have been able to imagine, even on her most bizarre day.

Her parents hadn't died in a freak car accident as she had always believed. They'd been killed, or as far as Cooper knew, were being chased at the time of the accident. Why hadn't anyone told her? Why hadn't they told her that this *organization* that targeted her kind had been after her parents? The same one that had held Noah for fifteen years. *Fifteen years.*

She was quite possibly feeling every emotion, good and bad, known to man right now.

All. At. Once.

Now she understood, or as much as she ever would, why no one rushed to tell her what she was. The tears ran down her cheeks, she ignored them.

What was she?

She was a shifter from a long line of non-diluted shifters. What did that mean? She didn't know exactly, but did know it meant the simple black and white world she thought she knew was as colorful as a bag of skittles. Cooper had briefly explained the workings of the clan and the alliance. *God,* to suddenly know there were normal-looking people that were really wolves, cat, bears and too many other species to name was inane.

Ed was an alpha and leader of this clan, and she was just finding out now. Well, she was finding out so much; Gage was one of Devin's two seconds, and apparently some kind of shifter equivalent to royalty. So, what did that mean for Gage? Would he be going off to be with Devin, wherever that was, when he took over?

Clutching her head, she closed her eyes, maybe she was just going insane and none of this was real. Would it be too much to ask to go back to her not knowing any of it?

"Kelsey."

Every muscle in her body tensed, he was still using her given name. "Is the rest going to be as bad, Coop?"

"Worse than finding out about your parents? No, it's nothing like that, I promise."

Exhaling loudly, she lifted her head and turned on the rock so she could look at him. "Okay, good, because I don't know how much more I can take. Really."

"When I said we would talk, I had meant about the changes you're going to go through. I hadn't intended to tell you everything just yet."

She looked at his amber eyes that were filled with so much sadness. Nodding, she exhaled slowly. "I'm glad you did, well, as much as I can be. All these secrets are things I should have known years ago…"

"But you do understand now why we didn't tell you right away?"

She didn't want to, but did. "Yeah, I do. I guess."

Cooper sat on a rock a few feet from her. "What I really wanted to talk to you about was how the changes you're going through affects the boys…"

She rolled her eyes, "God forbid they should be a little uncomfortable."

He gave her a look, if she didn't know him as well as she did, it would have been scary being on the other end. "That's why we're having this talk. It goes beyond just being uncomfortable. You're lucky they think of you like a sister."

She looked down at the blade of grass in her fingers, avoiding his eyes.

Letting out a low sound that was close to a growl, he started talking again, his voice low and serious. "When they're this close to a female that's going into the change, or even after during her cycle, every instinct in them tells them to, uh, well, the end result is to mark you..."

Her head came up with a jerk. "*Mark* me?"

He nodded. "It's a natural thing." He rubbed the back of his neck like he was uncomfortable talking to her about this. "It doesn't happen often now, unless there's a mutual attraction and consent, but in the past..." he blew out a breath, "let's just say many couples found themselves stuck with each other for not ignoring the signs."

She opened her mouth and then closed it for a moment. "So, even though they think of me like a sister..."

"But that's just it, you're not a sister and their cats *know* that."

"Am I supposed to just stay at the house then? To make it easier for them until this passes?"

Taking off his hat, he rubbed a hand vigorously over his stubbly hair. Placing the cap back on, he adjusted it a few times before looking back at her. "You could, but you'd be there a long while."

"I don't understand, Coop. Maybe my brain is on overload. Just break it down for me."

He ran his hand over the back of his neck again. She had never seen him so fidgety before, it made her more worried about what he was trying to tell her.

"Your body would have changed gradually in the next few years, if you'd stayed in the city." He shrugged. "It may have been a few years before you felt it, but..." Blowing out a breath, he shook his head like he was waging some kind of internal argument.

"But..." she prompted.

"It is changing, and now that you're around six males it will be fast and furious and nothing you can do will stop it. Staying shut up in the house might drag it out some, but it's still going to happen…"

"Do you think I'll shift fully?" She interrupted and was rewarded with an annoyed look.

"That's the least of your worries, sweetheart," he said softly.

Sweetheart? It had been years since Cooper had called her that. Not since just after her parents died. "Okay," she swallowed the lump in her throat, "what *is* my biggest worry?"

"Mating." He huffed out a breath like he was relieved he'd finally said it.

"Mating?" Her eyes widened. "You mean having sex?" Shaking her head, she tried to process what exactly this had to do with anything they'd talked about. "Uh, I don't…"

"Your cat is going to want to mate during your cycle." He said it slowly, maybe hoping he wouldn't have to explain further, she didn't know.

Her cheeks grew hot. This was one talk she hadn't ever pictured having with Cooper. "Uh, so what…"

Cooper stood up and rubbed the back of his neck again. "You're around six…" he shook his head, "five vital, young males, Kelsey…"

"Oh." She jumped up and stood there with her heart pounding in her chest faster than if she'd just run a mile. "You mean, she…" she swallowed, "me—I will end up with one of them?"

He blew out a breath and nodded.

"No." She turned away from him, the guys in question faces flying through her mind. "No. I mean, yeah, I guess they're all something most women wouldn't mind…" she spun around, "but Coop, they're like brothers. I've never…" her cheeks heated again when she thought of Gage, "for most of them, I've never even looked at them like *that.*"

He nodded and crossed his arms. "I know."

She stared at him; her heart racing so fast still then she noticed he had that look, the one that told her there was still more. *God, just push me off a cliff, please. I can't do this.* "What? What else?" She made a frustrated noise in the back of her throat. "Cooper, just tell me. Is this ever going to end?"

Moving over, he placed a hand on her shoulder and gave her a sympathetic look. "I know, sweetheart…"

Jerking, she stepped back. "Don't call me that! Anytime *that* word comes out of your mouth it's been bad news." Running her hands up into her hair she grasped it and rested her hands on top of her head, fists full of her own hair. "Just tell me, Coop, I'm one second from a meltdown here."

"It's about Gage…"

Dropping her hands, she gaped at him, a lump in her throat. "What about Gage?" Her mind was spinning out of control. "Oh God, does he want me to leave? I'm distracting all the guys and that's dangerous working with the equipment," she groaned, "I didn't even think about that…"

"Gage doesn't want you to leave." He laughed.

She stared at him, eyes wide. He was laughing? How could he laugh right now? "He doesn't?"

"No." He grinned and then shook his head as if he was trying to get rid of the smile. "No, Gage most definitely *doesn't* want you to leave ever again."

Exhaling as relief filled her, she let the muscles in her shoulders relax a bit. "Good, because honestly I don't know where I'd go…"

"When Gage growled at you earlier, it's because Noah was touching you." He said it quickly like he needed to get it out fast.

Frowning, she rubbed her forehead. "Well, yeah he caught me so I wouldn't land on my ass…"

"I know, and so did Gage, he'd been watching the two of you for several minutes."

"Then why did he growl? Was Noah supposed to let me fall on my ass?" She pointed a finger at him. "And F.Y.I *Noah* is able to completely ignore this mating…urge…stuff."

Cooper nodded. "I know. We all do." He crossed his arms over his chest. "Gage sent him out there so you wouldn't feel like a leper, so he *does* trust him around you."

"Then what's the problem?" She'd never had so much information dumped on her all at once before, lines were blurring and her normal logic was completely shot. "I don't get it, Coop." *Did I just whine that?* Now *she* wanted to growl.

Blowing out a loud breath, Cooper closed his eyes for a moment like he was drawing on the last of his patience. "Each of us has one true mate. It's rare to find them." He waved his hand around in the air. "And when, or if, you do, then the urges are ten times stronger."

"The urge to be with them, or mark them, whatever…" What did this have to do with anything he'd said today?

He nodded. "Yeah," his eyes flicked down to the ground and he didn't look back at her, "Gage found his mate years ago and has been waiting ever since."

She wanted to stomp on his foot so he would hurry up and just tell her. *Oh, God what if Gage has a mate?* Giving herself a mental smack, she realized those teenage fantasies about the son of the people that taken her in were the very least of her problems. "*And?*" She urged, not hiding the annoyed tone in her voice.

"He realized it was you when you turned sixteen, Kelsey." His serious eyes locked on hers and he didn't move, she wasn't even sure if he was breathing.

That was the first time she could actually *see* that he was a cat inside. Her brain felt like it was moving in slow motion, she couldn't process what he'd just said. It was there, but not. Cooper continued to look at her, not saying a word. She didn't know which part she was supposed to focus on, how Gage treated her from sixteen to now? Or, the fact that she was his mate and they didn't have a choice? That's where her mind stopped. If she was Gage's mate, then he didn't have a choice really, or her either, because of some sort of animal thing. "So… he, *we* don't have a choice in this?"

Cooper tilted his head like he couldn't believe after everything he'd just said that was what she said first. "That's all you have to say?" Shaking his head, he put his hand on his hips and looked all around them. "I can honestly say that's not what I'd imagined your reaction being for the last seven years."

"You knew?"

He nodded slowly, "We all did. When he had trouble coping, we ran interference..." he stopped and studied her. "You don't have a clue what I'm talking about do you?" Chuckling softly, he continued. "Of course, you don't, and it's our fault." Raising a hand, he offered her an odd smile. "I know you've got a lot to deal with right now and I truly am sorry for all of it, but..." he shrugged, "I have to ask, do you see Gage as your brother, Kelsey? It would kill him, but if he knew that, he would find a way to get through your change and give you time."

She opened her mouth slowly, changing her mind with what she was going to say. "What do you mean?" For most of her life she'd thought she was a fairly intelligent person, but today the only thing she seemed to be was clueless.

"This would be so much easier if he could talk to you himself, but he's having issues right now dealing with you finally being home and near..."

Kelsey nodded, even though she really didn't understand—again. "I've never thought of him as my brother," she felt her cheeks heat and wanted to curse, "but right now, with what you've just told me, I can't really think." She ended on a breath so soft she wasn't sure she said it loud enough for him to hear. "Maybe I should just go away for a while and..."

"*Jesus*, don't do that." He ran a hand over the scar that ran from his temple to his jaw. "If you were to take off because of this, it would destroy him." He stepped over to her and put his hands on her shoulders so she would look up at him. "Stay. We may be a bunch of males, but we all care and want to help you through all of this." He waited for her to nod, which she did numbly then he continued. "If you were to go off and then shift alone for the first time, sweet..." he smirked, "it wouldn't be good."

Blinking, she looked up at him. How could she have forgotten that part in all of this? "I can't imagine it, and I don't even want to try, Coop." Dropping her head onto his chest, she inhaled and noticed that his scent smelled familiar and made her feel a small amount of comfort. *God, I am what they're saying.*

He pulled her into his arms and held her for several minutes without speaking. "Let's get you home, Kitty Kat, I think a hot meal, a warm bath, and long sleep will help."

Nodding, she let him guide her back along the path that led to the shop, or the house, depending on which turn you took.

Sometimes your world can tilt a bit and throw you off balance, so you need to stop and make some minor adjustments. This—this wasn't tilting. Her entire world and everything she thought she knew had just spun out of control and flipped in more directions than she could count. She was numb, inside and out.

Chapter Eight

Gage smacked the top of the case again with the handle of the screwdriver.

"Maybe you have it backwards," Jake joked as he held the wires up out of the way.

Giving him a brief glance, he tried again. "If the crew that runs this equipment didn't try to fix shit they break, it wouldn't get bent out of shape."

"Want me to read them the riot act when I take it back?"

Shaking his head, Gage sighed. "Because they'd listen this time like they did the last ten times?" He heard it finally snap into place. "No sense wasting your breath." He checked the wires running from the side making sure none of them were pinched.

Jake straightened. "Hey, Coop's back."

"About fucking time," Gage muttered under his breath.

"Kels doesn't look so good."

Straightening up, he hit his head on the casing as he turned around. When he saw her, he started to go toward them but Cooper gave a quick shake of his head telling him to keep his distance.

Kelsey walked slowly as Cooper guided her, an arm around her slumped shoulders. Her eyes were lost and it made his heart jerked in his chest to see her looking so defeated.

He stood beside Jake, who was also dumbstruck by her appearance, and watched as Cooper helped her into one of the pickups.

"What the hell did he tell her?" Jake spoke in a hushed tone.

Gage inhaled, trying to breath past the tightness in his chest. "From the looks of it, everything."

"Holy hell," Jake shook his head, "it's heartbreaking."

Gage could only nod as he watched Cooper hug her where she sat in the truck. He wanted it to be him to comfort her, but he respected the elder's decision and stayed where he was.

Cooper closed the door and turned around, with a motion he called Jake over.

Jake looked at Gage.

He nodded. "Take her home, Jake." He wiped at the grease on his hand. "Don't leave until you make sure she's all right."

"Will do." Jake went over quickly and spoke to Cooper before he climbed in the driver's side.

Gage could see him talking to her as he turned the truck around. Jake would look after her.

Turning, he closed the access panel they'd been working on and waited for Cooper to come over.

"*That* was the hardest thing I have *ever* done," Cooper said with his voice breaking. "If your dad was here, Alpha or not, I'd kick his ass for keeping all of that from her." He shook his head, "If I could bring Phillip back from the dead, I'd kick his ass too." He stopped and stood there with his hands on his hips looking at the ground.

Gage squatted down and leaned back against a tire. "I take it you told her everything?"

Cooper dropped down and sat beside him, pulling his cap off and turning it over and over in his hands. "Yeah. She knows what happened to her folks, what happens when she hits her first cycle," he snorted, "how fucking nuts she's making you boys…" He pulled the cap back on with jerky movements, "and she knows she's your mate."

Part of Gage was thrilled to hear that but the piece of him that tensed wasn't sure if it was good. "Do I want to know any details?"

Cooper blew out a breath and stared across the yard. "Well she thought at first going away would fix everything."

Gage was sure his heart stopped beating as he gave the older man a panicked look.

"Don't worry; I talked her out of that." He gave him a sympathetic look. "If it means anything, she sees the others as brothers."

"And me?" Gage tried to swallow with a dry mouth.

Cooper shook his head. "Not you, but…" he held up a hand, "she's not going to just accept it. I can tell you that right now. *All* of this is beyond her control, not a damn thing she can do about it, but *you*…" He pointed a finger at him, "where things are going? She believes she has a choice."

Gage closed his eyes. "She does have a choice." He gave Cooper a serious look. "If it kills me, I will stay away from her if that's what she really wants." He exhaled in a slow steady stream, trying to calm his heart rate.

"She's not going to know what she wants for a while, Gage. Shit, she just found out about her parents, she'll need to mourn them all over again."

Nodding, Gage opened his mouth to speak when the truck came skidding back into the yard. Jake was out of it and slamming the door before it stopped. They heard his cursing as he stalked across the yard heading for the side gate, clothes strewn about as he went.

"Shit," Gage muttered and went to get up.

"Let him run it off. He may not be mated to her, but he loves her in his own way." Cooper turned and gave him a steady look. "We all do." Getting up slowly, he brushed the dust from his jeans. "You push her and you're going to end up with an uprising within the clan."

Gage dropped down to sit with his knees drawn up, resting his wrists over them. He looked up at the man who kept him steady at all times. "I know, Coop. I won't rush her, and I'll never hurt her."

Cooper nodded and looked down at him without speaking for several moments. "I think I'll go join Jake for a run and keep an eye on him."

Gage just nodded. If he didn't have a delivery coming, he would have followed them, but with Blair and Noah on a delivery and Gary gone to pick up supplies, he would have to stay in two leg form and wait for someone to return.

He sat for quite a while after Cooper vanished between the trees. This was not the homecoming he had planned for Kelsey. Pulling his phone out, he brought up her number and started typing.

Are you okay?

Clasping the phone between his hands, he hung his wrists off his knees and looked at the trees. His cat was strangely quiet and he wasn't sure why. It was unusual for him not to know exactly what his feline side was thinking. Shaking his head, he leaned his head back against the tire, since when was he and his cat two different entities?

His phone beeped, he almost dropped it trying to read Kelsey's reply.

No.

Cursing, he typed. He really wanted to go to her, but he didn't want to crowd her right now. Reading what he'd typed, he cursed again and deleted it. He retyped his message and hit send.

Call me if you need me. I'll come home.

Holding it in two hands, he stared at the screen willing her to answer him. It was taking every bit of restraint he had to stay put and not go see for himself how she was doing. The screen lit up.

It's okay.

What the hell did that mean? He squinted at the message. Holding it tightly, he hit the keys, his big fingers hitting the wrong letters making him even more frustrated as he had to keep correcting.

KELSEY IF YOU NEED ME PLEASE CALL

Nodding, he hit send and blew out a breath. Jerking his head around, he stared at the trees, what was taking them so long to come back?

Her reply came back, one word.

Fine.

Growling, Gage grit hit teeth and sent her one more.

Get some rest.

He wanted to punch something. He didn't need to see her to know how much pain she was in. Everything she knew had changed in the last few days. When Cooper had brought her back she had looked like she was in shock. As he was slowly getting up, it dawned on him that the frustration and anger wasn't even stirring his cat. Normally his cat reacted as soon as he saw her, hell, even thought about her. The fact that it was so quiet had Gage even more distressed. For years he'd been told about how connected mates were, but he thought they'd at least have to *be* mated for this to happen... *What is going on?* For the last several years he could always feel the animal inside and now it was nothing but an eerie stillness. Pacing across the yard, he kept an eye on the treeline, hoping Jake or Cooper came back soon. For once, it was frustration that had him needing to run.

When his phone rang, he dropped it trying to see who was calling. Cursing, he picked it up to see it wasn't Kelsey, but Devin. Exhaling, he answered it, "Devin."

"Gage. Have you heard from Calum?"

Gage frowned, it wasn't unusual for Devin to be blunt and get straight to the point, but he sounded urgent. Devin never sounded that way.

'No. Why?"

"I got a message from him last night saying he had found the location. I haven't been able to reach him."

Rubbing a hand across his forehead, Gage stared at the ground. "Maybe he's in a dead zone."

Devin made a sound of annoyance, which was pretty much how Gage felt too. "That's possible. He's in the middle of nowhere in some back-mountain country..."

"I'm sure he'll get a hold of you when he can." He kicked the dirt under his boot. It wasn't like Devin to chase people. In fact, he was known to go weeks, months even, without any sort of communication. Had Rayne changed him this much, Gage had to wonder. "Is something going on?"

Devin sighed loudly into the phone. "Yeah. Tomas has upped his game and has been making some new moves."

Gage straightened a chill going up his spine. "Like what?"

"He's not staying close to the boarder."

"He's done that before, Dev..."

"Not like this." There were voices in the background. "Listen, I've called in extra bodies to watch over the camp."

Squinting, Gage stared off toward the trees again. "He's that close?"

"A few attempts have been made close by."

Close by where Devin was could be hundreds of miles away. He didn't exactly live in a populated area. "Is everyone okay?"

Devin made a hissing noise. "Yeah. Several clan families have settled here at the camp, ones that don't have a lot of males..." That told Gage that Tomas was targeting females. "We're contacting all the alphas so they can take precautions."

Just what Gage didn't need right now, with his life already a mess. "Did you talk to Dad?"

"I just did. He's going to head over to Bruce's and stay with them. He said you'd keep an eye on things where you are."

It made sense, half the females from Gage's clan lived in a small town with Bruce, his father's second, overseeing things. Gage only had to keep an eye on five males. Kelsey would be watched over regardless.

"Anyone would have to have balls of steel to show up here."

"That's what I thought too," Devin agreed. "Rayne and I are going to be heading to a few remote locations," he sighed, "a few clans of mine aren't reachable by phone."

That wasn't shocking; wolves seemed to like it that way. "Are you traveling alone?" Gage may be distracted by his own personal issues, but he still knew his priority was to stand beside Devin.

"I don't want to pull anyone from here, the more of us keeping an eye on things the better. We'll be okay with just the two of us. I wanted Calum to meet us…"

"I could send Blair," Gage rubbed the back of his neck feeling the muscles bunch tighter.

"No. Keep everyone there." Devin chuckled. "I won't mind a bit of time alone with Rayne."

Gage felt a twinge of what he could only label as jealously go through him. He wanted what Devin now had.

Devin's tone was serious again. "I'd ask how things are going there, but your tone says it all."

Rubbing his neck again, Gage tried to ease some of the tension. "We told her everything, Dev." All muscles in his body tensed as he said it.

There was a long silence before Devin spoke quietly. "That's a lot to digest all at once."

'Yes, it is. She should have been told long before now."

"How's she doing?"

Turning, he looked in the direction the house was, as if he could see through the trees. "I'll have to get back to you on that."

Devin let out a loud sigh. "Listen, we're going to be near there next week, we could stop in…" Gage could hear a female talking softly in the back ground. "Rayne thinks if she talks to her it might help. She understands everything in your world suddenly changing."

Closing his eyes, Gage reached for a trace of calm. Not finding any, he opened them and nodded. "It can't hurt."

"Is Noah all right? If his being there is..."

"Noah's fine here." Gage exhaled loudly. "He had a rough moment last night, but..." he rolled his shoulders, "he has really connected with Kelsey," his cat finally stirred at that thought and Gage almost sighed in relief to feel it again.

"What do you mean connected?"

Staring down at the dirt, he kicked his toe in it a few times. "I think she's probably the first female shifter he's ever been near that's not afraid of him."

Devin muttered several obscenities under his breath. "Do you trust him near her, Gage? That's what it comes down to."

Clenching his jaw a few times, he thought about it. Reaching past the jealously and tension, he nodded slowly. "Yeah, I do. He's just as protective of her as the rest of us."

Devin sighed. "Okay, he stays there for now."

The sound of a truck had Gage turn toward the gates. Blair and Noah were back. "I gotta let you go. Keep me up to date, Dev. I may be distracted, but I still know my place."

"I will. If you hear from Calum, tell him to get his ass home."

Gage snorted. "Right. He's going to listen to me."

"I worry about him. He's a little *too* in touch with his wild side."

Gage thought about how much time Calum had spent in his cat form in the last few years. "I'm sure he's fine. You can't tell me you stayed on two legs all the years you hid in the wilderness."

"I wasn't..." there was a long pause, "point taken."

Gage shook his head. "Speaking of the wild..."

"Yeah. Go. I'll talk to you soon."

"Be careful."

"Always am."

Chapter Nine

Gage hung up and turned to the two men walking toward him. Noah had a guarded look on his face. Gage had no one to blame but himself after growling at him earlier.

The easy-going expression on Blair's face faded as they got closer. He was always able to sense another shifter's mood. "What did we miss?" he asked cautiously.

Jamming the phone into his pocket, Gage shook his head trying to decide where to start. "More than I'd like." He gave Noah a nod in greeting, hoping the informal acknowledgment would be all that was required to put him at ease again, or as much as Noah could be. "Cooper had a talk with Kelsey."

Blair paused in his step and looked at him. "What did he tell her?"

"Everything."

Blair swore under his breath. "Even about her folks?"

Gage nodded.

Noah looked from one to the other. "What about them?"

Blair looked to Gage asking permission, he gave an abrupt nod.

"Tomas senior's men killed her parents. We're pretty sure they were going for her mother at the time."

Noah spun, his back facing them and paced a few feet away. Stopping he put his hands on his hips and dropped his head down. "Fuck," he uttered viciously. A breath later he stiffened and was composed again.

Gage had to wonder if they'd beat him into masking his emotions or if he'd learned how to do it to cope.

"Is she all right?" Noah's voice shook as he asked.

Not sure how to answer, Gage decided the truth was best. "I'm not sure. It was a lot to take in."

"There's more?" Noah looked over his shoulder at him.

Nodding, Gage crossed his arms over his chest. "He told her about mating," he blew out a breath, "and about me."

"Well shit!" Blair shook his head, a look of disbelief on his face. "When I suggested telling her, I didn't mean everything in one sentence."

"I had Jake take her home..." he glanced at the treeline, silently hoping they'd come back so he could find out more, "he came back and took off." He motioned to the clothes on the ground.

"Shit!" Blair threw up his hands and then waved them around. "Have you talked to her?"

Gage shook his head. "No. I didn't want to crowd her. I messaged her and she doesn't seem to be in a talkative mood."

"Fuck," Blair gripped the sides of his head and closed his eyes. "Seven fucking years we tippy-toe around things only to have it blow up..."

"I'd like to go check on her." Noah interrupted.

Blair stopped and dropped his hands; he looked from Noah to Gage.

Gage ignored the startled look on Blair's face. He had fences to mend with the man now looking at him. He also knew Kelsey would be less likely to rip a strip off Noah because he hadn't been hiding secrets from her. He nodded slowly. "Let her know you're there, if she wants to talk, she'll come to you."

Blair gave him a startled look.

Exhaling, Gage dropped his hands and jammed them in his pockets. "Noah won't be on her blacklist," he waved a hand between Blair and himself, "we will be. We kept a lot from her for too long." Blair sighed, his expression fading into defeat. "And, if anyone will recognize Tomas's *associate's* scents, it's going to be Noah."

Blair's expression lit up, he nodded. "That's true."

Gage turned to face Noah. "If you scent *anything* that shouldn't be here, you let us know immediately."

Noah's shoulders straightened a look of determination on his face. "I will." He gave Blair a quick look and then turned to head to the path.

Both men stood there and watched him leave. Gage waited until he disappeared into the trees before turning to Blair. "Devin's put every shifter clan on alert."

Looking startled, Blair nodded. "Does he need any help?"

Gage knew that in his heart, Blair was a warrior, a force to be reckoned with when his easy-going persona was peeled away. It had always surprised him that he hadn't wanted to be alpha of a clan. "I offered him your protection, but he wants you to stay here. I can't say I'm disappointed with that. Kelsey's been through enough, having you here gives me a little less to worry about right now."

Nodding, Blair blew out a breath. "You know I'd tear *anyone* to pieces if they ever did anything to hurt her?"

The tone put Gage's cat on alert. Was he making a statement or was he warning him? Straightening to his full height, Gage looked Blair in the eye. Keeping his tone low, he gave him a serious look. "I know."

With an abrupt nod, Blair looked toward the trees. "Go run. I can sense your frustration and it's making my skin crawl."

With a half grin, Gage turned to head to the trees.

"Gage?"

He paused and looked over his shoulder at him.

"You should know..." Blair paused and took a deep breath, "if Kelsey accepts you, I'm going away."

Feeling like someone had just smacked him in the face; Gage turned around and looked at the man he'd known since he was two.

Blair gave him an uneasy grin, something that seemed so out of place on his face. "I won't interfere; I know true mates are rare." He shrugged. "I couldn't help falling for her" he gave a strangled laugh, "Who wouldn't? She stormed into the shop and bested us all on the rigs, never gave up..." he shook his head and looked down at the ground for a moment before straightening and giving him a serious look. "I know its shitty timing and all, but I thought you should know."

So many thoughts hit Gage all at once, his knees felt weak. "I, ah..." He puffed out his cheeks and exhaled all at once. "I didn't know." What was he supposed to say to shit like this? He'd been side-by-side with this man all his life and he hadn't noticed.

"You were a little preoccupied." Blair had never looked abashed before that Gage could recall, but he did now. "The guys know, well I'm pretty sure Coop suspects, but Gary and Jake know."

Heading spinning, Gage opened his mouth and then shut it again. His cat chose now to wake up completely. He was torn in half. He loved this man like a brother, but his mate, *his* mate...

"Look," Blair walked toward him, emotion playing across his face. "I didn't tell you to change things," he waved a hand between them, "I just wanted you to know, to understand..."

"It's a bit of game changer, Blair." Gage whispered in disbelief.

Blair nodded. "I know." He crossed his arms over his chest, looking uncomfortable. "I love you like a brother, I'd do anything for you, for our clan, but..."

Gage swallowed the lump in his throat. He knew what he was saying and his cat clawed at him that this man wanted his mate, but his heart pounded in his chest understanding what it must have taken for Blair to tell him. "I know." Taking a deep breath, he looked straight into Blair's pale eyes; he could see he was as conflicted as he was. "*If...*" he almost choked on the word, "if she doesn't accept me, I won't be able to..." he'd thought about it for seven years, but saying it was harder, "stay here or where ever she is." He swallowed again. "It will make it easier knowing someone..." He took another deep breath, shaking his head.

"I got it, Gage."

Nodding, Gage huffed out a breath. "I won't hurt her, Blair. I'd leave if it ever came to that."

Blair's jaw clenched a few times before he spoke. "I hope so." Waving a hand toward the trees, Blair blew out a breath. "Get out of here. I need some alone time."

No shit, was all Gage could think. As he walked toward the trees, he knew he was feeling a small piece of what Kelsey must be. He'd had no idea, never suspected once. All the guys loved Kelsey and until a few moments ago, he'd thought it was in a brotherly way. Shaking his head, he pulled his shirt over his head and tossed it to the ground. He'd known Blair talked to Kelsey often while she was away at school, but then all of them had called her from time to time. *All of them but you,* his cat reminded him.

He was thankful the clans, for the most part were civilized, if he'd had to fight Blair for Kelsey...well, it actually scared him to think about it. Kicking off his boots, he cursed fate. Would it have been too much to ask for to find his mate and make it simple? He reached for his cat as he shucked off his jeans, he wanted to run as fast and hard as he could, clear all of this from his mind, a short reprieve before he came back and faced reality, because he knew one thing for sure, it was going to be a bitch.

Chapter Ten

Gage fought to control the jealousy that hit him as soon as he spotted Noah sitting on the porch. He'd sent the man here for Christ sakes. Noah stood up when he saw him and came down steps toward him. Gage glanced at the house.

"I only saw her for a minute. She brought me out a sandwich and drink then went back inside." He motioned to Gage's truck. "I cleaned the inside of your truck to kill time." He cleared his throat and looked around. "Thanks for trusting me." He gave Gage and uncomfortable look. "I've...I never thought I'd feel," he shrugged like he couldn't find the right words, "protective like this." He motioned to the house.

It dawned on Gage then that he'd have to contend with Noah's feelings toward Kelsey as well as the rest of the guys. He snorted. "Yeah, seems to be going around." He rubbed his chest that still felt tight after Blair's confession.

Noah winced. "Ah, Blair."

Head jerking up he looked at him. "You knew?"

Noah shrugged. "His pheromones are off the charts whenever she's in sight."

Gage shook his head, he felt inadequate suddenly.

SCENT

Noah gave him a brief smile before a serious mask covered his face. "When you have to suppress the urge to shift, it seems to enhance all of your other senses."

Hearing that made him feel a little better, but not by much. He'd known Blair all his life and still had no clue how he'd missed all the signs, senses or not. "It's been a hell of a last few days."

Noah nodded. "You guys aren't boring, I'll give you that."

Grinning, Gage shook his head. "Apparently not." He gripped Noah's shoulder and squeezed before dropping his hand down. "Get out of here. I have to go face reality."

"It's been quiet for about an hour, I think she may have gone to sleep. She's distraught, Gage."

Gage nodded, not even questioning that Noah could hear what was going on inside the house. Later, when life settled a bit, or as much as it would, he had to find out more about this man he'd taken in. "Thanks."

Watching Noah leave, he sighed and turned and looked at the house. "Time to man up." He whispered out loud and he took long strides toward the porch.

He saw the wrapped sandwich sitting on the table. The idea that she'd made him one shocked him. He should have stopped and eaten it, after running for so long he was shaky, but he needed to see her before he could think about eating.

Using his sensitive hearing, he listened to see where she was. Heading to the living room, he stopped in the doorway and looked at her asleep on the couch. She looked angelic when she slept, face relaxed and so lovely. As he got closer he could see the slight puffiness around her eyes. He didn't know why it startled him to realize she had cried herself to sleep.

This wasn't what he wanted for her. He only wanted his mate to be happy, to not have a care in the world. Instead she was wrecked with shock and living under the threat that seemed to plague his kind more often than not. Pausing, he realized he'd have to tell her about what Devin had told him.

He could save her the worry, but keeping anything a secret from her at this point wouldn't do anything to winning her favor.

Blowing out a breath, he moved over and squatted down beside the couch. She was curled up on one end, clutching a pillow to her chest and his heart jerked with pain to see her that way. Her eyes opened slowly, fogged with confusion.

"Gage," she whispered.

Reaching out, his hand shaking, he brushed the hair back from her face. "I'm here."

"You should have told me." Her voice was hoarse with emotion.

He looked into her eyes and could see the pain and betrayal. Nodding, he dropped his hand away. "I know, honey."

She continued to look at him for several breath-holding moments. "I'll never forgive your parents for keeping this from me."

A chill went up his spine at sound of conviction in her voice. Not trusting his voice, he only nodded. As her warm palm touched his cheek, he closed his eyes for a second at the feel of her touch.

"I'm working in the office for a few days." She dropped her hand and slid up on the couch. "I don't want to see any of you right now."

Gage dropped to his knees as she avoided touching him and got up. He listened to her steps as she went up the stairs, not moving until he heard her door close. Well, that wasn't the outcome he'd wanted. Shaking his head, he pushed to his feet and stood up. The silence in the room engulfed him. Had he really expected her to be all right with everything? For seven years he'd deluded himself with the notion she'd find out and come to him with open arms. Clearly the real Kelsey was nothing like the one that had lived in Gage's head all these years.

Turning, he glanced at the door and then sighed. He needed to stay put for the night and going for another run wasn't going to change a damn thing. He trudged toward the kitchen. He had no appetite but had learned early on that if he didn't put food in at regular intervals, controlling his animal was a hard thing to do.

As he sat at the table, not even tasting the food in his mouth, he tried to sort through his thoughts. It was impossible as Kelsey, Noah, and now Blair swam around in his brain along with the threats of Tomas being on the prowl. Pushing back from the table, he growled in frustration and got up to head for the shower. Just having one thing go right would be a fucking blessing right now.

When she came into the kitchen, Gage kept his head down and tried to focus on the words on the pages in front of him. He'd felt her stiffen as soon as she entered the room. She had wanted space and as much as he'd give anything for her to have her wish, he couldn't back down when it came to her safety. All he had to do was figure out how to tell her that the nightmare didn't stop when her parents had died.

"Coffee's fresh," he said softly.

Sitting back, he watched her get a cup, her movements jerky. She was pissed he was here and part of him couldn't blame her. Closing the folder, he stood up. "Listen, I know you don't want to see me right now," his chest tightened, "but I need to tell you something…"

She turned and gave him a startled look, like she couldn't believe there was more.

He lifted a hand to get her attention before she started. "It's important, Kelsey, or I'd already be at the shop."

Nodding, she gave him an impatient look. She wanted him out of her sight, like ten minutes ago. "Devin…" he rubbed his jaw, "Coop explained who Devin was right?" She nodded, her jaw set. "Okay. Devin called and all of the clans are being put on alert…"

Her expression changed to concern. "You mean all the types of shifters or just ours?"

He had to give her credit for trying to understand. "All of them." He hesitated for a second trying to figure out how to explain this to her. "Tomas has been trying to abduct females…"

She physically jolted like he'd hit her.

Taking a few steps in her direction, he stopped and bit back the desire to shelter her in her arms. "I doubt he'd ever be near here, but we're not taking any chances. None of the clans will."

She took a shaky breath and hugged her arms around her waist. "Why hasn't something been done about these people? There *are* law enforcement…"

Gage shook his head. "And tell them what, honey? That a criminal organization abducts people that can shift into animals?" He lifted his hands motioning to her and then himself. "One-forms…" he paused when she frowned at him, "normal people that don't shift. They don't know anything about our world, Kelsey; it's safer that way, for both sides."

Rubbing her hands up and down her arms, she nodded and exhaled in an overwhelmed way. "I'll take your word for it." She stared at him from across the kitchen, but he felt like she wasn't really looking at him. "So, you're telling me this so I'll be cautious?"

"And, I'm not keeping anything from you again, even if I'm told it's for your own good." He almost held his breath waiting for her to reply.

The glazed look left her eyes as she focused on him. "Thank you, for that." She cleared her throat. "I'm going to go through the office and see if I can put my education to use and help the shop."

He nodded abruptly, "That would be great. I'm a bit of a dunce when it comes to all of that."

Her expression didn't change at the quip. "Is there anything else I *need* to know right now?"

There's the door, use it. He rubbed a hand over his chest; it was the hardest thing to stand this far from her. For years, he'd pushed her away on purpose and now he'd give anything to just hold her for a moment. "The guys will be lurking about keeping an eye on things, so don't hold it against them when they're under orders."

Kelsey regarded him for a long awkward moment before she nodded slowly. "Okay." She turned her back to him and went back to getting her cup of coffee.

Gage had never been dismissed so efficiently in his life. Staring at her for a few seconds, he turned and walked toward the door. How long would she be like this, he wondered as he stepped out onto the porch. It was hard enough finally being around her, but the icy aura just hurt, plain and simple.

Gage walked into the shop, looking forward to the distraction of work, to find all five men standing there looking at the phone Blair held. Frowning, he went over. "What's going on?"

Blair gave him a strange look. "I've been summoned."

He glanced at Cooper, he mouthed *Kelsey*. Gage's eyebrows shot up, he wasn't sure whether to be angry that she wanted to talk to Blair and not him or thankful that it was Blair and not him.

Blair exhaled loudly. "I think," he said in a quiet serious tone, "I'm about to have my furry tail shoved down my throat."

Gage couldn't even feel angry with Blair; he didn't envy him in this moment. Then again if Kelsey would at least yell at him, Gage was sure it would feel better than the cold shoulder she'd been giving him.

Tossing the rag on the tool cart, Blair gave him a skeptical look and then turned and walked out the door.

Gary whistled. "Kind of makes me glad I'm an antisocial, shy man."

Jake laughed. "If she's going to line us up and stab us one at a time, I'll make sure you're included."

Noah looked from one to the other. "You guys have fun with that, I'm going to go out and try to figure out the dozer."

Cooper laughed and patted him on the back. "I'll help."

Gage stood with the other two men and watched them leave. "I guess Noah's safe."

"How was she this morning?" Jake asked, moving over to the cart Blair had abandoned and picking up a wrench.

"Kelsey?" Gage asked, knowing exactly who he meant. He sighed. "I couldn't even see her for the six-foot-thick wall of ice she has surrounding her now."

"Shit," Gary muttered and left without another word.

Jake watched him leave and then turned to Gage. "This is going to get worse before it gets better, isn't it?"

Gage just gave him a blank look. He'd been stuck in worse for seven years, what was a little while longer? The only thing he hoped was that it wouldn't last forever.

Chapter Eleven

⊰⊱

Kelsey let the hot water run over her for a few minutes. She had hoped that it would feel soothing, but it wasn't working. As soon as Gage had walked out the door, she'd bypassed the coffee and climbed in the shower. When she'd opened her eyes this morning, it had been as if she was stuck in a strange world, one that felt suffocating. There was so much to digest; she didn't think she was going to be able to do it without choking.

Flipping the taps off, she grabbed a towel and got out. Wrapping another around her head, she stepped up to the mirror and wiped the fog off it. Studying her reflection, she didn't see anything she hadn't been seeing every day and yet she was supposed to believe that the face looking after her was some sort of tiger. What would she look like? Sighing, she turned around and began to dry off.

It was absolutely unforgiveable that all of this had been kept from her for so long. Yes, she understood the reasoning behind Ed and Beth not telling her right away. It probably would have crushed her completely at that point in her life, but to let it go on this long? There was no excuse good enough.

Tossing the towel over the shower rod, she stared at the wall. She couldn't believe the men that had been her whole world since she was fifteen had kept this from her.

Thinking about Gage, just made her feel more confused than ever, so she tried hard to keep him out of her thoughts completely. Gary, she understood, getting two words out of him on a good day was performing nothing short of a miracle, but Jake and Cooper? She was close to them. How could they go every day without telling her? And Blair? Oh, she saw red when she thought of him keeping this from her. They'd talked once a week while she was away, sometimes more.

That was three years of conversations. She'd only seen him a couple times when she'd come home and it hadn't been long enough, but he was good at his job so some crews requested him when Ed had to send someone, but still…

Pulling on her jeans, she scowled at the woman in the mirror. How could he talk to her about every bloody thing under the sun and never, *ever* once mention any of this? With a growl of frustration, she dug around in her housecoat for her phone. She didn't even pause when she brought up Blair's number and typed three words.

COME HERE NOW

She hit send and tossed the phone on the counter. Pulling on her t-shirt, she grabbed the phone and went back out to the kitchen.

It took some doing on her part to be sitting at the table looking calm when Blair slowly walked into the room.

"Hey, sweetie, how are you doing?" He glanced at the cup she held between both hands and in his easy glide, moved behind her to the coffee pot.

She sat there and waited, not saying a word. Actually, not even knowing what to say that wasn't going to come out sounding scornful and vicious. He came back around to sit at the end of table so they were only a foot apart.

He took a sip and then set the cup down and looked at her. His eyes moved over her face, she tried to read what he was thinking, but Blair was too good at masking his thoughts for her to get a glimpse.

He gave her one of his lopsided grins, "Are you all right? I wanted to come see you last night, but…"

"Why didn't you tell me? You of all people, the one I counted on the most…" she shook her head and looked down at her cup, "why?"

Blair blew out a breath and reached for her hand, she pulled it off the table and clasped it in her lap with her other one.

"I wanted to, I really did." He sighed and leaned back in the chair, watching her without blinking. If she hadn't been used to it, she would have been bothered, but it was just a Blair thing. "I almost did so many times." Running a hand across the side of his face, he sighed again. "I'm sorry, sweetie." He shook his head. "More than you will ever know."

In all the years she had known him, she had never heard him use that soft, angst filled tone. "I don't know what to think, Blair." She got up and went over to the counter and leaned against it. "Everyone that was important in my world…" she gave a frustrated growl when she felt her eyes tearing up again, "everyone that *was* my world lied to me." She squeezed her eyes shut and breathed deeply to keep control of her emotions. "You lied to me for years." She looked back at him.

"I never once lied to you, Kelsey." His eyes held hers. "I didn't tell you, but I sure as hell didn't lie to you."

Taking a deep breath, she held it and closed her eyes again. He was right, but that didn't make what he did okay. Opening them, she blew out the breath and glared at him. "I can't believe you didn't tell me."

He sat there, looking at her, a pained expression on his face. "What can I do?"

She shook her head, a sound of disbelief escaping her mouth. That was so typically Blair. He always thought he could fix things. Shaking her head, she hugged her arms around her waist. "I can't even sort it all out Blair, and you sure as hell can't make it all better."

Leaning forward, he rested his arms on the table and dropped his head into his hands. She could feel the anxiety coming off him, but wasn't able to stir up enough empathy at the moment to do anything. "Finding out about my parents was…"

His head jerked up. "You were devastated when you came here. How the hell were we supposed to tell you what really happened to them?" He motioned in the air. "How could we tell you without telling you everything after that point?" With his brows furrowed he studied her for a few seconds. "Could you have handled all of this when you were sixteen? Seriously, maybe finding out you were a shifter at sixteen would have been kind of cool, but finding out about your folks?" He made an exasperated noise in his throat. "How about finding out that a man was your mate? Not a teenager like you, but a fully-grown man?"

Kelsey knew he wasn't saying anything that wasn't the truth, but she still couldn't see past them not telling her when she was eighteen or twenty, even last year. "Maybe I couldn't handle it then, but I'm twenty-three now. I'm a big girl and *someone* should have told me." She yelled the last part at him.

Blair was on his feet, closing the distance between them in a few long strides. "We couldn't…"

Kelsey snorted. "Couldn't? That's *crap* and you know it!" He was right in her face then but she refused to back off. "I've been thinking I was losing my mind, Blair," she was still yelling, "and you of all people *knew* that!" She shoved at his chest, only getting more frustrated because she didn't even move him. "You talked to me every week for three years and said *nothing*." The tears were rolling down her cheeks now, but she refused to wipe them away. Let him see them, let him feel as helpless as I feel right now, she thought.

"I couldn't," his tone was low and controlled.

She stared up at him, his pale eyes blurring through the tears. "Wouldn't," she whispered and then turned her back on him to stare out the window.

Smacking his hand down on the counter beside her, he pulled her by the arm and turned her to face him. "*We* were under orders from our Alpha. I get that you don't understand how that works, but when your alpha gives you an order you damn well follow it."

She had never heard so much emotion from him before, his voice shook with it. Blinking, she brought him into focus as she struggled to understand what he was saying. Shaking her head, the tears flooded her vision again, she couldn't understand why Ed would do that to her. Her shoulders began to shake as she tried to control the sobs that were building inside her. "I..." She didn't get another word out before she was crushed against his chest, his arms surrounding her.

Later she would regret it, but she fell apart in the shelter of his arms, sobs wrenching from her body and tears flowing.

Blair just stood there and let her, his hand rubbed slowly up and down her back as he cradled her head into the warmth of his chest. "I'm so sorry," he whispered to her over and over.

Kelsey didn't know how much time went by until she couldn't cry any more, and then she just stood there feeling completely drained. Her cheek stuck to his wet shirt. "No one told me you were ordered not to tell me." She leaned back and looked up at him. "Why wouldn't you guys tell me that instead of letting me think otherwise?"

Lifting his shirt, he wiped her cheeks off with it and gave her a grieved look. "We're just dumb males, sweetie, who knows why we do half the crazy shit we do."

She smiled, she couldn't help it. Inhaling, she stopped when a strange smell came to her. It was nothing like she'd smelled before, wholly masculine but unusual. Leaning forward she fought back her embarrassment and sniffed at Blair's neck. He stiffened, his hands sliding slowly down her arms and then gradually dropping away. "Um…" she looked up at him again, his pale blues eyes watching her cautiously. "Why can I smell you?"

Taking a shaky breath, he stepped back from her and wiped a hand down over his wet shirt. "It's…" he shrugged but didn't look at her, "probably just your new senses kicking in a bit." Tucking his shirt into his jeans, he looked at her from beneath his long pale lashes. "I wouldn't worry about. It will come and go for a while and then you'll get used to it when it's enhanced all the time."

Blowing out a breath, she brushed the hair back from her face. "Well, at least you don't smell bad."

He smiled a stiff grin. "Good to know." Clearing his throat, he hunched down and cupped the side of her face. "Are we okay now?"

Inhaling slowly, she closed her eyes and stood there for a moment trying to see what she was feeling. Opening her eyes, she nodded. "As okay as possible right now."

Dropping his hand, he tucked his hand into his pocket and gave her one of his patented charming Blair smiles. "Good." His eyes searched her face for a few seconds. "You need to eat, Kelsey. You can't skip a single meal right now."

She nodded. "Yeah, Gage said something about that." She shrugged, "I'm not really hungry…"

"Doesn't matter," he looked around the kitchen, "even something light will be better than nothing at all."

Kelsey sighed. "I got it." Picking up her cup, she sipped to see if the coffee was still warm. "Is there anything else other than not eating that's a no-no?" Would the things she needed to learn ever stop, she wondered.

Blair cleared his throat and moved past her to the fridge. "Well, yeah there's…" he opened the fridge and leaned in it. Pulling out eggs, he set the carton on the stove and then grabbed the milk. "There's one thing," he glanced at her hesitantly over his shoulder.

"What?" She didn't know if she wanted to know with him being hesitant to tell her. Blair didn't do hesitant; he did straight on blunt, nothing less. Grabbing a pan from the cupboard, he knew where everything was here, she thought, he set it on the stove and then turned and looked at her.

"Don't, uh," he looked down at the floor for a second and then back to her, "don't go sniffing any of the guys right now," he motioned to her, "not smelling as inviting as you do." He shook his head. "Jesus, if Gage had seen that he would have snapped my neck before he even realized he'd moved."

Kelsey's cheeked went hot and her jaw dropped. She slapped a hand over her mouth and then dropped it again. "I-I didn't, I'm not sure why…" fanning her face with her hand, she stared at him, eyes wide.

"Hey," he moved across the floor and grasped her shoulders lightly, "Hey. It's okay. It's only me and you didn't know." He rubbed his hands up and down her arms a few times until she nodded, then he released her and stepped back over to the stove.

"I'm sorry, Blair, I completely forgot about *that*."

He chuckled. "You say *that* like it's a disease." Glancing over his shoulder he winked at her, "its animal magnetism at its best, babe."

Rolling her eyes at him, she leaned her hip against the counter and sipped the cool bitter liquid. "I guess I'm safe with you, huh? Nothing sexier than your little sister sniffing at you." She grinned, until he stiffened and turned slowly.

"I've never seen you as my sister, sweetie, just off limits."

She stood there with her mouth hanging open, not able to form any words.

"Close your mouth, flies will land on your tongue." He turned back to the stove.

Shaking her head, she set the cup down on the counter and moved to see his face. "You just decided to tell me this out of the blue?"

He shrugged and kept his focus on the eggs in the pan. "I wasn't going to give you another reason to say I lied to you or kept something from you." He glanced at her out of the corner of his eye. "But, as of right now, for years actually, you've always been off limits, regardless of my feelings."

In the last few days, she'd had all sorts of information dumped on her, but this honestly shocked her. "Because of this mate thing?" She hadn't realized she spoke out loud.

"Second thing that's a law you just don't break, after following an alpha order..." he made eye contact with her for a second, "is, you don't mess with someone's mate."

Sighing, Kelsey crossed her arms over her chest and watched him stir the eggs around in the pan. "I don't even know how to feel about that right now. It's still out of my grasp."

Turning the burner off, he set the pan aside and reached around her to get a plate. Scooping the eggs onto the plate, he held it out to her. "Never having found my mate, I can't tell you from experience," she took the plate as he turned her toward the table. "All I can tell you is your cat, *you*, will know if he's what you want."

She sat down and watched him get her a fork. Handing it to her, he turned back to the counter and grabbed her mug. She took a small bite of the eggs and waited for him to come back to the table. "I had a mad crush on Gage when I was seventeen."

Sitting in the chair at the end of the table again, he nodded. "I remember quite clearly."

Studying him, she took another bite and tried to recall if she'd said something to him to tell him.

He smirked. "You didn't hide your feelings, they were obvious to me." He shrugged. "And I was the lucky idiot that ran interference for him the most while he was struggling to let you grow up before he went all mate-like on you."

Her cheeks heated again. She'd never thought of that side of it. At the time Gage spent most of his time avoiding her or pissing her off. Sighing, she set the fork down. "I've spent years wondering," she glanced over at him but couldn't hold his stare, "I thought maybe he doesn't see me as a sister..." She shook her head not sure how to finish it.

Blair reached over and picked up her fork and held it out to her. "I know. In three years, I don't think you mentioned his name once when I called."

Taking the fork, she took another small bite so her wouldn't start feeding it to her. "I was that obvious, huh?"

He smirked and then tilted his head to the side and looked at her. "Only to me." With an exaggerated glare, he motioned to her plate.

Sighing, she took another bite and then played with the eggs, moving them around the plate. "I don't know how to feel now, Blair. I mean I always liked Gage, but finding out the things I have in the last few days changes my view on a lot of things."

"How so?"

She went to set her fork down again and then thought it would be best if she took a bite before she did. Swallowing, she sat back and studied him. He sat perfectly still, just watching her, noticing every move she made. It dawned on her that he'd always been that way and she'd never thought a thing about it, but now he looked like a predator. Sighing, she bit her lip for a second. "Before wanting to be with Gage felt like a normal..." she waved a hand around, not sure of the word she was looking for, "urge. Now, to find out it has nothing to do with anything normal and that I don't have a choice..."

He held up his hand and sat forward. "You *always* have a choice. He can't do a damn thing unless you accept him. If *anything* happens that you don't want, you come find me..."

"But you just said..."

"What I said was you don't mess with someone's mate, implying that it's a done deal. But if you don't want him, that's a *totally* different battle I'm willing to fight."

A chill ran down her spine, his whole posture had changed his eyes too and she could see he was a lethal man that she'd befriended years before. She thought of how he looked when he was his tiger and she smiled. "You're a very pretty cat, by the way."

Blair snorted and stood up. *"Pretty cat* is not what a man wants to hear." He looked down at her. "I should go. Are you going to be okay now?"

Shaking her head, she offered him a weak smile. "I have no idea." She didn't want him to go; she missed spending time with him the last few years. Everything was easier when he was there. Standing up slowly, she moved around the table and hugged him. "Thank you."

"Jesus, Kelsey, don't thank me." He hugged her back briefly and then stepped out of her reach. "I haven't done anything to deserve your thanks." Looking at her for a few more moments, he nodded and stepped back toward the door. "Make sure you eat, regularly." He stopped and exhaled in a long breath. "Don't make any rash decisions in the next few days; just let it all soak in for a while." She nodded. "Call if you need me, I'll always be there for you." With that he turned and left.

She stood there looking at the door. That had felt so final, but not. Sighing, she looked down at the half-finished plate of eggs. As she sat back down, she couldn't help but think of Blair not seeing her as a sister. Laughing quietly, she took a bite of her eggs. It would have simplified her life a lot if she'd known years ago. Blair was someone she could have been with then; he didn't have that dangerous feeling like Gage. She grinned, knowing he'd love that description even less than being called a pretty cat.

By the time she had finished eating she realized she felt a bit better. Whether it was the food or getting answers from Blair, she wasn't sure, but she'd take it. Cleaning up the few dishes she decided it was time to go tackle the files in the office and see if she could make any sense out of things. Clearly, she couldn't go anywhere, not with the unknown of this change she was going to go through, so she needed to find her place here again.

Chapter Twelve

For two days Kelsey climbed through the files and records in the office. She'd taken several pages of notes, had ideas and questions. The problem was she couldn't bring herself to call Beth or Ed, and wasn't ready to talk to Gage just yet either.

Hiding in her room each morning, she waited until Gage went to the shop before going down. She wasn't being cowardly, just needed time and space to figure things out. The feelings, or desires, she had for Gage had changed, yet hadn't at the same time. It left her with her emotions whirling around in circles inside her. One minute she would be humming quietly to herself as she read through the files and the next, she was in tears, or worse, mad at nothing. What she needed to figure out was why, before she threw herself in his path again.

One part she knew, as best as she could was that he had gone against his own instinct and let her grow up. For that, she was glad and owed him a certain degree of gratitude. Now, if she could just get through this change without incident, she'd be a lot happier. She knew she was ready for a man in her life, but when she thought of it along the terms of only one man forever, she wasn't that sure. None of her relationships had ever gone to a place of intimacy, a few times she'd come close, but there was always something missing so she stopped it there. Her roommate from school thought it was great she was still a virgin. Kelsey didn't feel like it was great to be a twenty-three-year-old virgin at all. To her it meant something was wrong with her, and that she couldn't seem to have a normal relationship.

Pushing away from the desk, she went over to the window and opened it. It was hot with very little air moving, but she still needed the fresh air. Keeping to herself was good, it gave her time to think things through. The problem was she was stuck, thinking over and over to the point of driving herself crazy. The only time she'd seen any of the guys since Blair had been here was when one of them went past the window. No one had come in, so she figured they were just keeping an eye on things, as Gage told her they would be.

She didn't even *want* to think about the organization that was taking female shifters. No one had given her details on the *family* that was responsible for her parents' deaths, but she saw the way Noah was, and knew he was a mess because of them. That was all the information she really needed to know.

Sighing, she turned from the window and headed to the door, needing to be outside. The air was muggy as she stepped out onto the porch. Running her hands through her hair, she debated on going back in and pull it up, only to decide down would be better, and she wouldn't get sunburned. Going down the steps she looked at the path across the yard that led to the ledge overlooking the lake. Her first thought was to go and get a bit of exercise, but the tone Gage used when he spoke about Devin's warning came back to her.

Spinning on her heels, she went toward the shop. Whether she wanted to speak to anyone or not, she wasn't foolish enough to put herself at risk by wandering off alone. Hopefully they weren't too busy today. Maybe Cooper or Blair had a bit of time to go for a walk with her.

By the time she arrived at the shop, Kelsey had a thin sheen of sweat covering her. Normally she didn't mind the hot weather, but today it felt heavier than normal.

As she hit the gate leading to the side yard, she noticed Blair and Jake working on a broken track on an earth mover. They had their shirts off and Kelsey paused to admire *that* for a moment. She didn't know if it was because of what they were, but well-formed muscles bunched as the two men pried at the dirt packed into the machine trying to clean it to work on it. If she wasn't so overwhelmed with other things in her life, she could have happily gawked at them for much longer. There was something sexy about sweaty, muscular men that she was pretty sure any female appreciated.

She was still a few feet away when both of them turned and looked right at her. A part of her wanted to believe it was coincidence, but the look on their faces told her otherwise. They had *smelled* her. Taking a deep breath, she smiled like it didn't bother her. "So much makes sense now." Tucking her hands into the pockets of her shorts, she looked at the rig like it interested her. "I could never sneak up any of you, now I know why."

Jake smiled to that, "Maybe you just walk heavy."

Blair chuckled, "Yeah, that's it." She noticed he looked at her denim shorts and worked his way slowly down her legs. "What's up, sweetie?" He looked back at her face, not giving away what he was thinking.

Kelsey tried to inhale without making it obvious to see if she could scent them like they did her. She didn't smell anything out of the ordinary. "I wanted to go for a walk to the lake lookout, but Gage told me about you guys keeping an eye out," she shrugged, "so I thought I'd see if someone wants to go with me."

Wiping the sweat off his forehead, Jake looked at the track hanging under the heavy machine. "We're going to be at this a while." He gave her a sympathetic look, "Gotta get it done today." He looked uncomfortable, trying to not look at her, but looking at her at the same time.

Shrugging, Kelsey smiled briefly. "That's okay." She looked at the shop. "Is Coop busy?"

Blair pulled a rag from his back pocket and wiped off his face. "He's on a pickup with Noah." He jerked his head toward the open bay doors. "I think Gary is waiting on parts though."

Biting her lip, she considered her options. She'd never been close to Gary, but then again, the man wasn't exactly the social type. She nodded. "I'll go see if he wants to." Turning she took a few steps in that direction when a strange feeling went up her spine. It wasn't an eerie one, just one of awareness. She glanced over her shoulder to see both men standing rock still watching her. "You guys should put your shirts on; you're going to get sunburned." It was a lie, they were both tanned dark already, but it made them aware they were staring and both jolted and turned back to the task they needed to finish.

Shaking her head, she went over to the bay. Was it weird she knew they were looking at her? Rolling her eyes at the thought she realized that was just silly, anyone could sense things like that, couldn't they? Stepping into the shade of the shop, she looked around and didn't see anyone. Pausing, she listened and heard voices coming from the office.

When she stepped through the door, both men straightened up and turned to look at her. *Might as well have bells tied around my neck.* Gary looked startled, where as Gage had a look of concern on his face. "Is everything okay?" He stepped away from the desk.

Giving him a puzzled look, she nodded. "Fine."

He exhaled, "You looked stressed."

She raised both eyebrows at him. "No, I've just noticed I can't sneak up on anyone today."

Gary flushed slightly and looked back down at the desk.

Grinning, Gage rubbed his jaw, "Did you need to sneak up on someone?"

Shaking her head, she crossed her arms over her chest and ignored how they stuck to each other. "No. I wanted to go to the lake lookout, just to stretch my legs but I didn't think it would be a good idea to go..."

"Alone." Gage finished for her. He looked at Gary for a moment, who stood there rod straight and looking down at the desk for no particular reason. Clearing his throat, he glanced at the door. "Jake and Blair should..."

She shook her head, "They're beating the hell out of the earth mover trying to get at the links."

"Noah and Cooper..."

"Aren't back yet," she raised her eyebrows and looked from him to Gary.

With his jaw set, he gave a brief shake of his head confirming what she thought, Gary wasn't comfortable being near her.

Exhaling loudly, she shrugged. "I can wait until later." Not giving him a chance to say anything else, she went back out into the shop.

"Kels."

She stopped and turned back to watch Gage come up behind her.

"I can go with you," he said it quietly, hesitating slightly.

"I'm just feeling cooped up today; it's probably just the heat." She avoided looking at his eyes, doing an internal assessment about how she felt being near him. It was still there, *it* being that overwhelmed feeling she'd always had around him. "I'll just turn up the air conditioning or something; I don't want to bother..."

"Our bodies run at higher temperatures, so hot days feel worse to us. You'll get used to it."

Looking up at him, she studied the patient look in his eyes, remembering what he'd done for years without her knowing. "Is that it?"

He nodded. "Feeling cooped up is something that will happen more often now. You're going to want to be outside."

Rubbing clammy hands over her arms, she looked down at the floor. "Yeah, I've been noticing that for about a year now."

"Come on," he touched her shoulder as he turned toward the bay doors, "Let's go for a walk. It will help you feel better. It's best to just go with what you want right now. You may not know what's going on or what you need, but your body does."

Not sure whether it was a good idea or not, she turned and walked outside beside him. "Gary is very uncomfortable around me now."

"He'll adjust to it, in time."

She noticed he was walking at a slower pace than he normally did, so she could keep up with her shorter strides. "Jake's struggling with it too, but doesn't make it too obvious."

"He'd walk through fire if it was for you, honey." He gave her a serious look.

Nodding, she tucked her hands into her back pockets and watched the ground in front of them. "Yeah, I guess I'm lucky that way."

He chuckled, "In the way that you have a whole clan of males that would do anything for you? I guess that *is* pretty lucky, most girls are lucky to have one cater to them like she was a princess."

Grinning, she smacked his arm. "You know what I meant." Looking away from the affectionate look in his eyes, she studied the ground. "I'm not a princess."

He shook his head. "No, you're not, but we'd still do anything for you." Leaning down, until she looked at him again he gave her a soft look. "*I* would do anything for you," his tone was low and gentle.

A heated shiver went down her spine. "I know."

"I'm really sorry for the way your homecoming went."

She looked up to see a real look of sincerity on his face. Stopping, she studied him. He was a beautiful man with his high cheek bones, deep blue eyes, and long lashes. She moved down his face and looked at his mouth, his lower lip was slightly plumper than the top lip. It wasn't fair that he had one of those mouths that you wanted to kiss.

"Kels," he said softly as his hand cupped the bottom of her chin, drawing her attention back to his eyes. "Unless you want me to kiss you, don't look at me like you want a taste." His voice was soft with a rough rasp and it sent heat through her.

Did she want a taste? Blinking, she was startled by where her thoughts were going. Stepping back out of his touch, she decided no comment was the best course of action.

Dropping his hand, he turned and started walking again. "How long are we going to pretend nothing has changed?"

Trying to keep her distance, she ducked under a branch so she didn't have to walk too close to him. "What do you mean?"

Shaking his head, he moved to the right side of the trail so she wouldn't be climbing through the trees. "You're almost in the trees to avoid being near me."

She wanted to deny it, but couldn't. Going back onto the path, she kept her eyes forward and off him. "I just don't know what's expected. I don't know what I should or shouldn't do." Closing her mouth quickly, when she almost told him what happened when she started sniffing Blair, which might not be something she should share.

Reaching over, he grabbed her hand and then continued walking like it was no big deal. "Nothing is expected of you." He smirked at her. "And if you do something out of place, it's okay. No one expects you to know everything about a culture you didn't even know existed until a few days ago."

Kelsey was trying not to notice how it felt to have him holding her hand. After years of wishing he'd do something as simple as that, she couldn't believe he was. His hand was warm, but not clammy like her own. The warmth seemed to spread up her arm.

"Are you all right?" He squeezed her hand lightly.

Stepping around a rock sticking up in the middle of the path, she walked slightly behind him for a few feet. He still held her hand. "I guess that depends on the definition of all right."

He chuckled. "There's more than one meaning?"

Nodding, she glared up at him. "There is in my world right now. There's all right as in I'm not dying or having a mental breakdown, and then there's I'm no better than I was thirty seconds ago, but could change in the next thirty seconds. Or..."

Tugging at her hand he pulled her closer and lean down, "I get it. Your mind is filled to capacity right now."

She didn't speak; she was trying not to breathe. He smelled so good to her, a dark spicy scent that just hit all the right chords in her body. Damn him for that, she had enough issues right now.

Gage stopped suddenly and went rigid. She stumbled into him and looked to see him inhaling and looking into the trees.

"Stay right here." He said it in a whisper but with a tone that had her nod in immediate agreement. "If I'm not back in a few minutes, you book it back to the shop and get Blair."

Nodding again, she touched his arm. "Be careful." Kelsey didn't know what to expect but she wouldn't argue with him right now. Squeezing her hand again, he let go and moved into the trees.

She stood there hugging her arms around her waist, waiting. It was so silent; she couldn't even hear him moving through the trees. Pulling her phone out of her back pocket, she noted the time. Looking back at the trees, she watched for Gage.

Before she had time to go into full panic mode, the branches moved. She held her breath and then Gage stepped back into sight.

"Just some people in a boat out on the lake."

Her eyebrows shot up. "You could tell from here?"

Nodding, he brushed a few pine needles off his arm and then tapped the side of his nose.

Kelsey frowned at him, "I can't smell anything but trees." She shrugged, "Maybe I won't change like you think."

Walking back to her, he grasped her shoulders and grinned at her. "Oh, you're changing, don't doubt that."

She rolled her eyes at him.

"Close your eyes, cover your ears and then turn slowly and inhale."

Her look was the equivalent of *you're nuts*.

"Just do it. Take away one sense and the rest are stronger…"

Inhaling, she exhaled in an exasperated way and then reached up and covered her ears. Turning away from him, she closed her eyes. Gage rested his hands lightly on her waist. Ignoring the warmth of his touch, she inhaled deeply and then paused before exhaling. She was just doing it so she could tell him he was wrong. It shocked her when she could actually smell different things. A week ago, she would have described it as the bush smell, but it was so much more. She could smell pine trees, birch and cedar. The smell of the dirt filled her.

Gage's hands gently guided her to turn to her left slowly. She moved and then inhaled again. This time in addition to the trees, she could smell a raccoon. She didn't know how she knew that's what it was, she just did.

With a firm touch this time, he turned her back to the right where she was able to smell the lake. It amazed her because she knew how far down it was, not to mention how many trees were between here and there. Yet, she could smell water.

With a smile on her face, she let him turn her again. His hand dropped away for a second before resting on her hips. Taking a deep breath, she waited to see what else she could smell.

Her eyes popped open when she realized it was Gage, a scent that was pure unadulterated masculine power. He was standing right in front of her, his eyes moving over her face slowly.

Dropping her hands from the sides of her head, she looked at his chest and kept her focus there. "I smelled the lake and a raccoon."

"What else?"

She looked up to see him grinning at her. Smiling back, she felt giddy. "Different kinds of trees, dirt," she thought about it for a second, "moist soil, maybe a form of moss or loam? And..." glancing away, she had almost said him.

He was nodding, "And?"

Inhaling slowly, she let the scent of him fill her again. "You," she whispered and then exhaled. His hands she realized were still holding her, they flexed slightly. She knew she should look away, step out of his reach but the way his eyes held hers had her unable to remember how to do either. His dark eyes are gone a shade of deeper blue.

"Kels," he whispered as he lowered his face closer to hers. "I'm going to kiss you. If you don't want me to, all you have to do is stop me."

She knew he spoke, his words registered slowly, but she didn't want to stop him, not when she'd been wanting him to kiss her for six years.

His lips brushed against hers so lightly she was afraid she imagined it. Reaching up, she placed a hand on his chest, the solid muscle flexed under her touch; she could feel his heart beating strong against her hand.

With a shaky breath, he touched her lips again, lingering longer. Kelsey moved her other hand up to his neck and raised up toward his mouth. It was all the encouragement he needed. He began to kiss her, tasting her mouth over and over again. If his hands hadn't been holding her steady she wasn't sure she'd be able stay upright.

His tongue slid over her lips, coaxing her to open her mouth. Giving in, she moaned as the kiss changed from cautious to demanding, as his tongue plunged into her mouth, rubbing against hers.

Heat flashed through her whole body, something she had never felt before. It was overwhelming, but exciting. She grasped his hair and held on as his mouth assaulted hers. Her knees felt weak, they weren't going to hold her much longer. Gage wrapped an arm around her and she was held tight against his body.

She wanted to grind her hips into him as an urgency to get closer to him shook her.

Never having had that urge before, she pulled back, breaking the kiss. Swallowing, she fought to regain her breath so she could speak.

Gage didn't say a word; he just held her against him and looked down at her with lust hazed eyes. His chest was moving as fast as her own as he tried to catch his breath.

Dropping down from her tiptoes, she slid her hand slowly down his shoulder until it rested on his arm. With a shaking hand, she touched her mouth, his eyes tracked her movement, and she could see the desire in them when they stopped where her fingers rested.

"I didn't mean to get carried away. I just…" he loosened his hold on her, putting a bit of space between them, "caught fire…" he said in a tone of disbelief.

Nodding, she couldn't deny that was exactly what happened. They had gone up in flames from a kiss. 'I've never…" she swallowed, not even sure how to say it.

Squeezing her waist once more, he dropped his hands away from her and placed them on his hips. Taking a deep breath, he released it gradually. "Neither have I." He lowered his head and continued to breathe deeply.

Kelsey blinked and looked at him. Was he admitting kissing her had affected him as much as her? She studied him while he wasn't looking. His hands rested at his hips, they were shaking slightly. Looking down she could plainly see his arousal under his jeans. A shocking flash of heat went through her, enough to make her gasp quietly.

"Christ, honey, don't look at me like that if you expect me not to touch you."

Startled, she glanced back at his face, a determined look was etched in his features, but it was mixed with pain.

He waved a hand in the direction of the lake. "Walk." Clenching his jaw, he took a deep breath. "I need to get my cat under control."

Eyes wide, she turned and started down the path. Alone.

Kelsey was sitting on her favorite boulder when he finally joined her. She was still working on settling her body down, not to mention her very vivid imagination.

Gage squatted down beside her and looked out over the lake. He gave her a brief look, his eyes having regained their usual sparkle again.

"Are you okay?" she asked hesitantly.

He gave her a lopsided grin. "Yeah, I've had years of practice getting my cat under control around you."

"Is that why you were such a dick to me most of the time?"

Chuckling, he glanced at her briefly again and then out at the lake. "If I acted like an ass, you stormed away and were out of reach…"

"You weren't an ass," she said softly. He looked at her, doubt on his face. "You were a dick and you know it."

Dropping his head down, he nodded. "Yeah, I was." He shrugged. "I won't apologize for it. It was for your own safety."

Sighing, she pulled her legs up and hugged her knees. "I know." He gave her a surprised look. "Blair explained it."

"I wanted to give you time…"

"I appreciate it," she looked at him, "really."

Nodding, he looked out over the lake again. "I don't know how much longer I can give you." He said it in such a serious tone, she turned and studied him.

"What do you mean?"

Sighing, he dropped down and sat on the grass between the rocks. "Every fiber of my body tells me to claim you," he gave her a pained look; "it may sound barbaric to you right now, but its part of the animal side. After you change you'll understand that."

Frowning, she tried to stay calm. "Why can't you just keep controlling it?"

He snorted and then shook his head. "It was hard before you went away to school, but now..." his eyes moved over her slowly, taking in each inch of her, "Now, even my cat knows you are mature."

Shaking her head, she looked away from him. "Tell your cat no."

Moving over, until he was in front of her, he grasped her chin and gently forced her to look at him. "If it were *that* simple, I would. It's like having razors clawing at my insides, Kels, telling me to claim you, to protect you," his eyes darkened, "to look after your every need or want." His touch lightened. "I'm fighting it, but I can't say for how much longer."

The last part sounded like an apology. If it were anyone other than Gage, she would have been afraid, but he'd picked up the pieces of her heart when her parents' death had devastated her, and she trusted him like she did no other. She'd never realized that before. "What if I'm not ready?"

His eye brows shot up and she knew he was remembering their kiss.

"Not like that," she chastised, "I meant emotionally, mentally."

Releasing her chin, he rested his arms on her out stretched legs. "Honestly, I'll have to leave."

She opened her mouth to say that wasn't right when he shook his head.

"You need to be around other clan until you understand everything and have completed the change."

"I really hate this, Gage. I refuse to accept I have no choice in all of this..."

Grinning, he dropped his head down. "Somehow that doesn't surprise me."

"It's not funny," she whined.

"Oh, I know. Not one bit of this is playing with my funny bone." He rubbed the back of his neck and then stood up. Exhaling in a slow stream, he looked down at her. "We better get back. Being alone with you out here surrounded by nature is not helping me." He held out a hand to her.

Letting him pull her to her feet, she gave him an exasperated look. "Oh, and living in a house full of beds is better?"

Tugging her closer, he leaned down and whispered close enough to her ear that she could feel his breath. "I don't need a bed to do what I want to do to you, honey, trust me."

Kelsey had never felt so turned on as she did right now. Turning his head slightly, she inhaled his scent and released a shaky breath. "Why couldn't it just be about sex? I could handle that without all this other stuff." *Liar.*

Gage's hand flexed around hers and he straightened up releasing it like it burned him. "Christ, don't say shit like that to me." Groaning, he grabbed her by the shoulders and spun her around. "Walk."

With a grin he couldn't see, she quickly moved back along the path. All of it was a nightmare to her, she was good and truly lost, but knowing Gage was suffering right along with her somehow made it a bit better. It was all she had to cling to right now.

Chapter Thirteen

Gage watched the door close and turned to head back to the shop. He hadn't meant to kiss her. Hell, he'd said he wasn't going to touch her, and then he reached out and grabbed her hand a breath after the thought.

Kissing her had been the best, and worst thing he'd ever done, as far as she was concerned. He hadn't expected them both to ignite. Oh, he'd heard it was all heat with your true mate, but didn't expect to get burned like that. Stopping had taken every ounce of restraint he could muster, and he had to dig *really* deep to find it.

His cat had almost ripped him to shreds from the inside. He rubbed a hand over his ribs, as if he expected to feel gouges covering them. It still hurt. It was taking all his restraint to keep walking away from her right now. Her taste was on his lips, her scent was all he could smell, and he could still feel exactly where her body had pressed into his.

He let out an exasperated sigh and looked down at the front of his jeans. Not that it was a new state whenever she was near. Or had thoughts of her. Now he had her flavor on his taste buds and he was damned for sure, because he had no desire to wash it away. He was screwed plain and simple.

With a scowl on his face, he stomped back into the yard. Halfway to the shop he spotted Gary, Jake, and Blair struggling to free up the broken track that was jammed in the wheel assembly of the earth mover. Obviously, the operator had tried to keep going after the links had snapped. That wasn't unusual around here.

An annoyed hiss left him as he walked over to help.

Blair and Jake were heaving on a long pry bar, and judging by the growls coming out of them, using their human *and* animal strength. Gary was literally beating the shit out of the wedged link trying to get it free.

He shouldered his way between the two straining men and grasped the bar with both hands. Pouring all his frustration into his efforts, he leaned on the bar and was rewarded with a loud snap as the track let go. Blair stumbled back as Jake hit the ground with a loud gasp.

Straightening slowly, Gary let the hammer slip from his hand as he exhaled loudly.

"Our own hulk," Jake muttered, trying to catch his breath.

"We just loosened it up for him," Blair quipped as he reached down to pull Jake to his feet.

Dusting off his jeans, Jake took a deep breath. "I didn't think the bitch was ever going to let go."

Blair mopped at the sweat covering his face with his forearm as he eyed Gage. "You take some extra vitamins today, Herc?"

Gary leaned back against the side of the rig, with a large bottle of water resting on his hip; he inhaled deeply and then straightened up, coughing. He gave Gage a wide-eyed look. "I don't think vitamins are responsible for his sudden increase in strength."

Gage watched the other two subtly inhale, then look anywhere but at him. He clenched his jaw, cursing the sensitive sense of smell of his kind. He clearly had Kelsey's scent all over him.

Blair was the first to make eye contact, and knowing how he felt about her, Gage could now see his pain. "So," Blair rubbed a hand over his sweat drenched chest, "Kelsey feeling better after her walk?"

Gage studied him for a moment; tension plainly visible in the way he held himself. Rubbing the back of his neck, he looked down at the broken track. "I showed her that her sense of smell is now heightened."

Jake grabbed the bottle of water Gary held out. "How'd she like that?"

Gage smiled as the image of the excited look in her eyes came to him as she explained what she'd been able to smell. "She was awed."

"Is she all right?" Blair asked quietly.

Turning Gage watched Blair, his jaw was tense. He gave him a serious look. "Yeah. She's still struggling with everything, though."

Blair picked up the bottle of water sitting on his shirt, "She'll get a handle on it," he took a small sip and hesitated, the bottle held away from his mouth. "There's nothing she can't do." Changing his mind, he capped the bottle and turned toward the shop. "I'll go grab the shit we need." The anger in his words hit Gage like a slap.

He watched him walk away, his stride long and not as smooth as it usually was. "Damn," he muttered under his breath.

"Give him time to adjust." Jake said quietly standing beside him.

"He had to know it was coming," running a hand through his hair, Gage looked from one man to the other. "If I could step aside, I would, but…"

Jake shook his head. "He knows it's not a possibility, Gage. His heart just hasn't caught up with his head yet."

"How did I not see this?" Gage said it more to himself then them.

Jake gave his shoulder a light smack. "You were blinded by the sudden drive to mate." He motioned to the door Blair had gone through. "Otherwise you would have noticed the pain radiating off him when you finally confessed why you were acting like a complete asshole toward Kelsey."

Glancing at him out of the corner of his eye briefly, he acknowledged his friend's lack of sugar-coating his words. "But he went to help Bruce…"

"Right after you told us." Jake shook his head. "That's why he did." Exhaling, he glanced at Gary who nodded. "He almost went fucking mad when he realized she was off limits."

Gage groaned and stood there looking at the ground. "Fuck." Taking a deep breath, he rolled his shoulders; the pounding desire to go to Kelsey was still riding him. "Let me know if he reaches his breaking point." He gave both a no-nonsense glare. "Blair in a full-blown rage is something that frightens even me."

Both men nodded they're agreement. Pulling out the phone, he checked the time. "When was the last time someone did a sweep of the boundaries?"

Gary motioned to the track. "I was just going to head out when they needed me."

Nodding, Gage glanced at the shop and then back to him. "I'll go. I need to burn off some frustration right now."

Jake squeezed his shoulder. "He'll get a grip on it, Gage. He doesn't have a choice; he won't risk Kelsey, if not being here puts her safety in question."

Gage closed his eyes, biting down on the anger that flared at the thought of a threat. "Any idiot that would even attempt to come here…"

Jake laughed. "Would be a *dead* fucking idiot."

Gage grinned, knowing the other men in Kelsey's life would all do everything to protect her. "A bloody slaughter could be therapeutic at this point."

Gary choked on his drink. "Hopefully it won't come to that." He waved his hand in the direction of the road. "Go check the perimeter so we can get back to work."

Giving him a mock salute, Gage started to turn. "Yes, sir!" Stripping off his shirt, he tucked it into his back pocket and turned, jogging out of the yard to the long driveway. Hopefully he'd sweat Kelsey's scent out of his system. Shaking his head, he knew there was about as much chance of that happening as there was for him to turn into a butterfly.

Passing the window, Gage told himself he was just checking for unknown scents near the house. Even he knew it was a lie. He'd already checked all but one, and hadn't spotted Kelsey anywhere in the house. Maybe she was in the shower... He came to an abrupt halt at that thought. *Don't think about her naked. Too late.* Groaning, he forced his foot to move and inhaled again, searching for unfamiliar scents.

As he passed the kitchen window, his heart stopped in his chest. Kelsey was leaning over the counter, pressing her face against it. Frowning, he stepped closer. What was she doing? She had changed into some sort of sundress that left most of her back bare. His groin tightened again.

Snapping his teeth together, he was just about to step away when she moved and pressed the other side of her face to the counter; a look of pain etched on her face. Without pausing, he was around the corner, leaping up over the railing, and rushing into the kitchen.

Moving toward her, he tried to ignore the bare legs on display beneath the little dress she wore, "Are you all right?"

She continued to press her upper body and face against the cold tiles. "No." she panted, "no, I think I need to go to the hospital."

Panic hit him in the gut. "What is it?" He leaned on the counter, afraid to touch her.

"I'm burning up, Gage. I've tried everything. My stomach is cramping, my skin is so hot..." she hissed out a breath and spread her arms across the tiles. "My clothes even hurt..." she made a sound of distress.

Gage fought his panic and took a deep breath, the last thing she needed was him freaking out. A scent hit him and his body almost convulsed when he recognized it. Her body was emitting pure female cat scent. It was one he'd only smelled a few times before when he'd been visiting Bruce and it usually meant... his brain shut down as his cat fought him for supremacy. *Shit.*

Kelsey made another sound of distress and both his man and cat froze. Slowly he went to stand right behind her. She may not shift yet, but he'd learned his lesson years ago when he'd almost lost half his face to a female's claws. "Let me help you, honey." He kept his voice soft and gentle.

He blew gently against the bare skin on her back. She stilled beneath him. His hand was shaking as he brushed the tips of his fingers from her shoulder along her stretched arm until he reached her hand. He held her hand flat against the countertop, feeling more confident now that she wouldn't be able to turn suddenly on him.

"Gage," her voice was filled with fear.

"Shh," he leaned forward, trying hard not to press his hips into her as he did. *That* took willpower he didn't realize he possessed. "I can make this more bearable for you." He ran his other hand down her back, blowing softly over the skin across her shoulders as he did.

She made a whining noise.

He knew he'd brought this on by kissing her, which is why he'd tried so hard not to. The dormant cat inside her knew she was near her mate, even if Kelsey refused to admit it.

"I don't know what's wrong with me."

He couldn't believe how badly his hands were shaking; his cat lay just under the surface knowing how cautious they had to be, lest they be rejected. "I do, honey," he whispered against her shoulder. Her skin was like satin. "Your cat needs something..." he didn't know how to explain this to her without being vulgar.

She groaned as he brushed his lips over her skin again. "Why? Why *now*?"

117

Her voice was riddled with pain and need; he doubted she realized the latter. "The change is close, Kels, she knows I'm near…" he paused as he ran his hand down the heated flesh of her rib cage, gauging her reaction.

She stilled, barely breathing. "I couldn't handle the water on my skin…" she gasped as he opened his hand and touched her with more than his fingertips. "How can you…" As he touched her hip, she pushed back into him.

Gage had to clench his teeth to fight against his need to pin her against the counter.

"Gage?" She whined, the panic in her tone causing him to sweat.

"Shh, honey, just let me help you." He lowered his bare chest against her and had to bite back a growl when her soft flesh felt like it was burning. He ran his hand up her bare thigh, *Christ, I'm going to die here…* placing it under her skirt. When she didn't freeze under his touch, he kept inching higher until he reached her hip. His fingers skimmed over the edge of the elastic of her underwear, resting over her hip. Swallowing, he traced his way along it to her stomach.

His cat was running wild, wanting to push, but knowing they couldn't go faster. Brushing his mouth along her throat, he paused against her ear. "Is this helping?"

His only answer was a soft mewling noise that sent more blood rushing to his already painfully throbbing groin. Running his finger under the edge of her underwear, he clamped down on the images flashing through his mind. One wrong move and her cat would reject him, and Kelsey would hate him.

As his hand moved under the material, she started clawing at the counter. Pausing, he released the the hand holding hers, then and grasped both of her wrists firmly. "Easy, honey," he murmured, moving his lips back to her neck.

Every instinct told him to mark her, but his cat paused knowing what a mistake that would be. Moving his hand between her legs, he cupped her lightly. She tensed and he froze, giving her time to adjust and, hopefully, accept him. When her legs opened further, he took that as consent. Barely able to remember to breathe, he moved his hand over her swollen flesh and almost swallowed his tongue when he felt how wet she was. Soaked would not have adequately described it. She hissed out a breath and pushed into his hand.

Fucking. Killing. Me.

Sliding his finger through her heat, he slid it slowly inside her. Her muscles clamped down. She was so tight his knees shook, her scent enveloping and choking him.

Moving his finger in and out with great care, he pressed his face into her throat, reveling in the incredible scent of her skin. *So tight...* he bit back a groan. A thought hit him like a splash of cold water. "Are you a virgin, honey?"

She thrust against his hand and moaned what took him a moment to realize was a yes.

Christ...

That helped keep his restraint in check. His heart pounded with an emotion he could only label as triumph. She would only ever be his.

Torturing himself while pleasing her, he thrust two fingers into her tight wetness while trying to keep his mind focused and distracted from taking her right there, right now. His cat was prowling under his skin now, knowing he'd have to show her tenderness before a true mating would happen.

Her erratic breathing and throaty moans were almost his undoing. He bit her shoulder and then froze and turned away quickly. The noises she made as her body clamped tight on his fingers as she came almost brought him to his knees.

Waiting as long as he could, he released her, kissing the side of her neck as he pulled his hand free from beneath her clothes.

Not trusting himself to speak, he straightened and backed up, leaving her sprawled on the counter as she attempted to catch her breath.

He turned and stumbled to the bathroom. He leaned back against the closed door, rubbing his shaking hand over his face, only to pause when he realized it was the same hand that had been inside her.

"Fuck." The scent made his body shudder. Hastily he kicked off his boots and ripped his jeans from his body. He grasped himself in a tight, almost painful grip as he fumbled to get the shower turned on and get into it as his hand began stroking the rigid flesh. He wasn't going to survive her change.

Chapter Fourteen

※

Kelsey straightened, lifting herself off the counter. *What the hell had just happened?* Her cheeks flamed. Well, she knew what happened, but why? And why did she feel better? *Oh God, what did I do? Or more precisely why did I let him do it?* Her body quivered as she replayed the moment.

She'd never... okay, she had but never from a man doing it. Heat rushed over her, she tensed afraid the pain would return. When it didn't, she exhaled slowly and stood, questions running through her mind.

Was that going to happen to her again? And she wanted to know how the hell Gage had known exactly what to do? It was like he'd... she frowned at the floor. Like he'd had to do it before...

That thought felt like a smack in the face and she wasn't sure why. Of course, he wasn't a virgin. Twinges of jealousy accompanied memories of the never-ending string of girls that hung around when Gage and the rest of the guys were in their early twenties. Still, she couldn't run to him if that horrible feeling hit her again. There had to be something that she could do about it.

Spinning toward the hallway, she almost ran into the bathroom. She stopped in front of the door, hand on the handle. She could hear the water running, but she could also hear more. Her cheeks flushed when she realized she could hear Gage in the shower, and what he was doing. Letting go of the doorknob as if it burned her, she stood there trying to decide what to do.

Before she could come to any sort of decision, the shower turned off. Counting to five, she hoped he had a towel close at hand. Bursting into the room, he was just wrapping a towel around his waist. The water dripped off his body, forming a small puddle on the tile by his feet.

Gage eyed her with a wary look on his face, but didn't say a word as he grabbed another towel to begin drying his upper body.

Kelsey tried to ignore the way his muscles flexed as he moved. Before she changed her mind, she forced her eyes to meet his. "What is wrong with me?" She ran her eyes over his exposed flesh briefly. "And don't give me some kind of juvenile answer please. I understand horny and that..." she pointed out the open door in the general direction of the kitchen, "*That* was not just horniness." She glared. "It hurt so much, Gage." She stopped there because she didn't know if she should be mad at him or cry with relief that he'd made it go away.

Tossing the towel at the clothes hamper, he pushed his hair out of his face with both hands. She looked down at the floor to avoid acknowledging how sexy he was.

Sighing loudly, he went to place a finger under her chin, raising her eyes to meet his. Connecting with her expression, he dropped his hand away. "That was you coming into the change, or your first cycle. One or the other happens first." He leaned against the wall; crossing his arms over his chest he studied her. "And it's worse than being horny; it's like you're on fire inside and out." He shrugged. "Or so I've been told."

She bit her lip, determined she wouldn't ask who had told him. His eyes looked at the lip her teeth held captive. She glared back. "So, it's gone now?"

He stilled before responding. "It will be back."

Her jaw dropped. "Why? We just..." she frowned, unable to say it out loud. "So how long will I have to go through this?"

Several emotions crossed his expression, but she couldn't tell what he was feeling.

"It varies, honey, there's many variables that could..."

"Variables? What am I a math equation?" She snapped. Considering all she'd been through, he'd just had to get over it. "How do I fix it?"

Gage looked at the floor, jaw clenched. It seemed like he was working through what to say. "There's only one thing that will ..." he looked at her, "*fix* it."

"What?" Did she hope there was actually a solution?

"*If* you weren't already mated, then lots of..." his lips twitched, "sex would do the trick."

She knew her cheeks heated, she loathed her readiness to blush at her age. "But?"

He moved closer to her, inhaling subtly as he did. "But you *are* mated, or are near your mate, so having just any man won't help you."

Scowling, she stopped him from moving closer with a look.

"You're going to have to accept what's happening, honey. Accept me and we can lessen this, make it a more comfortable, controllable experience." He shrugged. "Except for a few heightened times a year, that varies with each female..."

Shaking her head, she hugged herself. All she kept hearing was the *no choice* in everything she'd been told, and that went against everything she believed. "It's not fair..."

"Fair?" He stiffened; his tone made the hair on the back of her neck stand up. Gage rarely shared any emotions, always calm and steady. "This is not a children's game, Kelsey, fair doesn't play in to it." Clamping his mouth shut, he took a deep breath and then raised his palms, indicating he wasn't going to bark again. "Look, I'm a patient man. I think I've more than proved that."

She couldn't argue with that, so she gave him a little nod.

"When I went through the final change, it was liberating," He lifted his hands in exasperation. "I don't know what changed in you, one day you were cute little Kelsey." He offered her a weak smile, "I adored you, even then, the strength you had…" He shook his head. "Then the next day you were my mate, something our kind reveres, something many of us never find…" He swallowed like he was having trouble saying the words. "Some can go their whole life feeling like a part of them is missing." He inhaled sharply and continued. "But I had you, only I couldn't *have* you." He lifted his hands and let them drop on his hips. "It's been a long six years, Kels, and I *am* trying to give you all the time you need."

She was torn. The vulnerability made her want to hold and reassure him, but she still heard *no choice* in the back of her mind, like a chorus. "You've been with other women…"

He snorted. "What the hell do emotionless and disconnected fuck sessions where I was trying to get you out of my head have to do with this?" He swore under his breath as she saw her face blanch with his harsh words.

Swallowing the lump in her throat, she tried to process what he'd said.

"There hasn't been anyone in over three years…"

She held up her hand to stop him.

He ignored her and moved, leaning down close enough their breath shared space. "Kels, it wasn't as bad as it sounded. Most of the time nothing happened, I couldn't…"

She stepped back, not able to focus with him this close. "What do you mean?"

Running a hand through his hair, he swore. "I felt like a bastard, okay? I couldn't because my body wanted you…" He shook his head. "Don't make me say it to you, Kelsey, please." He looked at her and then sighed, "Look, how do you feel around other men?"

She gave him a confused look. "Fine…"

He gave her a look that told her that wasn't the answer he wanted. "Do they turn you on?"

She shrugged. "Some, I guess."

Smirking, he tilted his head and studied her. "Then why are you untouched?"

Kelsey remembered her answers when they were in the kitchen. Her cheeks grew hot. "I am not untouched, not completely." She shrugged, avoiding his eyes. "I just have the worst luck and go out with guys, who, once I get to know them..." she wasn't sure how to say it, "don't do a thing for me."

He stepped into her space again. "And *now?*"

She backed up and found herself against the wall. "Now what?"

"Is there anyone that *does* it for you?" He loomed closer.

Not wanting him too near, because his smell was making her shaky, she pushed him back, only to drop her hands when the feel of his bare chest sent a jolt of lust through her. "That's hardly a fair question; the only men I've been near are the ones I grew up with."

He placed his hands on either side of her head, letting his chest and hips brush against her with each breath. "And now?" He whispered.

She hated him right now. Hated the way her body reacted. She tried to find the words to deny it.

"You don't have to answer; I can feel your need." He gave her a look that was almost sad. "You won't admit it either, but that need is only for me."

She put her hands up and managed to push him back so she wasn't as caged in. "I am not, doing this. It's insane." She growled.

He didn't back away. "You don't have a choice." He gave her a hard look. "*I* don't have a choice."

"I refuse."

"Refuse all you want, honey." His voice had softened again. "The only choice in all of this is that ultimately, *you* choose when."

She shoved him, not wanting to hear what she'd been denying.

He held her head, she had no choice but to look at him. "I won't force this, so help me, if it kills me, I won't force your decision." His eyes roamed over face, tenderness was mixed with pain. "When you can't stand it…" he inhaled and closed his eyes. "When you can't stand it…" He opened them only to reveal a lust-filled stare. "When you want to peel the skin from your bones, come and find me." He brushed a feather-light kiss on her forehead, "accept me as yours and let me help you."

Gage stepped away so suddenly, she almost fell on her face. Glaring, she couldn't believe what he'd just said. She scowled harder, pushing away from the wall. There was nothing she could say, and he knew it. As she stepped out of the bathroom, he put his arm out to stop her.

"And Kels, in case your brain tries to cook up some loophole, don't. Please don't even try asking one of the guys to help you."

She really hoped her eyes were relaying the anger she felt, because at that moment she couldn't form words.

"If you do, you're signing their death certificates," he said quietly. Moving his hand, he looked down at her from his full height. "We have our own laws."

He shut the door so abruptly it lightly hit her in the back before she had moved away. She glared at the closed door. Inhaling deeply, she wanted to scream at him, something that would shock him until his spicy scent filled her system.

Shaking her head to clear it, she rushed toward the stairs. Running up as quickly as she could manage, she ran into her room slamming the door behind her before flinging herself on the bed in tears of frustration.

Chapter Fifteen

"You look like shit."

Gage spun around to see Cooper leaning against the fence, watching.

"It's been a long week."

Cooper looked at his wrist to check the time, he wasn't wearing a watch. "Since when do we work in the moonlight?"

Glancing back at the backhoe he'd been pressure washing he shrugged. "Just trying to get caught up."

Cooper came over and stood beside him. "And since when do we spit shine the rigs?"

Gage dropped the sprayer on the ground as his chin hit his chest.

"You can't avoid going home, son. She's still going to be there."

Gage turned off the compressor and glanced at him. "That's the problem."

"I figured." Cooper looked around the yard for a minute before looking back at him. "You have a fight?"

Picking up his shirt, Gage wiped his face off. "I don't know what the hell you'd call it."

Cooper chuckled. "Give me the word to define it then."

Gage squeezed the back of his neck trying to ease some of the tension. "Clusterfuck."

Cooper laughed, which should have pissed him off, but he found himself smiling.

"It's a fucking mess, Coop." He threw up his hands. "I kissed her when we went for that walk." He rubbed a hand across his forehead. "The heat shocked both of us, but I thought..." He shook his head. "I thought..."

"She'd do an about-face and come running into your open arms?" Cooper had a huge smile on his face.

"You don't have to say I'm a fool. I *know* I am."

"This is Kelsey we're talking about, Gage, have your hormones made you forget that?" Tucking his hands in his pockets, he stood there waiting.

Feeling awkward, Gage sat on the wheel of the washer tank. "She's in her cycle, Coop. Not full blown, but..."

"When?"

Gage looked down at his hands resting in his lap. "I was checking around the house..." he realized he didn't need to give him a play by play, "I found her pressing her chest and face against the counter trying to put out the fire."

"Shit." Cooper yanked his hat off and rubbed a hand over his head before jamming it back on. "Did you just leave her there like that?"

Gage noted how strained the older man's voice was. He was glad it was dark sure even he would blush before the end of this conversation. "No."

Cooper's head snapped up, his eyes boring into him.

Holding his hand up, he shook his head. "Not like you're thinking." He sighed. "I helped her out and threw myself in a cold shower."

Cooper nodded but didn't comment.

"She..." Gage lifted his hands, "demanded answers and..." he closed his eyes. "I gave her all the wrong ones. I'm pretty sure she hates me now." He leaned back against the water tank, trying to cool off, as he'd been trying to accomplish unsuccessfully for hours.

"I doubt she hates you." Cooper finally said quietly. "She's just pissed you're the main cause."

Gage snorted. "Is that supposed to make me feel better?"

Cooper shook his head. "No. I doubt anything I say will do that."

"You'd be right there." Gage started to wind up the hose. "I don't know what to do, Coop."

Cooper watched him silently for several minutes. "It's a lonely fucking existence without your mate, Gage. When you know who it is, but can't have her."

Gage's eyes snapped to him. That sounded as if he'd lived it.

Cooper shook his head when Gage was going to speak. "You're going to see her through her cycle, whatever she wants…"

"I…"

"Don't say you can't, because I *know* what every bloody cell in your body is telling you."

Gage closed his mouth.

"Whatever she wants, you'll be there for her." Cooper said softly.

"I don't know if I can do it without marking her."

"You'll manage." Cooper gave him a hard look. "Because you already know anything she agrees to when the heat has her won't mean a damn thing when she's thinking clearly."

Gage blew out a breath and nodded. Any male from his clan knew that, most learned it the hard way.

"Be what she needs, Gage. When it's all settled down, she'll come around."

"You can't know that, Coop. What if…" he couldn't say it.

Cooper rubbed his jaw and gave him a lopsided grin. "She's been mooning over you for years. She's just rebelling right now because we dumped a shit load on her and she needs to fight back, whatever way she can."

Gage's legs gave out and he flopped to sit on the wheel. "How do I not mark her?" He asked, his voice shaking.

Cooper blew out a breath. "Dig deep. You can't until she consents…"

"I know that. I just…" he dropped his head into his hands. "Fuck."

"Yeah." Cooper turned away and then paused. "Gage?"

Raising his head, he looked at him, but Cooper didn't turn back.

"Take it slow." Cooper stood looking into the darkened path that lead to the house. "She's all I have left of Katie." With that he walked into the shadows.

Gage stared into the dark that had swallowed him whole. Cooper had sounded so lost. Had Kelsey's mother been his mate? Why the hell had she been with Phillip then? Gage swallowed the knot in his throat. If he fucked this up with Kelsey, he'd end up with that hollow look in his eyes that Coop had. He didn't know how he knew that was what happened, but his gut said it was dead on.

"Gage?"

He almost growled, hearing Blair's voice in the the darkness. That was twice tonight someone had gotten close to him without sensing them near. He turned and watched Blair walk toward him. His movements were stiff.

"You all right, man? I got the drop on you."

Gage smirked, he'd hoped Blair wouldn't notice, but should have known better. "Yeah, my head's just a fucking mess right now."

Offering a sympathetic smile, Blair came over and leaned against the water tank. "I can relate." He cleared his throat. "Sorry about earlier…"

Motioning with his hand, Gage interrupted him. "Don't be." He ran a hand through his hair. "I get it." He sighed. "At least I do right now, which could change without notice though."

"Everything okay?

Gage studied his best friend for a moment. He guessed Blair was in was just as hard a place as his own. "Not by a long shot."

"It's been a while since you worked yourself to exhaustion to avoid Kelsey."

Groaning, Gage nodded. "Yeah. I'd hoped I was done with that."

Picking at the cap on top of the tank, Blair nodded slowly. "What's going on?" He rolled his eyes at him. "That kept you out here until midnight?"

Surprised, Gage hadn't realized he'd been *that* long. Sighing, he rubbed at the back of his neck, the exhaustion was finally registering. "Kelsey's hit her cycle."

Blair tensed, "Fuck."

Smirking, Gage nodded. "Yeah that's my take on it too."

Blair stood there, suddenly tense. "You want to bunk in with us?" He seemed to stop breathing.

Gage blew out a loud breath. "I don't think I can just leave her to suffer…"

Nodding, Blair stared off into the darkness. "I get that." He ran a hand over his face. "I don't want to, but…"

"I'm sorry…"

Glaring at him, Blair straightened and started to move away. "Don't be. Fuck, you found your mate. I…" He shook his head. "I'll live through it. Somehow." Turning, he stood facing the gate. "Get your ass home, Gage." He took two steps and stopped, letting out a long breath. "She has to think it's her idea." He gave him a sober look over his shoulder. "Don't say I never gave you anything." Snapping around he walked away, stripping off clothes as he went.

Then from just outside the fence, a large sleek white tiger turned and studied him with pale eyes that glowed in the dark. With a low chirruping noise, he spun off and was gone into the night.

Exhaling a breath, he didn't realize he was holding, Gage scanned the yard once before turning to go home.

Should have joined the fucking army when I turned eighteen, he growled inside his head. *Then my life would have been a walk in the fucking park. Facing bombs and bullets sounded a helluva lot better than the mess I'm sinking in here.*

Gage picked up his pillow and pounded it between his hands, trying to reshape it. The day had gone without incident. Kelsey hadn't avoided him, but had been cold toward him. Cold enough that Gage was sure if he looked closely there would be frostbite. He twisted the pillow again then dropped it like it was to blame for him flipping around in bed. Tossing the pillow against the wall, he ripped the sheet off his body and grabbed a clean pair of jeans out of his dresser.

Yanking them on, he went out into the hall. Maybe a few shots of whiskey would settle him down enough to get a few hours of sleep. Grabbing the banister, he froze when a whimpering noise came to him.

He looked at Kelsey's door. What was she doing awake? He'd checked on her after his run. If things kept going the way they were, he'd soon have to learn how to work in animal form. She'd been sleeping soundly.

He listened at her door. Soft, tantalizing sounds were coming from the other side. Quietly, he opened it a few inches and peered in.

She was twisting in her sleep, discomfort plain on her face. Thinking it was a nightmare, he stepped into the room when the scent of her heat hit him, catching him off guard. His nostrils flared, his body hardened in an instant.

Kelsey moved her legs as if she was trying to run, kicking the sheets off her body. He watched it slide to the floor and stood frozen in place. She was wearing one of those little baby doll nighties, her body barely covered in soft white material. He wanted to be that material rubbing over her skin.

Christ. He tried to swallow, his mouth suddenly so dry he could barely breathe. She gasped and then squirmed some more, he realized she was sensing him near and it only made it worse.

He continued to stand there, his eyes roaming over every inch of her skin. His cat, that he'd thought he'd exhausted, was rubbing against him trying to entice him him to go over to her, the scent was so fucking intriguing.

He should just let her suffer and maybe she'd stop being so pigheaded. Taking a deep breath, he knew he was being a dick, every instinct was telling him to take care of her, to fill all her needs and she was in serious need right now.

Moving toward the end of her bed, he was unable to take his eyes from her. The bottom of the nearly transparent pajamas she left little to the imagination. His heartbeat pounded rapidly, so powerful he could feel it in his throat, when he realized she wasn't wearing underwear.

Moving like a cat preparing to pounce, he lowered to his knees and rested his hands on the mattress. *Christ, how am I going to touch her without going too far?* She made a needy mewling noise in the back of her throat and he swore he heard the zipper on his jeans break apart, he was that hard.

Her legs started moving again, unconsciously, moving to rub herself. *Christ.* Shakily, he reached out and gently clasped one of her ankles. She stiffened, stilled, simply waiting. He looked up to see her eyes were still closed. Was she awake? Taking hold of her other ankle, he held her legs still. With a needy moan, she flexed her legs trying to move them to no avail, he held them tight.

The edge of her gown rode up further and he couldn't look away. He'd only intended to touch her, to comfort her cat with a bit of contact, but now he was looking at her swollen pink flesh open to him, so wet he could see it from where he knelt. He knew he was going to do more than comfort her.

Inhaling, he tightened his grasp and flexed the muscles in his arms, pulled her toward him until she was almost hanging off the bed. Reaching under her legs, he held her hips and blew on her dripping folds.

Please don't hate me, he prayed as he leaned forward and stroked his tongue over her. She stilled completely, but didn't attempt to move away from his touch, so he did it again. His eyes rolled back in his head at the sweet, potent taste of her. Doing this for her wasn't going to be a sacrifice in any way.

He pulled her thighs wide so he could bury his mouth in her flesh. Her hips lifted and thrust against his mouth as he applied more pressure. Her panting was increasing with each move he made.

Lifting his head, he straightened to pick her up off the bed. He still didn't trust she wouldn't claw him up. Lifting her legs bringing her hips completely off the bed, he nibbled along her inner thigh, making her gasp each time his teeth lightly marked her. It took all his restraint not to sink them in and mark her fully.

He plunged his tongue inside her and kept on until her breathing was an erratic mix of moans and gasps. He gently nipped at her engorged clit until she was thrashing around on the bed, pulling at her gown until her whole body was bare. He watched her breasts bounce with each movement, his own hips rocking into the end of the bed, driving him even more crazy for her.

When she started to make soft squealing noises, he knew he wouldn't be able to continue much longer without climbing on top of her and making her his. Grasping her nub with his lips, he sucked until she was shaking and louder than he'd ever heard a woman groan. It was killing him slowly.

When her cries quieted, he lowered her, licking at her with long strokes, wanting to take the taste with him. She lay there completely sated, her entire body bared to his eyes, watching him with glazed eyes. She was the most beautiful thing he'd ever seen.

Reaching, he pulled the sheet up and across her body. With stiff movements, he got up and looked down at her. "Get some sleep, honey." He whispered, his voice so hoarse with lust it was unrecognizable.

He didn't look at her again as he left the room, pulling the door closed softly.

Stumbling to the stairs, he almost missed a step that would have landed him at the bottom in more pain than he was already in.

The pain of his erection was so bad it actually burned, and he couldn't see calming it down, no matter what he tried. His body wanted its mate; no substitute was going to cut it.

With a curse, he headed for the back door. He'd have to run this off, even though he doubted the effectiveness of the only option he could think of.

Chapter Sixteen

Gage swore, tossing the folder onto the desk. He looked down at the mess and glared. His brain was completely A.W.O.L. He blamed that on only a few hours of sleep, seeing Kelsey's naked body splayed on the bed was playing over and over and over in his mind.

He'd left the house before she got up, not sure if she'd want to see him.

His phone rang, bringing his focus back to the now. Devin's number displayed on the screen. "Go ahead."

"Hey, Gage. We're going to be there tonight."

Gage closed his eyes, he'd forgotten he'd have house guests.

"Gage?"

"Yeah, sorry, I'm here." He rubbed the back of his neck.

"What's wrong?"

Sighing, he decided he should let Devin know what they were walking in to. "Kelsey's going through her first cycle. It's…"

Devin laughed, loudly. Gage was shocked, his friend wasn't a really laughing person.

"Sorry," Devin said, recovering his breath. "I just had flashbacks to the mind fuck I went through with Rayne."

Clearly, Gage thought, Rayne wasn't in hearing distance right now. "Yeah, it's something, that's for sure."

"Kelsey still unmarked?"

Gage wanted to groan, or maybe whine, but didn't. "Yeah."

"Are you going to be okay with me near her?"

Staring at the ceiling, he thought about it for a minute before answering. "I think so. You're mated and not even clan..." He fidgeted with the folders skewed on the desk. "Who knows? I'm having a bit of trouble with everything right now."

"Maybe Rayne talking to Kelsey will help."

"I won't hold my breath."

Devin laughed again and then paused. "Have you heard from Calum?"

"No."

"I still haven't heard from him."

"Well, he's in the back-country, and it *is* Calum..."

"Yeah. I swear I'm going to stick a tracker in him so we can see where the hell he goes."

"Where doesn't he go might be easier. Any more on what Tomas's crew is up to?"

Devin sighed. "They're all over the place. They're not being picky about the types of two-form they want, and they've tried to snatch from just about all the clans so far."

"Shit. I'd hoped he would have backed off."

"No such luck." He could hear voices in the background. "I have to go. We'll see you tonight."

"Okay. See you later." He hung up and then stared at the mess on his desk.

"Any luck?"

Gage looked up to see Jake leaning against the doorframe. "No. I need that damn invoice this afternoon."

"Did you take it to the house by mistake?"

Rubbing his forehead, he tried to remember. "I don't know."

"Why don't you give Kelsey a call and ask her to look?"

Gage didn't want to admit he was avoiding her. "Yeah." He sighed. "Devin and Rayne are going to be here tonight. Let everyone know so they don't freak out when they smell another shifter."

Jake grinned. "I'm looking forward to meeting her. She's all you and Blair talked about when you came back from the wedding."

Not wanting to discuss mates and weddings, Gage stood up "You get that brake line fixed?"

Straightening, Jake nodded. "Just waiting on Gary to lend me a hand to bleed the line before I sign off on it." He walked out of the office.

Sighing, Gage picked up his phone again. He dialed Kelsey, almost hoping she ignored it. She didn't, her soft voice teased his ear.

"Hey, honey. Can you go look in the office for an invoice?"

"I'm in the office, what am I looking for?"

He rhymed off the name of the supplier. "It may have got stuck in one of the folders I brought over last night."

"Okay, give me a second here..." he could hear her shuffling through them. "It's not here. Would it be anywhere else?"

Closing his eyes, he blew out a breath. "I doubt it." He pawed at the folders on the desk. "I can't find the bloody thing, and I need it."

There was a long pause on the other end of the line. "I can come to the shop and see if I can find it."

Gage realized what it was costing her to offer to come and help. "If you have the time, I'd really appreciate it. I can't finish this invoice without it and can't remember how much half the parts on it cost." He rubbed his jaw. "It's a huge account."

"Okay. I'll be there in a few minutes." She hung up.

Standing, Gage looked around the office and shook his head. She was going to climb up one side of him and down the other when she got a look at the mess.

Cursing at himself, he bent to pick up folders he'd stupidly knocked on the floor. As he straightened, he spotted Kelsey in the doorway. Her mouth was open in shock as her eyes surveyed the mess.

"Did a cyclone come through here?"

He opened his mouth with the first sarcastic quip that came to mind, then snapped it shut.

She stepped into the room, moving toward him slowly. He searched her eyes for a clue to her mood. "Where's the invoice you're trying to finish?"

Pointing to the computer, he decided he couldn't screw up a thank you. "Thanks for coming."

Moving past him, she went behind the desk and moved files to find the mouse and clear the screensaver. "I was running out of things to do at the house." Looking at the office, she raised an eyebrow. "The mess in here should keep me busy for a while."

Deciding he was safe enough, he winked at her. "Anything to keep you from being bored."

Holding out her hand, she looked at the folders he held. "You didn't randomly start pulling files, did you?"

Handing them over, he gave her a half grin. "Only the ones that were active when the supply delivery came in."

Glancing at the files, she frowned. "I can't believe you guys don't catalogue parts and prices in a database."

Pushing the folders out of the way, he sat on the corner of the desk. He'd have discussed anything with her, just to be with her without tension filling the space between them. "Mom and Dad tried it last year, but neither are really computer savvy."

She smirked and nodded. "I gathered that from the office at the house." She smiled, a real smile that had his heart pounding. "That's what I've been working on, cataloguing everything."

Turning, she started clicking away on the computer, Gage had no idea what, mostly because he watched her more than the screen, and he was one of those tech illiterate people. He could text on his phone and program arms on the equipment, but put a mouse in his hand and his brain shut down.

"So, I linked the database I started at the house to the shop…"

He looked at the screen to see what she was explaining.

"If you need to search for a part, you type it in, if it's in the database all the info will open."

Grinning, he read the screen and saw the supplier info, part specs, count and several other tabs. "You did all this?"

She gave him a cheeky grin. "All by my little self." She waved a hand at the screen. "It's not complete, not by a long shot, but it's a good start." Tapping the folders on the desk, she raised her eyes and looked at him. "As soon as I clean up your mess, I'll start entering stuff here. I'm only going back through the last year though; anything older would be useless."

He was so distracted watching the animation as she spoke, he didn't realize she was just staring at him. He cleared his throat. "You learn all this at school?"

Kelsey shrugged. "It wasn't part of my major, but I took a few classes on the side." She smiled. "So, I could finally show your dad the system I tried to talk him into using years ago."

Gage laughed. "Well, he won't be able to argue it if it's already done."

"Exactly."

She sat there looking so pleased with herself, it was hard for him not to reach out and pull her close. "I'm proud of you, Kels."

A surprised look appeared in her eyes. Shrugging it off, she motioned to the desk. "You get to help me go through all of this and refresh my memory for some of it." She stood up and patted his shoulder. "And then you get to get out of my way."

Moving past, he wondered if she realized she'd just touched him when she didn't have to. Standing slowly, he was afraid to do anything that would set her off, he lifted his hands. "What do you need me to do?"

Glancing up from the files, she was looking through she glared at him. "First, don't touch any more files from the cabinet. It's like you randomly threw them over your shoulder."

He grinned. "Close."

"Have a disagreement with the filing cabinet, Gage?"

They both turned to see Cooper leaning against the door.

"Ha ha, no." Gage grimaced.

Wiping his hands with a rag, Cooper looked at his hands. "I guess that means the missing invoice is still missing."

"That's why I'm here." Kelsey offered with a smirk, "and from the looks of it, I'm late."

Cooper chuckled and looked up. "Good, you'll get it *and* him sorted out." He looked at Gage. "Devin and the Missus are coming, Jake said."

Gage nodded, tucking his hands in his pockets. "Yeah, they'll be here tonight."

Cooper bobbed his head. "I'll tell Blair, he's on watch tonight."

"Thanks."

Looking around the room once more, Cooper tapped the side of his cap and winked at Kelsey. "Good luck, Kitty Kat."

Kelsey chuckled and shook her head. After he left, she glanced at him. "Devin's coming?"

She was biting at her bottom lip. Gage's stomach tightened as he dragged his eyes away from her mouth. "What's wrong?"

Her brow furrowed. "I don't understand the dynamics with Devin, what he is and how it works into my..." she sighed, "our world."

Perching back on the desk, he crossed his arms biting back a grin, since she'd finally admitted she was clan. He had to tuck his hands under his arms so he wouldn't wrap them around her. "Devin hasn't stepped into his father's place yet, so for now, and to us, he's just my friend Devin." He gave her a weak smile, "Calum and I are his seconds though, so when he does take over for his father the rules will change somewhat."

"So, I don't have to..." she waved her hand around, "bow to him or anything?"

Gage bit back a laugh. "Christ, no. Maybe later on in a ceremony or something, but not now." He chuckled. "I'd never hear the end of it if you did that. He doesn't like being who he is half the time."

She exhaled loudly. "See, I don't know. He's some kind of prince or something, but I still can't see the whole picture."

Gage sighed and stood up, this time he did go to lightly grasp her shoulders. "Relax. No one expects you to learn everything right now." He ran his hands down her arms and back up again, arguing with his cat that was pushing him to do more. "It's going to be all right, Kels."

"Promise?"

He almost fell into her amber eyes as she looked up at him. "Promise."

"Does Devin know about me? About..." she lowered her lashes and looked away from him.

"He does." Releasing her before he lost the battle with his cat, he let his hands hang loosely at his side. "His mate, his wife Rayne, is actually looking forward to meeting you."

Her eyes came back to his. "She is? Why?"

"Rayne just recently found out about her heritage..." he waved his hand around. "I'll let her go into the details, but she thought she might be able to talk with you and answer some questions."

Kelsey stood without moving for several seconds. He knew she didn't realize she was doing it, but it was so cat-like he was almost bouncing with joy inside.

Finally, she nodded, "I do have several..." she crunched up her nose, "thousand questions, maybe she'll be able to help."

Nodding, he stepped back, the scent he'd been almost able to ignore had just gotten stronger during their conversation. He swallowed and hoped they could get through the next day without her heat coming back, so he could have some quiet time to maybe renew her faith in him a little. At that thought, his cat reacted, almost scratching him raw on the inside; he wanted the heat, the she-cat. Trying not to shake his head, he pointed to the computer. "Please save me and help me get this invoice done before Gary has to leave."

Giving him a little smile that went straight through his heart, she nodded. "Okay."

The stupid invoice turned out to be on the floor, under the desk. Which made him feel like an idiot, but Kelsey seemed thrilled to have something to do.

Several times over the next hour, Gage had to clamp down on his cat. Kelsey was so in to this whole catalogue project, they'd ended up close together as he answered questions. He'd caught her inhaling his scent as they leaned near one another. He could have happily stayed in the office with her for days without complaint, even though he didn't give a crap about indexing each part.

He made sure the door remained open, so her cat didn't feel trapped. All the guys had wandered by slowly, but with a glare from Gage had kept moving away.

He was flipping through the files in the cabinet trying to find the stupid file they needed when Kelsey stepped in front to grab the file. Three seconds later, she had placed it in the drawer and shoved it closed.

"Done." Turning, she smiled up at him. "The mess is sorted, everything is filed, *and* your invoice is finished."

Grinning, he curbed the need to reach out and touch her. Being close to her was like some kind of self-inflicted torture. "I could mess it up again if you get bored."

Her eyes widened, "Don't you dare." She poked him in the chest. "From now on all receipts and invoices will be placed *neatly* in the basket so I can enter them in the computer and then file them."

"Yes, ma'am." He gave her a big grin. Almost reaching out to touch her, he moved to place his hand to hold the filing cabinet, concentrating on keeping it there. Kelsey had stilled in front of him, he tried to decide if he should step away, in closer, or what exactly would be the right move. When she leaned in and inhaled deeply, he had to will his hands to not grab for her.

When she reached out and ran a hand down his arm to his fist, he clenched his teeth together, not breaking eye contact with her. *Christ, don't move. Don't move.* Her amber eyes lightened to a golden hue as she lifted his arm then placed it on the other corner of the cabinet. The scent of her cat was filtering through his senses as he tried to stay completely still. He needed to see where she was going with this.

Biting her lip, she looked up at him, determination clear in her eyes. "Just…" she took a shaky breath, "just kiss me."

Her soft voice rolled over his skin like a caress. He gripped the cold steel and lowered his head toward her.

When he was close enough to taste her breath, she whispered. "Don't let go of the cabinet."

His heart was pounding inside his chest, his breathing already uneven, "I won't." She touched his jaw and stretched up the last few inches until their lips touched. He tried to kiss her softly, lightly, trying not to scare her, but all that changed as soon as he tasted her.

Turning his head, he deepened the kiss, his cat hissed in triumph when she grasped the back of his hair, pulling him to meet her halfway. Heat poured through him like flames. His whole body wanted to claim her, the desire more insistent than any force he'd ever felt.

She gasped against his mouth and pulled back slightly. Gage froze and stood there panting like it had been his first kiss. When he feared she was going to move away she moved closer and grabbed his head with both hands, pulling his mouth back to hers.

His arms shook as he fought to keep his hands on the cabinet. She tasted so good, he didn't want to stop. Even if all of his oxygen ran out, he'd still keep kissing her as long as she wanted him to.

With a groan, she tore her mouth away from his and stood there panting, looking at him with lust-heavy eyes. He fought to gain air as he stood there, not moving a muscle. Her hands slowly let go of his hair, and then left him all together.

Gage wanted to stop her, but he didn't, continuing to do what she'd asked of him.

Her chest heaving, she licked her lips, Gage just watching and saying nothing.

Placing a quick kiss on his mouth, she ducked under his arm and ran out of the office.

Gage dropped his head and closed his eyes, still trying to get his breathing under control. He wanted to pick up the filing cabinet or beat the holy hell out of something.

"Shit."

He didn't look up when Jake's voice came from the door. "I was walking past and damn near got my ass singed."

Inhaling, Gage lifted his head leaned against the top of the cool metal file cabinet, his hands still gripping the corners. "You saw?"

"Uh...I needed a spec book, but caught the gist when I saw her put your hand on the cabinet..."

Gage glanced over at him, Jake stood there, hands up in surrender, eyes wide.

"I didn't dare interrupt after *that*."

"Good. That would have ended badly."

Jake nodded. "Oh, I know." He leaned against the door frame, a puzzledlook on his face. "I don't know how you're not running after her right now."

Finally feeling like he was in control, Gage straightened and rubbed a hand over his face. "If I did that, she'd keep running just to spite me."

Jake crossed his arms over his chest, nodding thoughtfully. "Yeah, I can see that." He glanced awkwardly around the office, avoiding direct eye contact. "Coop warned us that she was in her cycle..." he chanced a glance at Gage, long enough for him to nod. "You must have the willpower to rival a saint. I remember what it's like..."

Gage interrupted him, not wanting to talk about the females they'd *helped* when they were younger. "It's not like that." He sat on the edge of the desk and studied the rough cement floor. "When it's your mate, you consider everything, not just the physical."

Jake blew out a breath, "You still need an iron will to resist."

Shaking his head, Gage glanced at him. "It's the hardest thing I've ever done. Truthfully, I'm scared to death that I'll fuck it up."

Jake stood and looked at him, so many emotions crossing his face that Gage wondered what the hell he was thinking. Finally releasing his breath, he came in and grabbed the spec book he needed off the shelf. With a half-hearted smile, he paused in the doorway. "I don't think I want to find my mate." He walked out, not looking back.

Gage continued to sit, trying to figure out why Kelsey had kissed him. Maybe Blair was right, and it had to be Kelsey's idea for him to get anywhere. Problem there was if he knew Kelsey, and he thought he did, she could stretch this into months before she put him out of his misery.

Chapter Seventeen

Kelsey stood watch at the door, gnawing at her lip, as Devin and Rayne got out of the car. Gage barely had time to greet them before Cooper and the other four men in her world came out of the trees from the shop. She knew Gage was aware she was standing there in the shadows, worrying.

Taking a deep breath, she opened the door and went down the porch steps. The smile on Gage's face encouraged her to keep going, even though her knees were shaking. Everyone paused and turned to watch. She glanced from Gage to Devin a few times. Devin's wife was so petite, even by Kelsey's standards, *and* she was absolutely gorgeous with miles of blonde hair, a pale complexion, and bright blue eyes. Her smile was warm and accepting, putting Kelsey at ease, a bit.

Gage stepped beside her, close enough she could feel his body heat, without touching her. Somehow his nearness made her feel better.

"Well," Devin grinned at her, "you're a long way from the brat that dumped oil on me."

Kelsey smirked, she'd forgotten that incident. "I didn't dump it on you. I told you to move," she shrugged, "you didn't listen."

Devin laughed then shook his head when Rayne gave him a questioning look. "Don't ask." Sobering, he gave Gage a questioning look.

Frowning, Kelsey glanced up at to see Gage respond with a quick, but tense, nod.

Devin stepped toward her with a smile on his face. His hug was friendly but brief. "It's good to see you again, Kelsey."

Kelsey blinked and tried not to look like she was sniffing the air, confused, she glanced at Gage as Devin stepped away. His expression turned to concern as he leaned down to her.

"You okay, honey?"

Letting out a quick breath, she nodded and turned her head to whisper, "He kind of smells like a wet dog."

Gage snorted and looked down, lips twitching. "You'll get used to it," he said softly.

She turned to see everyone, including Devin, trying not to smile as they looked anywhere but directly at her. "I guess I still have to learn a few things, huh?" Kelsey whispered.

Rayne stepped forward and pulled her into a sisterly embrace. "Just ignore the males, Kelsey. They're still too connected to their inner children to show restraint." She leaned back and smiled at her. "And you're right, he does smell like a wet dog."

Devin's jaw dropped as he looked at her.

She chuckled. "Which, it seems, appeals to me."

With a fake growl, Devin pulled her back beside him and pulled her tight against his side.

Kelsey decided right then that she liked Rayne.

Cooper cleared his throat, drawing everyone's attention to the men standing and waiting quietly.

Devin and Rayne turned toward them. Kelsey watched, still staying close to Gage without being too close.

Noah started to get down, on one knee from the looks of it, but Jake grabbed his arm and shook his head. She watched as all five men bowed their heads for a few moments as Devin and Rayne stood there in front of them.

When they straightened, Devin moved over and shook their hands. When he reached Noah, he stood there. "Noah, it's good to see you." He smiled. "You look good."

Noah averted his eyes and nodded. "I like being here."

"Good." Devin put out his hand and waited while Noah hesitated before finally shaking his briefly.

Noah looked over to Rayne and Kelsey watched as his whole posture went rigid. Noah's eyes were wide as he continued to just stand there.

Moving over, Kelsey stepped in front of him. "Noah, what's wrong?" She could see everyone looking at them.

Noah's troubled eyes finally looked down at her. 'I know her," he said in a shaky voice.

Kelsey placed a hand on his arm, she could feel his fear.

Eyes wide, she glanced at Gage. He frowned and came over. Blair was right behind him, concern etched in his features.

"Noah?" Gage inquired in a hushed tone.

"She was with Aiden Tomas," Noah uttered in an icy tone.

"It's okay, Noah," Gage assured him, "she wasn't part of it."

Noah's eyes darted from Rayne to Gage, he was inhaling slowly.

"Gage?" Devin's tone was wary.

Shaking his head, Gage lifted his hand telling Devin to wait. Turning back to Noah, he reached out and placed a hand on his shoulder. "Rayne didn't know, Noah. She's like Kelsey; she didn't know what she was until she met Devin."

Kelsey glanced at Rayne to see her give Devin a glare before he dropped the arm he'd used to hold her back. She walked over to Noah with sure strides, holding her head up and maintaining eye contact.

Gage moved Kelsey back so he was between Rayne and Noah, as Blair stepped up to place himself almost right in front of Noah, keeping Rayne a few paces from reaching him. Kelsey watched the expression in Blair's eyes harden, as without a sound, he let Noah know he needed to watch his step.

Rayne stepped closer, holding her wrist up toward Noah.

Hesitating, he glanced from Blair to Gage and then lowered his head, inhaling the scent from Rayne's wrist. Surprise lit his eyes.

"I'm…" he lowered his head, "I didn't…"

Rayne placed a hand on Blair's arm so he'd move back. She stepped in front of Noah. "It's okay. I had no idea. I've spent the last few months giving the Alliance every detail I can remember to help them get others out." She smiled at him. "If you could help by filling in any details, we could free more like us, Noah."

Straightening, he looked around at everyone, his eyes settled on Kelsey as she moved out of Gage's shadow. Nodding, she gave him an encouraging smile.

Noah swallowed and looked back at Rayne, "I can try. I don't know security codes, but I know a few places Tomas's men keep some of the women."

Rayne reached out and squeezed his arm. "That would be a great help."

By this time, Devin had moved to wrap his arm around Rayne and pull her back into his chest. "One piece at a time, Noah and we'll end his tyranny."

A relieved look appeared on Noah's face. "I hope so, sir."

Devin leaned down and whispered something to Rayne. Kelsey looked around; no one seemed to be able to hear what he said. She had to figure out all these new senses.

"Gage," Blair placed a hand on Noah's shoulder, "Noah and I are going to check the borders, he can chat with Devin when we get back."

Kelsey knew it was Blair's way of giving Noah some time to adjust, and she was pleased he cared enough to give Noah the break.

"Sounds good." Gage said over her head.

She could feel the heat from his body, he was that close to her again. Afraid it might start strange things happening inside her in front of the others; she side-stepped and glanced at him. "I'll just take Rayne in the house and show her around."

Gage's eyes searched her face for a moment before he gave her a brief nod.

"I'm thrilled to be here," Rayne said on a soft laugh, "some of the other stops we've made go through this intricate ceremony," she accepted the cup of tea from her, "most of which I still don't understand." She sipped the tea. "Then I have a grumpy man to contend with, because he hates all *that* stuff."

Kelsey leaned back and nodded. "Well, grumpy men I'm used to," she motioned toward the window where Gage, Devin, Cooper and Gary stood still talking, "But as far as how most things go, I know less that you."

Sitting back with the cup cradled between her hands, Rayne studied her. "I can't believe you," she shook her head, "Okay, both of us were around shifters our entire lives and didn't know." She played with the handle of the cup. "I felt like my parents deceived me, and I felt so betrayed when I found out."

Kelsey watched the pain flash in her eyes. "I still haven't decided who to be maddest at; my parents, Gage's parents, or all of the guys for keeping it from me."

Giving her a sympathetic look, Rayne ran a finger around the rim of her cup. "After seeing what Noah and the others that the Tomas family have survived, I understand better why my parents didn't tell me. They wanted me to grow up, feel normal and build a life of my own." She sighed. "Only I'm not sure what they expected me to think when I woke up one morning as a wolf." She grimaced, "It wouldn't have been a good start to my day."

Kelsey smiled. "Yeah, I still don't see why my parents never said. They had me here a lot, but I don't know how I didn't see the signs."

Rayne's eyes sparkled. "Yes, I suppose tigers are out of the ordinary in a normal world."

"Considering the size of some of these guys when they shift, yeah, they had to do some serious sneaking around." She sat there, questions running through her head, not sure which to ask.

"Just ask them, Kelsey. I'll try to answer as best as I can." Rayne said softly.

Kelsey took a deep breath and exhaled while trying to decide what she wanted to know the most. Closing her eyes, she blew out another breath before looking back at Rayne. "I haven't been able to bring myself to call Beth, Gage's mom, just yet, so the only perspective I have on any of this is from the guys." Rayne rolled her eyes to that, and Kelsey couldn't help but smirk. "This cycle, heat, or whatever it's called," she felt her face redden, "do you…have you…"

Rayne reached over and grasped her hand lightly. "I haven't been through it myself, yet." She winced. "But I have talked to others about it."

Kelsey sighed in relief. "Please tell me what you can." Rubbing her free hand over her stomach, her shoulders relaxed. "It's absolutely horrible. I thought I was dying, hot inside, hot outside and my stomach cramping…"

Rayne gave her a sympathetic look. "I hate to say it, but from what I'm told, the feline shifter has it worse than the others."

"Wonderful." Kelsey muttered.

"Have you…" Rayne looked down at her hand and then back up at her. "Have you and Gage been together?"

Kelsey shook her head as her cheeks flushed more. "He…" she searched for the right word. "helped me both times it's happened, but we haven't had…sex."

Rayne nodded, with an understanding look on her face. "Well, if it helps, let him." She leaned forward. "You don't have to do anything until you're ready though."

Sighing, Kelsey played with her cup. "When it happens, I don't have control of much of anything."

"I understand that." Picking up her cup, she sipped it a few times. "Tell Gage where you're drawing the line," she paused for a moment. "*When* your head is clear. I'm sure he'll do everything he can to make sure nothing else happens." She shrugged. "He is your mate after all, so his sole objective is your happiness and comfort."

Closing her eyes, Kelsey scrunched up her face. "That's part of the problem. What if I'm not sure I want a mate...right now?" She shrugged and looked back at Rayne. "I mean I've always had the hots for Gage, but I never saw the happily-ever-after scenario with him." She cupped her cheeks, knowing they would be flaming red by now. Dropping her hands, she gave Rayne a hesitant look. "I've never been with a man, and I don't want to be forever bound to one I'm not sure about."

Rayne sat there and looked at her. Kelsey was thrilled that she was actually taking time to think about her answers. "You can have sex without being marked. Tell him, Kelsey, he'll understand." She bit her lip for a second. "Okay, his animal isn't going to get it, but I think he'll try to understand for you."

Kelsey leaned forward and rested her head on her arms on the table. "God, I just wanted to come home and see Gage," She swallowed, "You know, see if there was anything between us and then figure out what direction I want my life to go." Tipping her head up, she looked over at Rayne. "Then everything happened and changed all at once..." she sat up and brushed her hair back from her face, close to angry tears. "I don't know how to handle all of this, I just don't." Dropping her hands in her lap, she waited for Rayne to speak, hoping she had some magic fix-it-all answer.

Finally, Rayne leaned forward, her arms on the table. "I understand all of that." She gave her a lopsided smile. "Let me tell you how I was initiated into this world of shifters, clans and far too many alphas." She gave her a wide-eyed look. "And then you will see how truly lucky you are to have a mate like Gage, who will wait as long as he has for you."

Kelsey nodded, just knowing that she wasn't completely alone in all this weirdness made her feel a little bit better.

Rayne started tracing an invisible pattern on the table as she spoke. "My parents sheltered me from everything. I barely knew anyone other than the two of them—and my father's employer, Tomas senior." Kelsey felt her eyes go wide, but she didn't interrupt. "When they were killed suddenly..." she paused and Kelsey knew, without asking, who was responsible for their death, just like her own parents. "Aiden Tomas was sweet and attentive...at first. He held my broken heart in his hands and I thought he was my savior." She glanced up for a second and took a deep breath, clearly struggling to find all the words. "We ended up engaged. He was my world, or as I realized, he controlled everything in my world." She waved her hands around. "I won't go into all the little details, but when I discovered he was a brutal man, I packed and left." She had a far-off look in her eyes, as if she was remembering as she spoke. "I picked a spot on a map. Drove from Chicago to this deserted campground a few hours past Timmins." She laughed. "I'd never driven more than twenty minutes in my life, and here I was embarking on a twenty-hour drive." She grinned. "That was interesting. I don't suggest doing it alone."

Kelsey sipped her tea, even though it had cooled, and waited for Rayne to continue.

"So, I bought everything you could possibly need to camp, even though I'd never done anything that barbaric in my pampered life." She rolled her eyes. "I thought I'd just hide out, examine my world and options, and then pick up the pieces," she shrugged. "*Then* I discovered that not only didn't I know a thing about setting up a tent or roughing it, but that I was trespassing on this extremely scary, anti-social, but potently sexy man's land." Kelsey waited while Rayne stared off into space. "I could go on and on, but some other time I'll share all the entertainment value of the story." She shrugged. "I was unnaturally attracted to Devin, even though I had just been devastated by another man." Her cheeks flushed lightly. "I couldn't keep my hands off him, and the feeling was quite mutual." Fanning her face, she gave Kelsey a look, one that only another female would understand.

Kelsey got the drift, even in her virginal state.

"Devin marked me as his mate before I was even aware of who he was, that I was his mate, or that I'd be a queen after being mated." She continued, an exasperated look clear on her face. "Needless to say, I broke. I thought the man was my savior, protecting me from Aiden's men when they came for me. Then I discover everything and that I'd been deceived by another man." Kelsey knew her jaw dropped, but she didn't comment. "I know, right," Rayne shook her head, a small smile appearing. "I'm clearly not the brightest when it comes to men." She looked down twisting the wedding band on her finger. "But you know what? Fate knows what she's doing. I was in lust with a man that was actually my mate, and now, I wouldn't change any of it. I feel complete in a way I never dreamt possible, and I feel loved and love him with every fiber of my being." She sighed and then glanced at Kelsey. "But that's just between you and I, he still thinks he'll be doing penance until he's gray for deceiving me."

Kelsey just sat back, her mind processing everything Rayne had just said. "I guess I am lucky that Gage hasn't done something before now."

"They can't help it, Kelsey, it's their every instinct to keep their mate safe and close."

Taking a deep breath, Kelsey looked up at the ceiling. Finally, she looked back at Rayne. "Thank you. That helped." She laughed and rubbed a hand over her face. "To understand a bit more at least, but I still don't know what I'm doing."

Rayne reached over and squeezed her hand. "Start by talking to Gage, while you're clear-headed."

Before Kelsey knew what she was doing, Rayne was on her feet and heading for the door. "I'll get him now. Get it over and done with."

By the time she could stand, Rayne was outside with the guys.

Chapter Eighteen

Gage glanced over to see Rayne walking toward them. His heart stuttered when he realized she was focused on him, not her mate. Glancing at Devin, he noted he realized it too.

"Gage?" Rayne's voice was soft.

He frowned, then answered. "Yes?"

She smiled, which made him realize why Devin could never say no to her. "Do you have a few minutes? Kelsey needs to speak with you."

His heart stopped. With a nod, he realized he was already heading to the house. "I'll be back."

As he stepped into the kitchen, he kept talking to himself. *Just breathe, it's okay, it's nothing bad. Everything is fine.* When she wasn't in the kitchen, he had to stop and inhale to find where she had gone.

She was in the living room, looking out the window. "Honey? Is everything all right?"

She gave him a look. "That's a loaded question, Mister Lockman."

Gage nodded, rubbing his jaw. "I suppose it is right now." He swallowed, loudly. "Rayne said you needed to speak to me?"

"Yes, but I don't know where to begin."

Gage tried to ignore his pounding heart. "Is something wrong?" He inhaled subtly to see if he could determine her mood. She stamped her foot, exasperated. Slowly, he stepped further into the room. "Okay, that was a dumb question ..."

"Ya think? That's only part of it." She turned so he could see her face. "This was so much easier when I was talking with Rayne."

"Do you..." he hesitated, "do you want me to go get her?" What he really wanted was to scream, *just tell me what's going on!* But he dug deep and tried not to freak out.

Kelsey sighed, just looking at him. Each second felt like minutes before she started to speak again.

"I'm overwhelmed with all of this, Gage."

He wanted to pull her into his arms, her voice held so much pain he only wanted to erase it. "I know, honey..."

She laughed quietly, shaking her head and he was even more lost, not sure what was wrong.

"I wanted to come home," she hugged her arms around herself, her expression hurt, "for the last year, that's all I wanted. To come home." She looked at him again, her amber eyes forlorn. "I wanted to see if I was still attracted to you, to see..." she blushed, "to see if there was anything between us, now that I'm older."

Gage swallowed, not sure if he was supposed to comment or just let her talk through it all. He decided the longer he kept his mouth shut, the better his chances would be.

"I'm not sure how to say this, without inflating your already large ego..." she shrugged, "but you were the object of all my fantasies for years."

He opened his mouth and then shut it, and jammed his hands into his pockets. How long did she expect him to just stand here and not touch her when she was telling him all of this?

She made a little noise in the back of her throat, he was pretty sure it was one of surprise, but continued before he could figure it out.

"Now, I don't know if what I feel is some residual thing from my adolescent fantasies, or what is from this mating stuff..." she waved a hand indicating herself. . "I just don't."

Gage struggled to get the idea of fantasies out of his brain and focus on her. To know she wanted him for all the years he'd been waiting wasn't helping him keep his feet planted in place instead. "What are you saying, honey?" He shrugged, "I'm not getting it."

She rolled her eyes. "Well my lack of explanation instead of simple random thoughts probably isn't helping." She took a deep breath and he watched as she released it, slow and controlled. "I don't want to be mated or with someone *forever* when I don't even know if there's anything real between us."

His breath caught in his lungs and he stood there, struggling to breathe without letting on that he felt like she'd just stabbed a knife into his chest. "I see." Crossing his arms, he gathered himself. "So, what do you want to do?" His cat was close to clawing through his skin, trying to force a more assertive position. This was *his* mate, and his cat didn't intend to take this quietly. Gage only knew if he listened, he'd lose her for good, so he tried to show her understanding all while he died a little inside.

"I don't..." She crossed her arms over her chest and shook her head. "What if what we're feeling is just the," she gave him a look, "animal thing..."

Ignoring his better instincts, he went over to stop right in front of her. Reaching deeply, he aimed for patience. "There's a lot more to us than just being mates. You didn't even know what a mate was, or any of this that you've learned when you were younger and throwing yourself into my path at every opportunity." When she flushed, he wanted to bite his tongue off for phrasing it that way. "If I'd been stronger, I wouldn't have had to run the other way..."

She sighed. "I know you only did that to give me time."

"Yes." He nodded. "And maybe giving me some time too. I was only twenty-one when I realized you were my mate," he shrugged, "a part of me didn't want to be mated that early in life. I'd just started to..." he stopped when he realized he'd been about to reference other women.

"I know what you're trying to say, Gage."

Almost sighing in relief, the look he gave her was relieved. "Good thing." He studied her face, wanting nothing more than to reach out and touch her soft skin, her silky hair... "I don't know of a solution that will suit both of us, honey, I really don't." He felt like he was falling into her tawny eyes. So many emotions were flooding his system, all while he tried to keep his animal half under control.

"I can see how conflicted you are, even though you're saying you understand."

Rubbing his jaw, he looked away. "I'm trying. It's hard."

"Because of your cat?"

Nodding, he looked back down at her. "What do you want me to do, Kelsey?" She bit her lip, and he couldn't look away. *Does she know doing that drives me crazy?*

"I've never even been with a man, Gage."

He supposed shouting *halleluiah* would be wrong, so he just bobbed his head and hoped she'd talk so he didn't have to.

"I want to..."

Frowning, he held up his hand. "If you're going to say you want to be with another man, I'm afraid that's where my cat will push past all the control I have..."

Her eyes widened. "No, that's not what I was going to say."

He let out a sigh of relief.

"I want to be with you..." her eyes held his, as if she was expecting rejection. He clamped his jaw tight and stood, inhaling slowly through his nose waiting for her finish. "But..."

But...yeah, saw that coming like a tidal wave. Christ, I'm going to need Coop to tranq me soon.

"But I don't want to be marked. I don't want us to be stuck with each other if it's only the heat or some metaphysical fate that's drawn us together."

He blinked, once, twice, then looked up at the ceiling for another blink. *Keep it together. Don't. Fuck. This. Up.* Lowering his eyes back to hers, "I know there's more, honey, but if you want to wait..." he almost choked on the growl his cat was trying to voice. He started to lift his hand, to touch her cheek, then changed his mind and jammed it into his pocket. "Then, we wait." Gage hoped the last few words sounded better to her than they had to his ears. Inside his cat was screaming *WAIT?*

When she smiled, a real smile, with relief flooding her face, he felt like crying himself.

"Okay, good." She let her breath out quickly, like she'd been holding it through the whole conversation. "So, if it turns out to just be a physical thing between us, then we won't have to worry about being saddled to each other for the rest of our lives. We can go our separate ways, right?"

With a frozen smile on his face, he kept his jaw clamped tight. Knowing there was no way he could speak without it coming out as a growl, he nodded. *Not in this lifetime are we screwing and then going our separate ways, my dear Kelsey.*

Grinning like he'd just handed her the best gift *ever*, she gave a little jump and hugged him tight around the waist. Hesitating to make sure he still had a strong hold on his cat, he wrapped his arms around her, hugging her soft body into his.

Leaning back, she kept her hands on his waist. "I'm going to get dinner started. We have company, remember?" Stretching up, she lightly kissed his mouth and then was gone from his grasp, heading into the kitchen.

What. The. Fuck. Just. Happened? She was in the kitchen humming. Humming! While he stood here feeling like she'd just beat him upside the head with a wrench. He wasn't going to survive this. In the last six years he thought he'd gone through some emotionally and physically demanding moments while waiting for her, but here she was and things just kept getting worse.

Rubbing the back of his neck, he frowned at the floor trying to sort out what exactly he'd just agreed to.

"Gage?"

Looking up, Kelsey was standing in the doorway.

"Maybe you could go out and ask if the guys want to join us? I'll defrost some steaks in the microwave and we could have a barbeque,"

With his head still swimming, he nodded and gave her a quick smile. "Sounds good." Moving fast, he walked past her, dropping a kiss so brief he almost missed on the top of her head before going outside to invite every male in their lives to dinner with his mate in the middle of her first friggin' cycle. He was going to go get the tranq gun and bring it to dinner too.

Stomping he went over to Cooper and Devin.

Cooper glanced up. "Gary took Rayne over to the shop to show her…"

Gage growled. "We're having a barbeque, go invite everyone." He headed in the direction of the trail to the lake lookout.

"Guess that talk went well." He heard Devin mutter to Cooper.

"Yep," Cooper responded.

No one had to be tranq'd during dinner, although Gage had to issue more than one warning look when someone got too close, or looked too long, or smiled in her direction… Now he sat on the porch with Devin, nursing the same beer he'd grabbed for dinner. He couldn't taste anything right now, so it didn't much matter. At this moment, he wasn't even sure what Devin was saying, he couldn't focus on anything as his conversation with Kelsey just kept playing over like it was an audio loop.

"Gage?"

He jumped and saw Rayne giving him a strange look. *Shit, did I miss something?*

"I don't think Kelsey's feeling well." She looked over at Devin, giving him a look Gage couldn't figure out.

Getting to his feet quickly, he took a few steps toward the door, not sure if he was supposed to go check on her, whether or not they believed he should.

"Gage?"

He paused and looked over at Rayne as she stood on the top step.

"Is there somewhere *secluded* where I could go for a walk with my mate?" Her tone was no more than a whisper.

Gage stood there and watched Devin almost fall on his face trying to get to his feet and over to his mate, a really big grin on his face. Just seeing the almost king was ruled by his mate made Gage feel a slight bit better. "Take her and show her the lookout over the lake, Dev."

Devin gave him a grin over his shoulder as he hugged her into his body started down the steps.

Watching them for a second, Gage opened the door and went into the kitchen. "Kels?" She wasn't there. Making a bee-line for the stairs, he stopped when he saw the bathroom door was closed. He stopped outside the door, tapping gently. "Kelsey?"

Chapter Nineteen

He could hear water running. Leaning against the door, her scent enveloped him and his legs almost gave out, the heat was back. "Honey, open the door." He tried to keep the growl out of his voice, but his cat was raging. Biting his lip, he focused on controlling his animal. They had to be careful or be rejected. That got his attention.

"I-I'm f-fine, Gage."

He scowled at the door. *Why did she sound like she was shivering? Christ, she wasn't...* "Kelsey, sitting in cold water isn't going to help you." He fought to keep his voice soft and gentle, even though he wanted to roar. *Does my cat even roar?* Shaking his head, he leaned his head against the door. How did he get her to open the door without scaring her? When he realized, he felt like a dumbass. "Baby, we're alone, open the door."

There was splashing on the other side, he waited. The door opened a crack and she looked out at him. "Where are Rayne and Devin?"

Placing a hand on the door, he gently pushed it open. "They went for a long walk. I think they wanted to be alone." His heart jerked in his chest when the door opened to reveal her tear-stained face as she stood wrapped in a towel, shivering. "Christ, Kelsey. What were you trying to do?"

164

She shook her head. "I didn't want anyone to see me like this."

"You should have called me." He gripped the door frame rather than grab for her; she looked like she was going to bolt, despite their talk earlier. Knowing how scarey it could be for a woman in her first few cycles, he stood quietly blocking the door, fighting to not make any sudden movements that would scare her more. "Kels, you need me…" He watched a tear roll down her cheek. "*Nothing* is more important than you are to me."

She nodded, but still didn't move.

"Let me kiss you," he coaxed softly, "let me touch you and help you." He tightened his grip on the doorframe, wanting nothing more than to grab her and sweep her into his arms. "Come here," he whispered. "It's not mating, baby; it's letting me help you." When she nodded and took a hesitant step toward him, he squeezed the wooden frame harder. He didn't know what else to say to ease her fears.

It took every ounce of restraint to control his cat when her hand touched his waist and slowly slid up his chest. Breathing her scent in, his whole body tightened. She pushed her nose into his chest and took deep breaths. *That's it; let your instincts take over. Please.* Using both of her hands now, she shoved his shirt up and rubbed her cheek against his chest. *Christ.* Gage flexed his hands and felt the wood of the door frame give into the pressure he exerted.

When she licked across his pec, he released the frame and ripped the shirt from his body. His cat was vibrating inside him, just like he was from the tension and need this woman created. He moved his hand slowly up her arm and across her shoulder, until he was able to cup her head. She lifted her mouth from his skin and looked up at him. The need in her eyes undid his resolve.

Grasping her hair, he reached to pull her tight into his body as his lips crashed down on hers. Her mouth assaulted his in return. Tearing his mouth from hers, he captured her gaze, "Let me take you upstairs." She nodded, her hands moving all over his chest like she couldn't bear to not feel him.

He pulled the towel free from her body and lifted her up. "Wrap your legs around me." He hissed out a breath he hadn't realized he held when her hot flesh melded with his. He tried to keep his balance and focus as her legs squeezed the breath out of him, her teeth blazing a trail across his shoulder and neck. When she bit his neck, he had to stop and brace himself against the wall half way up the stairs. *Christ, yeah.*

Grasping her tightly, he gently pulled her head from his neck. "As much as I fucking love that," he growled, "keep your teeth to yourself, or I'll return in kind and you'll find yourself marked." It amazed him that he managed to force the words out. Nodding, she pulled free and proceeded to lick her way up his throat. Stifling an exasperated growl, he stumbled his way to his room, without them hitting the floor.

Setting her gently on the bed, he kicked his boots across the floor while ripping at the zipper of his jeans. He couldn't stop looking at her, she was so fucking perfect. Her skin was dusted with freckles, and he planned to kiss each one. Her waist was trim and toned, but just enough to look soft and womanly, not muscled. If she kept devouring him with her eyes, he was never going to get these damn jeans off his body.

"I don't know what to do," she whispered breathlessly when he finally crawled onto the bed.

He crawled up her body, tasting all of her flesh he could manage without stopping. "Your body does, listen to it."

He got no further than her breasts. Breasts he'd tried to picture a thousand times in his mind, yet he'd never come close to the real ones he was about to taste. She had deep rose-tinted nipples, now completely erect. He licked over one slowly and she moaned. *Christ, going slow will kill me.* Lowering his body between her legs, he sucked the other nipple into his mouth and growled.

She almost came undone beneath him when he switched to the first. His hands glided over every inch of her skin, he couldn't seem to touch her enough.

"Gage," she moaned, "it's burning, so bad."

Lifting his head, he couldn't believe he'd forgotten the heat. *Shit. How am I supposed to be gentle and deal with her heat at the same time?* He kissed his way up her throat, and she began clawing at the sheets. He groaned. *And keep her cat from ripping my skin off?* Grabbing her wrists, he held her hands against the bed and crushed her mouth beneath his.

God the way she kissed him, responded to him, gave new meaning to being eaten alive and he loved it, but knew he had to look after her.

Tearing his mouth away, he released one arm and rolling in one move, until she was on top of him. "You control this, baby." Grasping her hips, he pulled her up to straddle his body, aligning them. He kissed her again. "I want to do this right, but your heat isn't going to let us go slow, and I don't want to hurt you."

When she leaned down to bite her way up his chest all while grinding against him, he gripped her hips and fought to just lay there and let her move, keeping his teeth to himself. He could do this, for her; give her a first time that is slow and gentle.

"Gage," she gasped, "it burns..."

He could see she was ready, her rubbing up and down over him left no questions. Grasping her hips, he lifted her and aligned their bodies so the tip of his throbbing erection pushed slowly into her heat. *Christ, so fuckin' wet.* He ground his teeth and lowered her slowly, trying to stop her from thrusting down and impaling herself. "Kiss me," he told her trying to distract her to maintain some control. She leaned down and attacked his mouth, he decided if he died at that moment, he'd be the happiest man ever. With each thrust of her tongue, he lowered her hips a bit more. *She's so tight, Christ.* He didn't think he was a big man, but he was worried he really would hurt her. *Kil..ling...me.*

Lifting her head, she moaned deep in her throat, almost causing him to lose control of the pace he had set. Gripping her hips tighter, he knew she'd be bruised, but couldn't help it. Holding his breath, he thrust up past the barrier and then froze. *So tight. Holy fuck.*

When she began to fight against his grip on her hips, he relaxed his hands to let her move the way she wanted. She sat up and began to ride him in slow movements, experimenting as he fought to breathe and lie still, letting her adjust to him at her own pace. He had to squeeze his eyes shut, watching her gorgeous body move over him would cause him to lose control and take over.

Dropping forward, she rested her hands on his chest and dropped down onto him. The moan that came from her had his eyes popping open. *Fuck it, I'm watching.* He thrust in time, trying to match her movements. Kelsey began to make sweet mewling noises in her throat as her breathing came in short gasps. When her fingers dug into his chest, the sharp pain brought him back to reality.

Grasping her wrists, he pulled her hands off his body and clasped them together, showing her how to use his braced arms as leverage. She began to move more frantically, and if he hadn't just taken her virginity he would have wondered where she learned such a thing. Lowering her head, she opened her eyes and looked down at him; he lost his breath when he found himself looking up into a stunning pair of golden cat eyes.

Christ, her cat is trying to come out. He glanced at her hands to see the start of claws where her nails had been. *Not now.* If he stopped now, she'd hate him or scratch him to a bloody pulp, neither of which he wanted.

Growling, he lifted his hips and flipped them over, so she was pinned under his body. Pinning her wrists in one hand over her head, he leaned on his elbow lifting himself from the reach of her mouth as he began to slam his hips into her. She spurred his movement on by making the sexiest noises in her throat.

Gage was sweating and trying to stay in control when she began thrashing her head from side to side. He had to fight to control his cat from biting and breeding her when she started to make little squealing, gasping noises. controlling his thrusts, he kept himself restrained, growling when her body squeezed him so tight; his orgasm was ripped from him before he could take a breath.

Slowing, he slid in and out of her until she went lax under him. His head was floating; he couldn't focus on any thoughts. Smiling down at her, her hair all over the place and a light sheen of sweat covering her skin, he waited until she caught her breath. As her eyes opened, he tensed and the fog in his brain was gone. Her eyes were still those of her cat. *Shit.*

Pulling out of her, he leaned on his side and ran his hand up over her stomach. "Honey, you need to grab some track pants and top."

"What?" She was breathless and sounded so sexy; a shiver went over his skin.

He looked up at her hands he still held. There were still claws. "Baby, your cat is trying to come out. We have to go outside."

With wide eyes, she looked at him. "Is that why I can't focus?"

He nodded and released her wrists, hopping off the bed and out of reach all in one move. "Yeah, come on, we don't have much time." This was not the way her first time was supposed to go, he wanted to scream.

With a confused look, she rolled to the other side of the bed. Gage opened a drawer and grabbed a pair of his sweats and a t-shirt and tossed them at her. Grabbing his pants, he pulled them on and then went over to help her. She was shaking so badly she couldn't stand still long enough to dress. He didn't know if the shaking was from sex or the change, but really didn't want to hang around in the house to find out.

When he pulled the shirt over her head, he leaned down and kissed her softly. "I promise next time we'll do it right."

Eyes wide, she looked up at him, his cat prowled across his skin, recognizing the

Cat eyes were looking up at him. "That was wrong?"

Grinning, he wrapped his arm around her. "Oh, no honey, that was right, but it will be better next time."

She chuckled quietly. "If you say so."

Chapter Twenty

Gage kept his arm around her, she was still shaking and he was pretty sure it was because she was changing. The heat and sex had just drowned out the beginning, which was a damn good reason for his missing the signs.

He started to take her on the path toward the lake and then remembered Devin and Rayne. Turning in the other direction, they hadn't gotten far when Kelsey gasped.

"Gage?" she stopped and hugged her arms around her middle. "What's happening?"

Rubbing his hand over her back, he encouraged her to keep walking. He wanted her in the open when she changed, he didn't want to lose her in the trees. "It's okay, honey, don't fight it, just let it happen." Even as he said it, he was remembering what it was like that first time your cat moved inside you. It was eerie and awesome all at the same time. "It feels weird, but as long as you don't fight it, it won't hurt."

They were almost to the yard of the shop. He stepped in front of her and ran his hands up and down her arms. Tilting her head up, he kissed the tip of her nose. "This wasn't what I planned after our first time together."

Kelsey leaned into him, drawing his scent into her system. "Well, we're not exactly predictable people."

He chuckled. "No, I guess we're not." She looked up at him, again he was struck by how stunning her yellow cat eyes were.

"Gage, I'm scared."

Pulling her into his arms, even though his instincts told him to stay out of the reach of her claws, he held her tight against his body. If he had his way, he'd keep her there forever. She was shaking harder now and it he was trying not to show her he was concerned so she didn't tense. Kissing the top of her head, he gripped her shoulders and leaned back. "Don't fight it, Kelsey, embrace it head on like you do everything else."

She gave him a small smile. "I'm trying. It's…" she bent forward and rested her head against his chest, taking long, slow breaths.

Gage tightened his jaw as her tiny claw tips dug into his forearms. "Come on, honey, let's find you somewhere private so you can take off the clothes."

Straightening up, she took a deep breath. "The clothes?" Closing her eyes, she blinked a few times. "Got it." She looked up at him again, "these eyes are kind of…"

He grinned. "You're going to love the full package, trust me." Taking her elbow, he guided her around the fence to the small opening where the guys preferred to change. As they went through the trees, Jake came out with his boots and shirt in his hand. Gage shook his head so he wouldn't speak. Jake's step paused as his eyes moved over Kelsey slowly. His eyes widened a bit as he saw her eyes.

Kelsey stiffened, until Jake gave her a big grin and a brief encouraging nod. With that, Jake kept going, leaving them alone in the clearing.

Kelsey's breathing was growing more rapid. "Gage."

He rubbed his hand down her back. "You've got this, honey." He wanted to hug her again, but knew better. "Just let it happen," he whispered, leaning as near to her as he dared.

Focusing for a second, he let his cat roll over his skin, so hers could scent him. Being with clan helped the change happen smoothly. Kneeling in front of her, he pulled the track pants down her legs, wincing as she grasped his shoulder for balance and her claws dug in his flesh. Kelsey didn't even notice.

Tossing the pants to the ground, he stood up. She looked so sexy in his t-shirt that hung down her thighs. Giving himself a mental smack, there was no time for *that*. "Close your eyes for a minute, Kels, feel for your cat. She's right there waiting." He stood close, letter her breath him in again. "When you're ready, well get down on our knees and take off your shirt."

With her eyes closed, she nodded. He knew she wouldn't realize it, but her breath kept fluctuating between a human's pattern and feline's, scenting the air around them with each breath. When she held her breath for a moment, Gage knew she had just felt her cat for the first time. He could smell the female scent much stronger than before. "There she is, honey."

Making a soft moaning sound, she backed up and got down on her knees. "Off," she panted.

Remembering how sensitive his skin had been during his first few shifts, he nodded and reached over to help her take the shirt off. Her movements were stiff and jerky; it was almost time as her limbs were getting harder to control. "Get down on all fours, baby, it's easier."

He could change in mid-stride, but those first few times, hell, for the first year he'd had to get down or fall down when changing. She groaned in pain and he heard bones snapping as her hips made the transformation first.

Kelsey held her breath.

"Breathe through it, Kelsey." Her breathing shallow, gasp after gasp, he smelled her panic.

Dropping to his knees, he leaned by her head. He knew this was breaking the first rule taught, but he couldn't stay out of the way. This was Kelsey, dammit, and even though what she was going through was as natural as taking a first step, he couldn't just stand back if she was afraid or in pain. "Breathe through it and it will happen faster, honey."

He heard more bones snapping into place as she continued to gasp, struggling to keep her breathing steady. "That's it."

Leaning back to give her more space, he watched as her skin began to darken. She was focused on her breathing and doing so well he didn't want to speak or move in case he startled her.

He'd seen it happen more times than he could remember, but never had it meant as much to him as it did right now. The popping came closer together, like popcorn, and a few seconds later, the most exquisite golden-orange tiger stood in front of him. Gage smiled into the fur covered face of his mate as she took a few cautious steps, testing her balance.

When she stretched to her full length, he was in awe. For such a tiny package, she was much larger than he thought she'd be. She had to be close to seven feet long. Sniffing the air in an almost regal way, she turned and looked right at him again and then took a few steps to close the distance between them.

"You're stunning, Kelsey, the most beautiful she-cat I have ever seen." He whispered, his voice thickened with a gravelly husk. Reaching out, he touched the side of her face. "Give me a second and I'll change and then we can go for a run."

Kelsey jolted and crouched down as she scented the air rapidly. Gage immediately let his cat closer to the surface and checked for himself. There was something off. Another shifter's scent was in the air, and it wasn't any of his clan or the two visiting wolves. "Kelsey," he said using his brusquer, more dominant tone. "Stay right there. Let me shift and check this out."

Her ears flattened and he cursed softly. Using that tone on *her* when she was in her cycle was possibly the dumbest thing he could ever do. "Honey," he got to his knees, trying to keep his tone soft, "there's another shifter out there..."

She hissed and swatted at him, Gage felt the claws slice through his chest and flinched but tried not to react any more markedly than that. Kelsey backed away, inhaling toward him, she could smell his blood. With a throaty yowl, she turned and took off into the trees.

"Shit." Gage jumped up.

Blair came running from the other direction. "Gage, Gary was out..." Blair froze, his eyes stopped on Gage's chest.

Pulling the track pants down, Gage turned in the direction Kelsey had gone. "Get everyone. Kelsey spooked and took off."

"Fuck." Was the last thing he heard before four paws hit the dirt and he tore off after his mate.

Gage hadn't realized there was a breeze until he tried to follow Kelsey's scent. There was just enough air flow that he had to stop every hundred feet and adjust his direction. The fact that he hadn't caught up to her, let him know she was fast, more so than he'd have liked at this moment.

He didn't pick up the strange scent again, which settled his nerves just enough to allow him to focus. Listening to see if he could hear her, he couldn't. Later on, he'd be proud that she was able to move silently though the bush. A noise to his left had him pausing to turn. Before Blair came into view, Gage picked up his scent.

Blinking, he stopped and watched Blair moving through the trees, hauling what could only be the track pants and shirt that Kelsey had been wearing. It was quite the sight to see a six-foot white tiger prowling along with clothes hanging from his mouth. He'd be sure to tease him later, after he thanked him for thinking of it in the first place.

Noah and Jake came bounding out of the trees to Gage's right, they slowed long enough to run beside him for several strides and then separated, heading back into the trees.

Gage scented the air, her scent was getting stronger. Increasing his stride, he crashed through an area hidden behind thick brush and paused mid-step. Off to his left, Gary was in his cat form staring up a tree. Chirruping, he got his attention. Gary turned and looked at him and then up into the tree.

Twenty feet up in the air Kelsey was sprawled along a large limb, looking down at him.

Cooper came out from behind the tree and Gage knew exactly what the old cat was thinking, there was no way he was going up after her. They were both too heavy. He began to pace back and forth, trying to figure out how to get his mate safely out of the damn tree. Leave it up to Kelsey to go up a tree the first time she shifts.

Going over, he stood beside Gary and looked up at her once more. Why did he feel like she was laughing at him?

Blair came up beside them and dropped the clothes, he looked up at Kelsey and then back to Gage. Every male was too heavy to go up after her. If he didn't know better, he'd think she picked that tree just for that reason alone.

Blair walked around the tree and then began to prowl back and forth, agitated. Gage watched Cooper pacing the outskirts of where they gathered scenting the air, he'd let them know if anyone was nearby that shouldn't be.

Looking up at Kelsey, he tried to decide how she would react if he demanded she come down. He didn't finish that thought, he knew just how well *that* would go. As he sat there weighing options, Noah came charging out of the bush, running straight for the tree. With a move Gage wouldn't have even tried, he vaulted off a fallen tree and launched himself up into the tree at the point where it branched out, a good ten feet in the air.

At first, he thought the crazy cat was going to try going higher, but instead Noah stretched up to his full length of damn near eleven feet, from whisker to tail, and clawed at the tree above him. All the while he was making soft chuffing sounds up at Kelsey.

She stood up and looked down at Noah. When Gage saw her crouch, her muscles bunching, his whole body tensed as she prepared to jump down. He was going to tear a strip off her, simply for scaring the hell out of him.

Surrounding the tree, Cooper, Blair, Gary and Jake watched as she came down the tree, one terrifying jump at a time. When she was just above Noah, she leaned down and playfully swatted at him. Noah sat down in the 'y' of the tree and chuffed at her a few more times before turning and jumping to the ground with a heavy thump when his paws hit the ground. Walking away, he stopped and looked back at her.

Kelsey moved down to where he had been sitting and then looked over at Gage. Crouching again, she pushed off only to land a few feet in front of him. Gage moved cautiously toward her. This was his unpredictable mate, and while Kelsey was still in control inside the cat, he wasn't taking any chances. She moved forward and rubbed along his side. Before he could turn to her, she took off at full speed back they way they'd come.

Grunting his annoyance, he went after her. This time he was able to keep her in sight, just barely. The rest of the clan spread out and ran shotgun behind him. He knew Blair could outrun him any day, but was glad that he was showing him respect and letting him deal with her. He was still planning on giving her hell when they got home.

When he reached the yard, she was lying by the gate, her sides heaving. He could scent her fear and the chastising he'd been planning was washed out of his mind with concern. Going over to her, he licked her face to reassure her.

Blair came running up behind him, dropped the clothes and then was gone again. Whether the rest were staying out of the way for Kelsey's modesty, he wasn't sure, but after checking around them he was sure they were alone.

Backing up, he kept Kelsey looking at him as he shifted. Without taking his eyes off her, he pulled his sweats on and went over and knelt closer to her. "Just let it happen, honey," he assured her.

Blinking a few times, she closed her eyes and her breathing slowed. He caught himself holding his breath as she changed back, the reverse much faster than her shift. Normally it took up to an hour to let the change happen. When the last of her fur retracted and she was lying there, Gage went over and picked up the shirt and went to her.

As she sat up, she smiled at him. Pulling the shirt over her head, he helped her to her feet and then hugged her into his body. "You're amazing, honey."

She squeezed him and then looked up at him. "*That* was wicked."

He chuckled. "*That* was not how your first shift and run are supposed to go."

Shrugging, she hugged him again. "You know I've always sucked at climbing trees…"

Laughing, Gage tightened his hold on her. "Don't do it again, you scared the hell out of me." Looking over, he watched the five cats come slowly out of the trees. "I don't think they were impressed either."

Kelsey turned and then pulled free of his arms. Gage looked around for the sweat pants, not liking that she stood there in front of them wearing nothing but a t-shirt. Noah stepped into the trees and came back a few seconds later, dragging the sweats along with him.

Kelsey took them and paused to run her hands along Noah's back. "I hope I'm as pretty as you guys are." Blair noticeably jolted and stared at her.

Kelsey laughed. "I don't care what you think, Blair, you're pretty." Pulling the pants on, she moved from one to the other, running her hands along their fur.

Gage stood there with his arms crossed, clenching his jaw. He was barely able to stand still, but had to allow her this greeting into the clan. Normally each cat would greet her while she was still in animal form, but with her in her cycle, it was safer this way, so he fought the rage of his cat and stood there, watching.

When she'd run her hands over the other males, he went up to wrap his arms around her, pulling her back into his chest. "They need to go check the borders, honey." He made eye contact with Cooper, knowing his silent message was relayed. Find out why I could smell another shifter, was the message.

"Looks like we missed the fun."

Devin and Rayne came across the yard, arms entwined around each other.

"Oh my, look how pretty all of you are," Rayne said with wonder in her voice.

Kelsey grinned and looked over at Blair. He chuffed and turned, running into the trees.

Gage leaned down and kissed Kelsey's neck and then went over to Devin. "I picked up another shifter's scent."

Devin's relaxed posture was gone. "Which way?"

Gage shook his head. "I can't be sure. Kelsey was shifting and I lost it when I had to go after her."

Devin turned and inhaled. He closed his eyes for a moment. Shaking his head, Devin opened his eyes. He glanced over at the cats waiting behind Gage. "I'll go out with them if that's okay."

Gage nodded. "I'll take the girls back to the house and wait for you there. Kelsey's going to need some food before the shakes start."

Devin kissed Rayne quickly and began unbuttoning his shirt.

Putting his arm around Kelsey, Gage gave Rayne a nod and the three turned to cross the yard.

Chapter Twenty-One

Kelsey sat there staring out the window. The house was quiet and she didn't want to go down the stairs and wake anyone when the steps creaked. She wasn't sure when she'd fallen asleep, only knew that she woke to silence and darkness. Gage must have brought her up, because she'd been far too exhausted to make it on her own.

After he'd made her eat two sandwiches, still shocked that she was able to eat after a steak dinner, they'd sat on the porch and waited for Devin to return.

Gage didn't relax, even after learning the guys hadn't picked up the strange scent again. That's the last thing she remembered.

It was so dark outside, but she was able to see and hear things she knew she wouldn't have before, and with her newly improved senses she knew it was oddly quiet out there tonight.

Glancing at the clock, she sighed. Why was she awake at three in the morning? Kneeling by the window, she rested her arms on the ledge and inhaled deeply again. Other than trees and dirt, she couldn't smell anything out of the ordinary. She wondered if she'd scent more if she was in her cat form.

Grinning, she shook her head. The fact that she'd shifted still had her mind reeling. She'd been a large orange tiger that could run faster than her first car could go downhill; at least it felt that way. And, to her delight, she'd climbed that tree she used to stand beside and wish for a way up. Much to everyone's surprise and displeasure she'd done it. She was a tiger shifter. There was no denying any of it now.

Glancing over her shoulder, she looked at the clock again, so restless it was unnerving. You would think after everything that had happened, she'd be unconscious deep in an exhausted sleep. She'd had sex with Gage, was no longer a virgin. Add in the tiger part, and the night had been one of many firsts. Sighing, she looked at the door; she really didn't want to stay in her room right now.

Gnawing on her lip, she stood and took a few steps toward the door. Her mind wanted to remember everything that happened, and as hard as she tried, she couldn't stop it. What she'd done with Gage had been something else. Too bad she couldn't hold onto a lot of the feelings, being lost in the heat blurred her memories, the only part she regretted. For too many years, she'd wondered, daydreamed, and fantasized about what it would be like to be with Gage in *that* way and she had been robbed of the emotions.

A twinge of heat moved through her and she stiffened; after assessing it was just good old lust and not her cycle, she relaxed. It excited her to realize she wanted Gage without the pull of the shifter thing. Picturing him naked made her smile, his body was much more perfect than she'd dreamed it would be. He was so fit, in *all* the right places, and she hadn't thought he would be as patient as he had been. Not that she was complaining, but she had to wonder if things would have been different if she hadn't been consumed by the heat at the time.

Thinking about this was just making her antsy, not to mention turned on. Biting her lip, she stood there and stared at her closed door. What would he do if she went to him when she wasn't out of her mind with animal heat?

Taking a deep breath, she exhaled and decided she was now going to find out. Not knowing when the cycle was going to consume her again, she wanted just one thing to be in her control.

Stepping out into the hall, she moved toward his door, careful not to make the floorboards creak. Devin and Rayne were downstairs in the guest room, but she still didn't want to alert anyone to her movements.

Turning the doorknob, she opened the door and went in, closing it behind her just as quietly. When she turned toward the bed, Gage bolted upright.

"Kelsey? Are you all right?" He inhaled deeply and then looked her up and down.

She didn't have to ask what he was sniffing for, he'd know better than she what her body smelled like. "I couldn't sleep."

Moving to the side of the bed, he swung his legs over the edge, pulling the sheet over him as he did. "What's wrong?"

No doubt he could sense her nerves, as her heart tried to pound out of her chest. Swallowing, she took a few tentative steps in his direction. "I was thinking, so much happened tonight..." She watched his shoulders stiffen.

"It wasn't the way I wanted things to go..."

"I know. I wasn't blaming you." She let her eyes roam over all the skin the sheet didn't hide. His chest and abs were so toned, not overly muscled, but more than enough to stir her awareness. She watched his chest rise and fall as she stepped in front of him, close enough to reach out and touch him. He continued to sit there, tense and immobile, as if he was waiting to find out why she in his room in the middle of the night. "I woke up and couldn't help thinking..." biting her lip, she looked up his nakedness until she reached his eyes, "wondering..." she didn't know how to say it.

His chest expanded as he took a deep breath, awareness lit his eyes. "Come here," he wove his fingers through her hair and pulled her toward him. "I'm glad you came to me." His lips brushed over hers, so lightly she shivered with need. "I've been laying here driving myself crazy," his mouth moved down over her jaw, "walking away from you when I put you in bed took all my restraint."

Everywhere his mouth touched caught fire; it felt like lava moving through her veins. "I don't want your restraint now," she whispered, dizzy as his masculine scent filled her senses.

He paused, his lips against her ear, "What do you want, honey?"

Running her hands up over his shoulders, she felt his muscles clench under her touch. "I want to be with you when it's *my* choice."

He let out a ragged breath and she couldn't be sure if it was relief, but then his mouth moved back to hers, his lips close but not touching hers, "Let me show you how it was supposed to be." He didn't wait for her to respond before his mouth took hers in a kiss so sensual and consuming it made her head spin.

His tongue stroked over hers slowly, as if he was memorizing her mouth, her taste. She felt his hands move to her waist and pull the pants she still wore down over her hips. Deepening the kiss, he pushed the material down her legs. Kelsey grasped his head, not wanting him to stop kissing her as she stepped out of them.

Gage hands molded to her skin as he moved up the back of her legs until coming to rest on her hips. Tearing his mouth away his hands moved up over her ribs, she made a sound of frustration, not wanting him to stop..

Lifting her shirt up, he pulled it over her head and tossed it on the floor. She felt self-conscious being exposed, but the way his eyes caressed her kept her standing in quietly. If he didn't touch her soon, she was going to collapse on the floor in anticipation.

His hands slid down her arms, leaving her shivering in awareness when he grasped her wrists, pushing her arms behind her pinning them together in one of his large hands. With a feather-light touch, he ran the back of his free hand over her shoulder, trailing it slowly to her breast. Her nipple puckered tighter, almost painfully, as he lingered. She gasped and closed her eyes, focusing on the sensations his touch created.

"You're so beautiful, I feel like the luckiest man on earth."

Opening her eyes, she watched him move toward her body. When he licked across her nipple, she moaned and felt her knees weaken. "So responsive," he whispered against her breast, the breath across her nipple going straight to her core.

Releasing her hands, he gripped her waist and without hesitation had her on her back on his bed, his body covering hers. "I want to taste every inch of you," he said before dipping his head down to run his tongue along her throat, stopping to bite her gently in the curve of her neck.

Gage growled low in his chest and heat shot through her. Kelsey caught her lip and bit down.

"Fuck," Gage's mouth crushed hers, his tongue thrusting inside, possessing he mouth completely. Kelsey grabbed his head, not wanting him to pull away again. Each time their tongues touched, she felt more heat pour through her. She wanted more, hotter, wanted the flames to consume her.

Shifting she moaned as his bare flesh burned into hers. Releasing her mouth, he trailed his lips down her throat in rough kisses using his teeth and tongue.

She tried to bring his mouth back to hers, but she couldn't hold him as he dragged it from her grasp and moved down her chest. When he sucked a nipple into his mouth, her back arched, offering him more. With each pull a pulse between her legs mirrored his attentions and she began to rub against him trying to relieve the ache even though his weight held her in place and mostly still.

Kelsey's breaths came in staggered gasps as his mouth burned her skin as he trailed down her hips and stomach. She quivered with a need she barely understood yet desperate to sate. He shifted and moved his head was between legs, she held her breath as his hot breath was brushed against her inner thighs and she shuddered, knowing what was to come.

Tenderly he stroked his tongue through her wet folds as she hissed out a breath, lifting her hips to get closer. Chuckling, he gripped her thighs and held her down on the mattress. "Not so fast, baby." He whispered against her heat. "I plan on savoring you."

She made a mewling noise of frustration, she didn't want to be savored, she wanted to be devoured. Now. She tried to tell him what she wanted, but each time she opened her mouth to speak, his tongue took all thoughts away.

Her body was coiled and reaching for release, he kept her hovering on the edge until she gripped his head and ground against his mouth. With a strong arm across her hips, he limited her movement, lifting his head to look up her body. His eyes were heavy with lust, almost black in color. Blowing against her throbbing clit, he moved to his knees and grasped her hips, lifting her with him.

"Look at me," he growled, his breath brushing over her pulsing need.

Opening her eyes, she looked up at him, trying to focus through a haze of lust.

"You're mine." His eyes held hers for a moment as if she was going to argue.

Unable to speak, she couldn't have even whispered at that moment. She nodded.

His mouth crashed against her wet center and she cried out as her orgasm washed over her without warning. Struggling to breathe, she gripped the headboard, trying to pull from his grasp as oxygen was sucked out of her lungs. Gage held her to him, she couldn't move while his tongue and teeth played with her body in ways she hadn't thought possible.

Then the aftershocks went through her, one right on top of the other; like jolts of electricity. Gasping, she tried to catch her breath. She thought he would release her, but he gripped her thighs and forced her legs further apart and lowered his mouth once again. An animalistic groan torn from her lips as he teased and tormented her again with his mouth. Just as she braced to explode, she found herself lowered and flipped over on her stomach before she could focus.

Wrapping his arm around her waist, he lifted her hips off the bed, using his muscular thighs to push her legs, opening her body to him. Kelsey came violently as he thrust deep into her in one fast movement. Screaming into the pillow; she was helpless as he continued to pound into her. Her convulsing muscles clenched around him so tightly, she could feel his entire length as he slid from her and then back, filling her tightness again.

As she started to catch her breath, he shifted his weight to lean over her. A hand moved up and began to squeeze her nipple; suddenly she was feeling him everywhere at once.

She could feel his sharp teeth moving over her shoulder, and it made another rush of wetness. Growling, Gage stopped moving, his whole body tensed. With a curse, he pulled from her and flipped her onto her back.

Pushing her legs open, he slid between them and was back inside her with a groan. Kelsey was helpless to do anything as her body obeyed his every want. Clinging to his shoulders, she gasped each time he slammed into her.

He grabbed her knee and pulled her leg up over his shoulder. "You're so hot..." he groaned against her ear, "come for me again."

Kelsey wanted to say it was impossible, her body was spent but as he began kissing her, she started shaking in response. When her tongue brushed along his sharp teeth, she realized they were his feline teeth, and he was as out of control as she was.

Reaching down, he slipped his hand under her hips and lifted her while his movement slowed, deep thrusts bringing the heat to hit her again. Moaning into his mouth, she clung to him as another orgasm moved through her.

Gage's thrusts were now almost bruising, suddenly jerky movements before he tore his mouth away from hers and tensed on top of her, a low, guttural moans echoing though the room, as she was clenching around him as he pulsed inside her.

She lay there, soaked in sweat, trying to catch her breath and relishing the weight of his lax body on top of her. *So,* she thought when some of the fog cleared, *that was worth waiting for.*

Lifting a bit of his weight off her, he trailed his tongue up her throat. "Was I too rough?" His voice was low and breathless causing another aftershock to run over her like a wave.

"No," she panted. Truly she had no idea, at the time it was just what her body wanted, what she needed and hadn't even realized. Then a thought hit her. "We didn't use..."

Propping his body up on his elbows, he brushed hot lips over hers before raising his face to look at her. "It's okay, honey." He gave her a lazy smile. "You can't get pregnant, unless I allow it," he chuckled softly at the confused look she knew was on her face. "The males get to control something, at least." He kissed her quickly and lifted more of his body from hers.

With a gentle thrust of his hips, he pushed against her sensitive flesh eliciting soft gasps. "And I plan on a lot more of this," he thrust again, "before we even consider anything else."

Kelsey wanted to ask what he meant, but he began to move in and out of her slowly. She didn't think he could, but she felt him growing harder inside her with each stroke. Heat flashed through her. Her eyes moved to his, giving him a surprised look.

Grinning, he lowered his mouth to hers. "I'm not done with you yet, honey." He brushed his lips against hers as her mouth opened with a silent gasp. "I'll be gentle this time, baby, let me show you."

Her eyes drifted closed as the sensations went through her, she was more than willing to let him do whatever he wanted.

Chapter Twenty-Two

Kelsey had never been as happy as she was the next morning. She was surprised she didn't feel tired, or sore. Gage had made love to her until the sun had started to rise, then with a growl he'd carried her to her own bed saying if she stayed in his, they'd still be going at it at noon and he had three jobs to complete.

She had breakfast with Rayne and Devin, Gage being long gone, but then apologized and headed down to the shop to see if she could help.

When she got there, the guys were neck deep in repairs that had to be finished by the end of the day. Ignoring the heated look from Gage as his eyes tracked her every move, she'd told him to put her to work.

The look he shared, told her he was reliving every second of their time together, just as she was while trying not to let her eyes roam all over his body. Tormenting him with her mouth was added to her to-do list as she watched his large chest rise and fall, no doubt scenting her just as she was him.

Finally, he'd given her a huge grin and sent her out to help Blair, Jake and Gary where they were struggling to replace half an engine some newbie operator had all but blown up.

An hour later she was wishing she'd stayed in the house and found something to do. She understood that the guys were essentially still adolescents at heart on a good day, but if they dropped one more not-so-subtle insinuation about her and Gage being together, so help her, she was going to feed them a wrench.

Wiping the sweat from her brow, she shifted and looked up into the cab Jake was hanging out of. "Try it again."

Nodding, he ducked back in and turned the engine over. It caught for a second and then choked out again. Waving at him to kill it, she waited until the purr of the ignition went off.

Pulling the screwdriver out of her pocket, she leaned in and began making minute adjustments.

"Gage is in one hell of a good mood today," Jake said louder than necessary looking at Gary. "I haven't seen him smile this much since…"

"Ever," Blair finished for him with a smirk.

Rubbing the back of his neck, Gary nodded with a smug smile.

"What did you do to him, Kels?" Jake continued. Glancing up from under her lashes she hoped he caught her drop-it look. He didn't.

Winking at Blair he grinned. "I'm thinking you should do it again, twice, maybe three times for good measure."

Gary chuckled along with Jake.

She waved her hand to motion him to try the engine again. He did. After a second the engine rumbled to life. Kelsey listened carefully to make sure there were no hesitations. Happy it was running smoothly, she signaled to shut it off.

"Great work," Jake said as he climbed down. "I'd forgotten your talent is in making anything you touch *purr* so sweetly."

Clamping her teeth together, she gave him a brief smile. Blair gave her a hand down and then handed her a rag. Exchanging the screwdriver for the piece of cloth, she focused completely on her hands for a moment. "So," she began, keeping her eyes shielded from all of them so they couldn't see her thoughts, "I've been giving this mating thing a lot of thought."

Jake snorted. "Is that what you call it? Thought?"

Glancing briefly at him, she smirked, raising her brows dismissing his pathetic quip. "Yeah." Looking back down, she feigned a shrug. "I was thinking I should make sure Gage is *the* one." She noted that all three were quiet now, she looked at them innocently.

Cautiously, Blair raised a bottle of water to his mouth, most likely to avoid commenting, she thought with a smile. Turning, she eyed each one slowly. "I think I should kiss each of you…" she smiled, "just to make sure."

She was shocked she managed to sound as serious as she did, and still keep a straight face. In hindsight, she thought, she should have had her phone out to record their reactions. Gary dropped the wrench he held, his jaw going slack. Blair spewed a mouthful of water in Jake's face as Jake stood there stuttering.

Keeping the serious look on her face, she watched them for a moment. Wiping off his face with frantic movements, Jake gaped at her.

A low rumbling growl sounded, and Kelsey turned to watch as Gage stomped in their direction. Glancing behind him, she saw Cooper and Devin laughing, they'd all caught what had just happened. "You guys deserve what you got," she said with an overly dramatic sigh and then turned on her heel and headed toward the house.

"Kelsey," Gage growled from behind her.

The sound sent a shiver through her, in that moment she hated that it did. Sighing, she stopped and turned around to glare at him. *His* buddies and only he could deal with them, she thought. How she did, she didn't know, but she felt her cat roll over her skin as a growl rumbled out of her throat from somewhere deep inside her.

Gage froze, his eyebrows raised. With a quick look at the men behind him, she shook her head and turned back to the gate.

"Honey, wait."

She kept walking.

"Ah, shit." She heard Gage spit out as she reached the path to the trees.

Watching his mate disappear into the trees, he put his hands on his hips and looked down at the ground. Turning around he gave Blair, Jake and Gary a quick once-over. "Did you guys leave your brains in bed today?"

No response, just three identical sheepish looks.

"Shit." Turning he glanced back at the trees Kelsey had just passed through. Clenching his jaw, he took a deep breath, wondering how much groveling he was in for to make up for his friends' idiocy. "How could you not sense her agitation?" He looked back at Blair. "I could feel it from all the way in the shop."

"I…" Blair closed his mouth and looked at Jake.

Jake gave Gage a wide-eyed look. "I got carried away," he finally said, head low and shoulders bowed.

Gary just shook his head, and refused to make eye contact.

Growling, Gage rubbed a hand over the back of his neck. When he looked back, Gary's head was still hanging down; his shoulders slumped in a submissive posture. "Fuck." Turning he looked over to Cooper, not having the slightest clue what to do next.

Cooper motioned to the trees lining the path to the house. Devin crossed his arms and nodded in agreement

Glancing back at his friends, he grimaced. "I may be back to rip your hides off later," he grumbled as he jogged toward the path.

When he reached the porch, Rayne sat there, with an odd look on her face. Women were so hard to read. She pointed to the door and mouthed *good luck*. Wincing he tentatively went in the house, his steps silent. Kelsey wasn't in the kitchen or living room. Taking a deep breath, he went to the stairs.

Stopping outside her closed door, he inhaled but didn't pick up any scent that gave him a clue to her mood. He listened, nothing. "Kelsey, honey?" He waited but she didn't answer. *Shit. Damn. Fuck.* Holding his breath, he tried the doorknob. It was open. Slowly he opened the door and looked in. "Kels?"

Something gripped his arms and spun him into the room. Before he could react, he found his back slammed against the door and Kelsey pinning him there with her body pressed into his.

"Our friends are assholes," she said in a low snarl.

Gage nodded and looked down, still not sure if he should let out the breath he was holding or brace for...*what?* Her amber eyes were bright and his pulse pounded in response to the way she was looking at him. In a move he didn't see coming, she tore his shirt open, sending the buttons scattering across the floor. The breath he held whooshed out all at once. Gripping her waist, he stared down into her eyes, still not sure what the right move was.

"Growl for me," she panted.

Inhaling, he finally scented her arousal and was stunned he hadn't caught that sooner. Grinning down at her he emitted a low growl and leaning down beside her ear as he did. He felt her shudder against him.

"Why does that happen?"

Her voice was breathless and he felt his body harden as a result. "Our cats know who we are to each other, honey." Her hands slid up over his chest and clasped behind his neck. He felt her tense and then she jumped up, gripping his waist with her knees. Grasping her hips, he held her there and was once again stunned by her actions. *Christ, my mate is a handful.* With uncommon sense today, he kept the grin off his face.

She nipped her way up his neck with sharp teeth and he had to bite back a groan. "So, if I growl does it affect you the same way?"

He swallowed. "Not the way you did back in the yard, that one was definitely a back-the-fuck-off growl." She made a soft sound in the back of her throat.

"I don't know how to do it," she whispered her lips brushing over his pulse.

Gage wanted her in a way he couldn't ever remember feeling before. "Try," he dipped his head down and inhaled the scent that was pure Kelsey. She squirmed against him, making him harder and his knees go weak.

Leaning back, she looked at him with passion-heavy eyes and he couldn't look away. Slowly she inhaled, as she breathed out a low rumbling sounded, it was the most erotic sound he'd ever heard.

"Christ, yeah," he grinned at her, "you better be careful when you do that, baby, it's a sure way to get yourself fucked." Gripping her hips, he pulled her tight against his body and rubbed her up and down his hard length.

Gasping, she clenched her fingers in his hair and pulled his mouth down to hers.

Bracing his legs apart, he held his shoulders against the wall, keeping her tight against his body with one hand as he took hold of her hair with the other and kissed her like he was starving. He was never going to get enough of her, this much he knew. All he had to do was convince her there was no one else. It had taken everything he'd had last night not to mark her, he'd come damn close when her body had been pinned beneath his on all fours. She took his control and shredded it, erasing all his patience.

Right now, she was rocking into him and devouring his mouth, biting like she needed to consume him, and damned if he wasn't willing to let her do everything she wanted. When she suddenly slid down his body until her feet were on the floor, he was momentarily dazed until she took her mouth from his and began to move down his chest.

Christ.

Dropping his hands to the side, he let her move at her own pace. pressing them against the wall to stay standing and let her do as she wished. As she undid his belt and zipper, he had to suck in a breath, knowing where this was going and afraid to do anything that might change her mind. When her hand closed around his hard flesh, his knees almost buckled, which was ridiculous, this wasn't his first time. He felt her breath brush over him. Everything was intensified ten times with her, bless this mating shit was the last coherent thought as her lips closed around his throbbing head.

Gripping her hair, he thought to guide her and was almost blinded as she led without his help. Closing his eyes, he leaned his head against the wall, his whole body engulfed in the feelings she was creating. With a groan, he looked down to see him disappearing into her hot mouth. *Fuck, I'm not going to last much longer.* "Baby," he groaned when she increased the suction, her tongue rubbing under the head. "You better stop…" His breath shuddered out of his mouth when she clamped down on him harder, swallowing him whole. Bracing against the wall, he growled as he exploded with such force into her mouth, it was almost painful.

Fuck. The only thought in his mind as he tried to catch his breath, pulling her up his body and holding her close. Inhaling slowly through his nose, he tried to fill his lungs. Her arousal filled his head and he felt his body awaken in response. *Christ. We'll kill each other if this keeps up.*

He wanted to throw her on the bed and bury himself inside her, but he knew it was the middle of the day and once she settled down, she'd realize everyone would know what they were doing while they were doing all the work. Able to breathe, he pulled her up on her toes and kissed her deep and slow. He had to control this as much as he could, or they wouldn't be leaving her room today. Pushing away from the door, he turned and grabbed her by the shoulders until she was facing the door. "My turn," he growled against the side of her neck.

She whimpered and it took him a second to get himself under control. Opening her jeans, he pulled her tight against his chest. Turning her head, he began kissing her as he shoved his hand between her legs. She was dripping and so hot, he debated again if they could spend the rest of the day in bed.

Shoving his tongue into her mouth, as he did the same with his fingers inside her, he felt her knees buckle and had to wrap his arm around her to keep her still. She moaned into his mouth as he began to move two fingers in and out, grinding the heel of his hand against her swollen nub as he did.

He wanted to bring her over the edge as fast and hard as she did him, but knew Kelsey wasn't quiet. Loosening his hold on her waist, he checked to see if she was going to be able to stay standing as he increased the speed his hand worked her over. He grasped her head and leaned around her, keeping his mouth over hers.

She began moaning into his mouth and he had to squeeze his eyes shut to remember he couldn't rip the jeans off and plunge inside her. Adding a finger, he stretched and filled her more, she was gyrating against his hand and making wet, smacking noises as flesh connected.

When she clamped down on his hand and began convulsing, he almost came in his pants, remembering how it had felt. She gasped against his mouth and made squeaky mewling sounds that drove him crazy. He practically collapsed against the door with her clutched tightly to him when she finally settled down again.

Neither of them could speak. He braced his hand against the wall and wrapped his other arm around her to keep them both on their feet.

"Sorry," she panted.

Opening his eyes, he lifted his head and looked at the door, trying to figure out what she could possibly be sorry for. "For what?" he finally asked.

"Reacting like that because the guys were being jerks."

Grinning, relieved that he wasn't the one in trouble, he shook his head. "I expected them to razz me about it, but they are idiots for giving you a hard time." He paused and thought about it. No, they were complete asses.

"Gage?" Devin's voice boomed through the door.

Clearing his throat, Gage turned Kelsey into his arms and held her close. "Yeah?"

"I just got a call, we have to go."

Frowning at the urgency in his voice, he helped Kelsey put her clothes back in order and quickly zipped his jeans. Dropping a kiss on her head, he shifted position and opened the door wide enough to see Devin. "What's going on?" He expected Devin to have a knowing smirk on his face, saying he knew exactly what they'd just been doing, but serious blue eyes captured his.

"Two women are missing from one of my packs. They disappeared early this morning."

Gage felt Kelsey tense against him, he ran his hand down her back. "Let me get changed."

Devin nodded abruptly. "I want to get there and see if we can pick up the trail before the Alliance team arrives."

Gage nodded and closed the door. Turning, he pulled Kelsey into his arms. "I have to go with him, honey, it's my job to protect him." He could see the fear in her eyes. Kissing her mouth lightly, he tried to reassure her. "Once the Alliance team gets there, we'll be back."

She nodded and he knew she didn't like it, but she kept those thoughts to herself.

Touching her cheek, he smiled. "I better go change." He looked down at his shirt and grinned. "Someone just destroyed my shirt." Her cheeks flushed and she gave him a gentle shove toward the door.

Chapter Twenty-Three

Kelsey stood on the steps of the porch beside Rayne and watched Gage speaking quietly to Cooper and Blair. Their easy-going demeanor was gone; their bodies were rigid and alert. Twice Blair nodded and glanced over at her, his expression deadly serious. Devin stood beside Gage and the expression on his face sent a shiver of fear through her.

When Blair nodded to Devin and then glanced back at them, Rayne sighed softly beside her. "I have a feeling you and I are going to be under house arrest, with fanged guards."

Kelsey's eyebrows shot up as she looked at her. "What do you mean?"

Motioning with her head to where the men were standing, Rayne gave her a look and rolled her eyes. "The Alphas are going all alpha."

Gage suddenly turned, taking long strides in her direction. A shiver of awareness moved through her as she watched him approach. What it was about she didn't know, but this wasn't the time to be thinking about *that* sort of thing. Stepping off the steps, she met him at the bottom, pausing as Rayne moved past her to go to her husband.

"Noah's going to come with us," he said softly, "Coop has to help Gary and Jake get those repairs finished." She nodded, not sure why he was giving her a lineup. "Blair is going to stay here with you and Rayne."

Kelsey glanced around his large body to where Blair stood a cold look on his face. "If he's needed at the shop, we'll be fine."

Gage shook his head. "We're not taking any chances, Kelsey." He closed his eyes briefly and then opened them and studied her. "Please don't fight me on this. It's hard enough leaving you right now."

"But you have to go." She wasn't sure why she whispered it.

He nodded. "Yeah, I do. If anything happened to Devin…"

"All hell would break loose."

He smirked. "Something like that."

Hugging her arms around her waist, she nodded. "Be careful."

"Gage." Devin stood beside the truck watching him.

Glancing over his shoulder, he nodded before looking back at her. "We'll be back before dark." He rubbed the back of his neck and let out an uneasy breath. "You call if you need me."

Kelsey tried to offer him a smile, but knew it didn't reach her eyes. "Okay." She stammered out. "I'll behave, I promise."

Grinning, he headed in the direction of the waiting men. "I somehow doubt that." Then he turned on his heel and came back to her. The look on his face left no doubts that he really didn't want to leave right now. She was just about to ask him what was wrong when he stopped and cupped the back of her head, dragging her halfway up his body. His mouth cut off anything she was going to say. Gripping the front of his shirt with both hands to keep her balance, she returned his kiss in a way that was going to make her blush whenever she thought of it.

As quickly as it began it was over as he dropped his hand from her, his blue eyes burning into hers as he spun back to climb in the truck.

With her head spinning, she glanced at Rayne who had a grin on her face, and to Blair, who was looking everywhere but in her direction. She watched the truck pull away and finally let out a shaky breath. Well, she had wanted to keep things with her and Gage discrete, but they'd just demolished that plan.

Tucking her hands into her pockets, she glanced at Rayne. "Now what?"

Rayne sighed. "We wait."

Blair moved over to stand with them. "If there's any scent to follow, they'll find it." He crossed his arms over his chest. "Gage can track anyone and Noah will be able to smell any of Tomas's guys from miles away."

"How old are the women that are missing?" Kelsey tried not to imagine their fear.

Rayne's eyes lowered. "Neither have had their first change, but they're close."

A chill ran up Kelsey's spine, she didn't want to say, but knew they were all thinking that Tomas wanted them close to exert more control. Taking an uneasy breath, she glanced from Blair to Rayne. "I'm going to make some lunch and take it over to the shop."

"I'll help," Rayne turned to follow her.

Rubbing a hand over his messy hair, Blair gave her a look. "I'm going to circle around in the tree line until you're ready to head out to the shop."

Nodding, Kelsey turned to follow Rayne into the house. Was this what she had to look forward to in this new life? Being guarded and always watched over? She thought about the women that were missing, not able to grasp what they must be going through. Closing her eyes, she prayed that Gage and Devin found them before any harm could come to them.

Rayne wiped her hands again and laughed, shaking her head. "I think I like playing with greasy wrenches and motors."

Kelsey took a sip of the water and then nodded. "Yeah, there's something to be said about getting covered in grease and oil."

Rayne examined her nails. "That it ruins a good manicure?"

Snorting, Kelsey shrugged. "Okay, that too." Taking a deep breath, she glanced over at the guys that were all working on the last engine to repair. "This is better than sitting in the house and wondering."

With a sigh, Rayne tossed the rag onto the bench. "Yes, it was. Thanks." She looked over at the men. "Although I think I frustrated them with my helping." Looking at her hands again, she rubbed them together. "Now, I'd like a shower."

Getting up off the stool, Kelsey nodded in agreement. "I'll go tell them we're going back to the house." She grinned, "and they love it when women get in their way and make them look bad." She caught a few grunts and curses as she moved toward them.

Cooper glanced up, a light sheen of sweat on his brow as he braced the bar against the pulley trying to give Jake and Blair enough wiggle room to get the belt off.

"Rayne and I are going over to climb in the shower."

Jake glanced up at her, opened his mouth and then shook his head, lowering his eyes back to the belt he was working on.

Rolling her eyes, she ignored him and looked over at Blair. She could see he was weighing his words carefully as he struggled to help Jake.

"I'll take one of the pickups and we'll go straight inside."

With a grunt, Blair glanced at Cooper who gave him a small nod. "I'll be right behind you." He paused and looked at her. "Lock the door, Kelsey."

Nodding, she turned and moved back to stand by Rayne before they changed their minds. Grabbing the keys off the rack, she motioned for Rayne to follow her out the door.

After their showers, they sat at the table staring into their tea. Kelsey looked at the door. "I don't do house arrest very well."

Rayne grinned. "Me either." She glanced at the door. "Think we'll get grounded if we sit on the porch?"

Biting her lip, Kelsey debated. It was the porch, five feet from the door with the lock. She sighed. "I don't see it being a big problem; we can see the drive from it and most of the treed area."

Nodding, Rayne picked up her cup. "Agreed." She turned to head out the door. "I don't do walls very well anymore either." With a laugh, she held the door open for Kelsey, "which is weird considering I lived in a posh, heavy on the security apartment, until I ran from Aiden."

Setting her phone on the table, Kelsey leaned back and put her feet up. "I almost went stir crazy my last year at school." She grinned into her cup. "My roommate thought I was nuts when I'd go out for a long walk every night, no matter what weather." Sighing she shook her head. "It all makes sense now." Kelsey's phone rang. Leaning forward she glanced at the screen and then rolled her eyes at Rayne as she answered it. Blair, she mouthed. "Hey." She nodded and rolled her eyes again. "We're just sitting here. I'm sure we'll be fine for five more minutes, Blair." Nodding again she hung it up and gave Rayne a stiff smile. "He's freaking out, thinks Gage is going to kill him for leaving us alone for half an hour."

Rayne laughed and then froze, the sound of tires on the gravel driveway reached them.

Kelsey set her cup down, grabbed her phone and stood up. Maybe Gage was back already. When a large, dusty truck came through the trees, she glanced quickly at Rayne. She sat there, her back stiff. "They're probably looking for the shop." She shrugged. "It happens all the time."

Rayne stepped beside her, Kelsey could feel the anxiety rolling off her in waves. The truck came to a stop and the two men inside sat talking, one was shaking his head as the other continued speaking. Kelsey tried to hear what they were saying, but the engine and the music hid all of their words.

The driver's door opened and a tall man with a rough beard climbed out. He leaned back inside, grabbed something and then straightened up. Kelsey's eyed what he was holding, relieved to see it was a map.

"They're lost." She glanced at Rayne and turned to the steps. "Happens all the time when there's only one main road and a lot of back roads that are not on most maps."

Rayne visibly relaxed and hovered at the top of the steps for a second before following her.

The man tipped his head at them. "Sorry to bother you ladies," he glanced back at his friend in the truck. "But we are hopelessly lost." He gave them a bashful grin.

Kelsey wanted to laugh, that was something you didn't see men admit often. "Not a problem, it happens all the time around here." She glanced at the man in the truck to see his head down like he was looking at something. "Where are you trying to be?"

Looking over his shoulder again, he turned back and started unfolding the map. "I don't think it has an actual name, I can show you." Turning, he flattened the map on the hood, running his finger down it trying to locate the place. "I don't think half the roads we've been on are even on this damn thing," he said, more to himself, as he squinted at the map. With a sigh, he looked up to the man in the cab and motioned with his head to join him. "I can't even find it, I'll let my not so skilled navigator show you."

Kelsey stood back with Rayne at her shoulder, they both watched the shorter man get out of the truck. He was quite a bit younger than then his friend, and looked like he wasn't happy about any of it. Shaking his head, he walked around the truck and practically tore the map out of the other man's hand.

"I keep telling him there's not a direct route," he shook his head and ran his hand down over the map, going from side to side. "but what do I know…"

Rayne felt sorry for him when she sensed the frustration coming from him. "Unless you're born here, there's no way to know." She shrugged and gave the tall one an understanding look. "I think they just randomly clear roads where ever they want." Stepping up beside the man frowning at the map, she looked over his shoulder and then pointed to where they stood. "You're here right now."

The younger man glanced at the map, then looked over his shoulder at her before giving the other man a look she didn't understand.

Stepping back, she moved closer to Rayne. When she glanced at her, Rayne's eyes had darkened and she was inhaling slowly. Glancing at the phone in her hand as a distraction, Kelsey took a quick breath through her nose. Before she had time to assess what she could smell, her cat rolled over her skin and sent a wave of panic through her.

Chapter Twenty-Four

Gage swore under his breath as he ducked around another branch that Devin had let go of too quickly. He looked over at Noah in his cat form, as he paced along beside them. "Noah's not picking up shit."

Pausing, Devin turned around, his eyes searching the ground. "How could the tracks just fucking disappear?" He growled out his frustration.

Gage shook his head and inhaled deeply, again. Nothing. He was picking up nothing. When his phone vibrated in his pocket, he pulled it out and then frowned at it. It was Kelsey. "Hey, honey." He listened and she didn't reply. "Kels?" With brows furrowed, Devin stopped and stared at him. "Kelsey?" Gage's heart started to skip in his chest. Looking at Devin, he shook his head. "Call Blair."

Pulling his phone out, Devin dialed it and they both stood there waiting for him to answer. There was still nothing on the end of the phone Gage held to his ear.

"Blair, where are the girls?"

Gage didn't need to hear his answer through the phone, he could hear pounding footsteps through Kelsey's phone.

"Hello?"

It was Cooper on her phone.

"Coop, where the *fuck* is Kelsey?" Gage turned and watched as Noah shifted quickly back to his human form.

"Gage," he could hear Blair and Jake in the background, hear the porch door slamming. "Fuck," Cooper swore, "they're not here."

Every muscle in Gage's body stiffened. "What do you mean they're not there? She dialed my number…"

"They were helping us at the shop, came back to shower." He swore under his breath again. "Blair just called her as he was heading over."

Gage heard the cry of a cat through the phone and recognized it as Blair. "Never mind talking to me, go find them." He glanced at Devin, who was already plowing his way through the brush. "We'll be there in an hour." He shouldered his way through the branches, not even flinching as thorns scratched across his cheek. "Coop, just fucking find them." He jammed the phone into his pocket and started to jog. Noah's cat bolted past him. With a curse, Gage lengthened his stride. She had to be okay. Nothing could happen to her.

Kelsey opened her eyes slowly and then closed them quickly. Her stomach rolled as she tasted something sweet and chemical on her lips. *What the hell?* She heard a soft moan beside her and turned her throbbing head to see Rayne rubbing a hand over her eyes.

"What happened?" Rayne whispered. "And what is that taste?"

Closing her eyes, Kelsey fought another wave of nausea. "I think we were drugged." She could feel the cold floor on her arms and legs, but didn't want to move.

"Lovely." She heard Rayne moving around but didn't want to open her eyes. "Are you all right, Kelsey?"

Exhaling slowly, she pressed the palms of her hands against her temples, and cautiously opened her eyes again. "I'll get back to you on that."

"Do you hear anyone?"

Squeezing her eyes shut, she tried to listen despite the pounding in her head. "I don't think so."

"Come on," Rayne's cool hand touched her arm, "We have to get moving to get whatever this is out of our systems."

She knew she was right, but Kelsey really just wanted to lay there and not move. A moment later she realized that alone told her there were still drugs coursing through her system, she never had a laid-back attitude. Grasping her head in her hands again, she rolled slowly until she was on her knees. Sitting up made her feel dizzy, her stomach roiled, and her head want to shatter into a hundred pieces. Opening her eyes, she was finally able to focus on Rayne. She was leaning against the wall, clutching her head between her hands. "Well, this is fun."

Rayne's eyes opened and she squinted at her. "Can you smell anything other than whatever they rubbed in our faces?"

Lowering her hands slowly, Kelsey straightened up. She could feel her pulse in her temples, and wanted nothing more than to lie back down and close her eyes until the throbbing stopped. "Give me a minute." Pushing herself, she squatted and then slowly straightened her legs until she was standing, although hunched over. Each step she had to pause to keep her balance; everything she saw was weaving back and forth. When she reached the wall, she leaned against it and took a few deep breaths, trying to move without making the pain worse. She opened one eye and tried to peer between the boards nailed over the window. She couldn't see anything.

Resting her cheek against the rough wood, she lifted her nose to a small crack and inhaled slowly. It took her a minute to dismiss the smell of the wood itself, but then she was able to pick up several others. Exhaling, she closed her eyes and tried once more, concentrating harder. The scents were familiar, but she still had trouble filtering through them with the pain throbbing in her head. Squatting down, she lowered her head to her knees and tried to concentrate. "I can smell..." Lifting her head, she looked over at Rayne's expectant stare. "I think we're at a quarry."

"A quarry?" Rayne gave her a bewildered look. "Like Flintstones kind of quarry?" She gave her a shrug. "Sorry, pampered city girl here." Resting her chin on top of her knees, she sighed. "I can sniff out a shoe sale like there's no tomorrow, but this whole outdoors thing is still new to me."

Kelsey turned her head and rested her cheek on top of her knees, she could still see Rayne but wasn't using any energy. "I can smell the equipment, or at least the odor lingering from it, the dust from gravel..."

Rayne waved a hand in the air. "Oh, I believe if you say it's a quarry." Lifting her head, she looked around the small space. "Judging by the boarded-up windows, I don't think it's still in use though."

"Yeah," Kelsey looked to see faded marks on the wall where charts once hung. The floor had worn traffic areas and then others where desks and shelves probably had rested. "Any idea how long we were out?"

"No." Rayne inhaled loudly and lifted her head to rest it back against the wall. "Why?"

Kelsey groaned and lifted her own. "I'm trying to think of any abandoned pits, but I haven't been around here in a few years, so we could be anywhere."

"Well that's good news," Rayne mumbled dryly. Pushing to her feet, she stood with a hand braced against the wall. "Let's see if we can find a way out."

"You think they're dumb enough to put us somewhere we can get out of?" Holding her head, Kelsey stood and waited for the spinning to stop before uncovering her eyes and looking over at Rayne.

"We can hope." She watched Rayne go over to the door. "There's one thing that is very consistent with the male personality." She ran her hands around the edge of the door.

Turning, Kelsey tried to pry her fingers under the boards. "They're horny?"

Rayne sighed. "Okay, two things. They constantly underestimate helpless little woman."

With a grin, she looked over her shoulder and met Rayne's bland look. "Yes, they do."

After going around the room twice, they both collapsed onto the floor. "My head isn't as bad now," Rayne said quietly.

"I think the effects have worn off, now I'm just pissed."

Rayne sat up straighter and looked at her. "How in touch with your cat are you?"

Kelsey gave her a hesitant look. "I really don't know. She's there and then she's not, it's all foreign to me still. Why?"

Rayne bit her bottom lip and looked her up and down. "So, you don't think you could partially shift?"

Eyes wide, Kelsey looked at her. "I don't even know how to fully shift without Gage's coaching, so I'm going to say no."

Rayne looked disappointed. "That's too bad. One of your paws would be so much more powerful than one of mine." She sighed and started to pull her shirt over her head. "I'm afraid my only weapon is my teeth and perhaps, my speed."

Scrambling to her knees, Kelsey watched her take off her clothes. "What are you doing?"

Rayne glanced around and then moved a few feet away from the door. "We are going to get out of here." She took off her Capri pants and set them on the floor, and then went to lie down on top of them. Holding up her shirt, she waved it around. "Come and cover me as much as you can with this. I don't want to give them an eyeful."

Going over she placed the shirt to cover as much of Rayne as she could. "And the plan is?" Kneeling beside her, Rayne bit her lip once more.

"You are going to raise a ruckus, tell them I'm sick, or whatever, to get them to open the door." She exhaled loudly, resting her hand on her arm. "Hopefully, only one of them comes through the door," she gave her an apprehensive look, "if not, slow down the second as long as you can." Taking a deep breath, she let it out and closed her eyes. "Just give me a second to focus, and then start pounding on the door."

Nodding, Kelsey stepped back and stared down at her. She closed her eyes, trying to see if she could feel her cat. A prickly feeling moved over her skin and she smiled. She may not know how to shift on short notice, but her cat was here with her. "Here we go," she whispered to let Rayne know she was ready.

Stepping up to the door, she smacked her palm against it. "Hey! Is anyone out there?" She smacked it a few more times. "There's something wrong with my friend." Her heart was pounding faster in her chest. "Someone, help me!" She kept smacking it until she heard keys on the other side.

"Just hold on."

It was the voice of the shorter man. She looked over at Rayne, who looked like she was asleep. "Hurry, please. I don't know what's wrong with her."

She stepped back when she heard the key in the lock. Moving to the side, she clasped her hands and tried to look like she was panicking, even though she wasn't really acting to feel that emotion. The door swung open and the man gave her a look. Pointing behind the door, she waved her hand. "She was burning up, so she stripped and then just passed out." Stepping forward she grasped his shirt in her fists, "Help her, please."

As he gave her a gentle shove back, she looked out the door to see he was alone. "Just sit over there and let me look."

Nodding and taking hasty steps back, Kelsey kept her eye on the door. Where was the tall one? Glancing over at Rayne, she watched as he knelt down beside her and leaned close to her face. She could see his rib cage expand as he inhaled slowly. Before he could do anything else, Rayne was in wolf form standing over him, his throat clamped in her jaw.

Kelsey jolted and scrambled over to Rayne holding him still. "Where's your friend?"

Rayne growled without releasing his neck.

"I think you better answer," Kelsey said trying not to grin, as the man's eyes bulged in fear.

"Supplies," he croaked, "he went for supplies."

Nodding, Kelsey looked around and then spoke to Rayne. "Can you keep him here for a second? I'm going to see if I can find something to tie him up." Rayne growled again. Kelsey darted through the door and down the stairs, wincing as the grated metal steps cut into her bare feet. The stairs led into a larger room that had to be the tower. Spotting a door, she opened it and discovered a closet. Rushing to the other door, she opened it quickly and ran outside.

Spinning in a circle, she tried to think where supplies might be found. An old rusted tool shed, half collapsed was on the other side of the narrow road that led down into the pit. Rushing over, she opened the creaking door and looked inside. A couple of forgotten pails were filled with chain. She went in and grabbed the pail with the heavy linked chain. It was going to have to do.

Securing his arms behind him, Kelsey struggled to get the hook through both links of the chain. "Well, it's not the best, but it will hold him unless he's Hercules." Glancing at Rayne, she went over and picked up her clothes. "Let's find somewhere to put him."

"My partner will be back any second now." He dragged his feet when Kelsey gave him a little shove toward the door.

"Then you'd better hurry along with us."

Rayne moved over, her ears flattened back and shoved her muzzle into his crotch, growling in a tone that even made Kelsey shudder.

"Okay, okay." The guy looked over his shoulder at her. "I'll move." Stepping back, Rayne backed toward the door, pausing to be sure he followed.

Releasing a silent breath of relief, Kelsey walked along behind him. "There's probably some old water drains around the pit, we could put him in one of those." He gave her a wide-eyed look over his shoulder, but continued to walk. Rayne stopped and waited for him to move past her and then stepped in behind him, emitting another warning growl.

Kelsey stumbled along behind them, barely able to believe any of this was happening. A week ago, her life had seemed so boring and normal, now it was neither boring nor anywhere near normal.

Chapter Twenty-Five

Stumbling into her, Rayne swore softly. "Sorry, I'm a little shaky after shifting."

Kelsey turned and put a hand on her shoulder. "It's okay." Taking a deep breath, she looked around, nothing but trees, no matter where she looked. "I wish I could see more, maybe then I could figure out where we are."

Rayne bent over, resting her hands on her knees and took a few breaths. "Where we are, is the middle of an endless forest." Lifting her head, she gave her a lopsided smile. "I loved the trees. When I first arrived at Devin's they were so peaceful." Standing, she sighed, "trees even saved me when I was stranded in a storm," she shook her head when Kelsey gave her a curious look. "A long story that I don't have the energy to tell right now." Groaning, she bent over and lifted one of her feet. "You know the next time we're going to be kidnapped, remind me to put shoes on first."

"I'll make a note of that." Kelsey looked up at the tops of the trees. It would be easier to travel on the road, but they had agreed that it would be a really great way for the tall partner to find them when he returned to the pit. Using the trees as cover had seemed like a great idea. "I completely suck at climbing trees, or I'd shimmy my way up and see if I could find us a landmark." If she'd been wearing jeans, she might attempt it, but in shorts and bare feet, not a chance.

Rayne chuckled. "Shimmy is a dance to me, so I'm afraid I'm less than helpful there too." She frowned at Kelsey. "I'm feeling very inadequate today."

Shaking her head, Kelsey grinned. "Well, your wolf was more than helpful, so you're forgiven." She looked up at the tree tops again. "Rayne?"

"Hmm?"

She looked over to see Rayne turning and looking through the bush. "Could you talk me through a shift?"

Rayne gave her a look full of doubt. "I don't know. I've only been on the receiving end myself, until I went all wolfie on that guy back there."

Pulling her shirt over her head, she dropped it on the ground. "Gage is going to kill me, he told me to stay out of the trees."

Rayne picked up her shirt and then held her hand out for her shorts. "I'm sure he'll be very forgiving in this instance."

Kelsey rolled her eyes at her. "You don't know Gage."

"No, but I know men, and I know my own mate isn't going to let me out of his sight, or possibly his arms for the next year or so after this. So, the sooner we find our way back to them, the shorter the trail of dead bodies is going to be."

Shooting her a shocked look, them thinking a few seconds more, Kelsey nodded. "Good point." Exhaling, she got down on her knees in the pine needles. "Let's do this." Closing her eyes, she reached for her cat, hoping they could do this. With a prickle of familiarity, she realized her cat was right there with her, moving against her, ready. "Okay," she whispered and put her hands on the ground. "Let's do this."

She focused on the cat that felt like it was prowling along the inside of her body, Rayne's voice was a soothing melody to her ears as she told her to relax and let it happen. This time she expected the snapping bones, and they shifted, but she still gasped each time it happened. Her body felt like a puzzle that was shifting into place. It wasn't painful, but it was such a weird feeling that it still freaked her out.

Blinking, she looked down and realized she was seeing the world through feline eyes. Everything was so different, more detailed and vibrant. Stretching, she looked up at Rayne.

"Well, you are positively gorgeous," she frowned, "and huge." Sighing, she tilted her head. "I'm really feeling insignificant right now."

Shaking her large head, Kelsey moved over and rubbed against her. Rayne laughed and ran a hand over her shoulder.

"Go get to shimmying and find out where we are." She backed up and then sat down.

Kelsey sniffed and could smell Rayne's exhaustion now that she had shifted. They had to get out of this bush. Turning, she walked towards the trees, sizing them up. She needed one that was tall enough that the branches would support her as she climbed higher.

Moving over, she walked under the low branches of some pine trees. She wasn't a tree expert by any means, but was pretty sure these were white pines, taller than most trees she'd seen. Then again, she was standing at the bottom looking up. With a quick glance behind her to see Rayne sitting there watching, she crouched down and prepared to jump.

The first few leaps were easy, there were plenty of branches to choose from, but the further up she went they started to thin out. Fortunately the trees were close enough that branches from multiple trees overlapped and were entwined with the one she climbed. Digging her claws in, she aimed for a group of large branches on the tree next to her. As she neared her target, she extended her claws and hoped for the best.

If Gage were here now, she would be in so much trouble, she'd be lucky if he didn't take away her shifting privileges, or whatever the equivalent of *bad kitty* punishment was. When the tree began to sway with each jump, her heartbeat picked up and she slowed down, worrying how much higher she should aim for. Looking down was a huge mistake. She was at least a hundred feet in the air, or it looked that far down. Getting down was going to be a whole new nightmare.

Panting, she licked across her sharp teeth. She could taste pine in her mouth. Bracing her body to adjust for the movement of the swaying tree, she stretched up and looked around. There were no roads that she could see, and only a few paths free of what would possibly be trees. She did see a few cleared areas that contained buildings. Looking the other way, she tried to find some landmark that would be familiar. Off to left, there was a large rockface. There was something familiar about it, but she couldn't be sure.

How long would it take them to get there? Slowly moving back to consider, she looked through the growth at Rayne. Could Rayne shift again? They'd probably make better time as animals, and that didn't hurt the paws like traveling on bare feet did.

Gathering her nerve, she started making her way down the tree. With any luck, she could climb down much of the way instead of jumping. Jumping up onto a branch was way easier than free-falling down to one.

Stopping halfway down, she paused to regroup. The branches were getting too thick to climb through. She didn't have a choice, she had to plan some jumping. Crouching down, she plotted her path through the dense needles and pushed off. As she landed, she had to scramble for a good hold or continue falling.

With twenty feet to go, she turned and aimed for a larger grouping of branches, hoping she didn't over shoot the jump. Before she could dig in, her hip bounced off the side of the tree and her body was crashing through the limbs. When she hit the ground, she landed on her side and just laid there, panting and assessing any damage done. So much for cats landing on their feet.

Opening her eyes, she saw Rayne standing over her with her hand on her mouth. "Are you all right?"

Getting to her feet, she took her time and shook off the effects of the sudden stop. She wasn't going to win the graceful kitty award, that was for sure. Nudging Rayne's leg, she turned and starting heading through the trees in the direction of the rock formation. Even her cat instincts agreed with that decision; the familiarity meant something and that became her goal. Trees grew and changed, rocks did not, that they looked like somewhere she knew gave her some hope.

"Kelsey, wait," Rayne called out behind her. "I'm on two legs, remember…"

Rayne cried out making Kelsey freeze and spin back to her. She was bent over, holding her foot. Moving back to her quickly, she stood there. Communicating in this form wasn't going to work out. As Rayne continued to swear under her breath, something about sticking a pine cone up somewhere to the guys responsible for taking them, Kelsey moved to a shady spot and laid down.

Focusing on her breathing, she closed her eyes and tried to relax and let her body change back. The pops were quieter, closer together than earlier. As pine needles digging into her hip registered, she opened her eyes to see that her vision was normal again. "Toss me my clothes." Her voice was a little rough.

Rayne glanced at her, and then threw her clothes to her. "Sorry about slowing us down," she grimaced. "My tender feet are not used to this."

Kelsey shook her head. "I don't think anyone's feet could get used to walking on all this." Pulling on her shorts, she motioned with her head in the direction she'd been going. "I spotted a large rock formation that way. It looks familiar. If we can get there, we'll at least be safe when it gets dark." She pulled her shirt over her head, then had to bend forward and breathe deeply to wait out the dizziness.

"You're going to be a bit light-headed until you eat." Rayne limped over to stand beside her. "It doesn't bother the guys as much to shift back and forth because of their body mass…" she shrugged, "or something like that."

"Sucks to be small I guess." Standing up, she paused to see if the dizziness had passed. "We better get moving, I have no idea what time it is, and I don't want to be stuck out here if it gets dark."

Rayne grinned. "We *are* the predators, remember."

Laughing, Kelsey began to walk. "I forgot. I guess we are the big bad now."

"Wolfed out or not, I don't think I'd like to face a bear though."

Glancing over her shoulder, Kelsey shook her head. "Yeah."

Rayne kept pace with her. "We're both going to have to eat soon." She panted and brushed her long hair away from her face. "At least I am."

Still feeling a little woozy, Kelsey nodded. "Me too." She looked around, trying to decide if anything was edible. "What are we going to do?"

Rayne glanced at her sideways and slowed down. "How does rabbit stew sound…" she cringed, "minus the cooking and stew part?"

Swallowing, Kelsey put her hand on her arm to stop her. "You're kidding, right?" The look on Rayne's face gave her the answer. "Eww." She shrugged. "Maybe my cat is a vegetarian."

Rayne raised an eyebrow at her. "I *am* a vegetarian…"

"Fine, but let the record show that I am objecting to this, even if my cat isn't."

Rayne sighed and unbuttoned her capris. "Noted, and I agree, but if we're going to make it, I don't see we have a choice."

Chapter Twenty-Six

Gage paused and bent down to pick up a rock, then looked around the swampy area. Where was she? If she so much as had a scratch on her, someone was going to pay. With. Their. Life. Growling, he leaned back and whipped the rock across the boggy pond. The cracking as it smashed against a tree echoed through the silence.

Closing his eyes, he inhaled deeply, praying the air would carry her scent.

"Kelsey have Bengal coloring when she shifts?"

Gage jumped at Devin's voice coming from the trees at his back. Turning, he frowned. "Yeah, deep orange, why?"

Devin exhaled and then leaned over, placing his hands on his knees. "Thank god." He let out another breath and then straightened. "Sometimes mates can project what they're seeing and I just got a flash of a really big tiger running like a demon through trees."

Gage's heart pumped so fast, he had to catch his breath. "They're in animal form, running?"

Devin nodded.

"So, they got free?"

"It looks like."

Gage wanted to scream in relief. "What did you see? Was anyone chasing them? Anything that would help us know where they are?"

Devin put his hands on his hips and stared at the ground.

Gage balled his hands, trying not to grab and shake him so he'd hurry up. Even in his panic and seeing red that someone had dared touch his mate, he still knew grabbing the future king and shaking the bejeezus out of him was bad. Friend or not, they were long past the age where crossing lines was forgiven.

Devin squinted at the ground. "There was a lake on the one side, nothing that is helpful." He cursed. "Wait, there was a huge rock face, still in natural formation, no drilling or digging..." he stopped and looked at him and then threw his hands in the air. "I don't know enough about this area to even suggest a direction."

Gage blew out a breath, trying to keep a handle on his anger. His animal was clawing to go find his mate. According to Cooper, both Devin and he needed to stay in two-legged form or they'd lose it completely. Regardless of how many legs he had, he was close to rampaging.

"Fuck," Devin kicked a rock across the clearing. "If you'd marked Kelsey, she'd be able to show you where they were."

Gage glared at him. "Yeah, and how well did marking your mate *without* consent go for you?"

Devin crossed his arms over his chest and studied him. "She came around."

Shaking his head, Gage paced over to the edge of the pond and stared out over it. "Obviously, you're forgetting what you went through *before* she came back..."

Blair came bounding out of the trees and stopped abruptly. He looked from one to the other and then shook his large white body.

Basically, Gage thought, he'd heard them bitching at each other and decided to abandon searching to play peacekeeper. Gage rubbed the back of his neck and stared back at the pale feline eyes studying him. "Rayne sent Devin some images through their *mate* connection," Blair blinked and that was the only reaction he gave away. "The girls are in animal form running hell bent through trees…"

Blair stiffened and glanced at Devin before looking back at him.

Gage nodded. "Yeah they've gotten away somehow." He briefly glanced at Devin then continued. "He saw a large rock formation that appeared untouched by man and machine. Does that ring any bells for you?"

Blair gave him a look that Gage was sure meant 'duh' and then he turned and ran into the trees.

Devin jolted. "He knows?"

Gage nodded and then ran into the trees. "Looks like it." Running as fast as two legs allowed, Gage pushed himself to keep Blair in sight. When he lost the visual, he picked up the pace and slid around a large boulder. Skidding to a stop in the loose soil, he looked up to see Blair standing on top of the large rock. Huffing out a breath, he pulled himself up until he stood beside him.

Blair's look was sarcastic, before he turned his head to the left.

Gage glanced in the direction and then froze. Off in the distance was the old drop-off they used to climb when they were younger, before any of them could shift. He heard running feet coming up the path. "Dev, up here."

He stood up and waited until his friend started to climb up the rock. Reaching down, he dragged him up. He pointed to the cliff. "Is that what you saw?"

Out of breath, Devin turned and squinted. "I think it is." He shook his head. "Not from the same angle, but the tree grouping at the top looks the same."

Gage patted Blair on the shoulder. "Go find Noah and Gary and meet us back at the truck."

They both watched Blair leap down and take off into the trees.

"How far is it?" Devin looked back at the large rock area towering over the tree tops in the distance,

"We can't run the whole way there; it would take about three hours," he rubbed his hand over his jaw, "too many detours around swamps and bogs. We can take the truck and get within ten miles by road." He glanced at their destination. "We can be there by dark."

Nodding, Devin turned and started climbing down. "Let's go."

Standing beside Rayne, Kelsey looked up at the rock face. "Now I know why it looked familiar, Blair used to bring me here."

Rayne raised both eyebrows. "For what?"

Kelsey grinned. "To climb."

Shaking her head, Rayne looked up to the top. "I guess when you don't have a mall to hang out in; you might as well climb a cliff."

"I think he did it to get me out of Gage's way." Kelsey moved closer, trying to figure out where the best place to start would be.

"Oh?"

She shrugged. "When I was seventeen, I decided Gage was the one my hormonal body wanted."

Rayne Chuckled. "I guess that fantasy has been realized."

Kelsey felt her cheeks heat. "It has now." Finding a good handhold, she searched for solid footing. "Gage knew I was his mate, but refused to go near me until I was older." She watched Rayne follow her up. "Or so I've been told." She paused to let Rayne catch up.

"Ten points for Gage," Rayne grunted as she pulled her body up further, "for not being a jerk and claiming a child."

Turning, Kelsey looked at the rough surface a few inches from her face. "Yeah." Reaching up, she felt around for another good hold. Now wasn't the time to think, she needed to focus on not falling off the face of these rocks.

"Kelsey?"

Finding it, she brought her foot up and pulled herself up higher. "Yeah?"

"Are we…" Rayne huffed out a breath, "climbing to the top?"

Pausing, Kelsey looked down at her. "No. There's a nice dry, safe shelf about…" looking up, she tried to guess how far, "another thirty or so feet. We can stay there." She went up a few more feet before Rayne commented.

"Will they think to look here?"

Resting her forehead against the rough stone, Kelsey closed her eyes. "I think Blair will." She opened them and felt around for another good finger-hold. "I used to take off and end up here when I was upset or moping, and Blair always found me." She lifted her leg and winced as her knee scraped along a jagged edge.

"So, you and Blair were close when you were younger?"

Kelsey knew Rayne talking to keep their minds off the reality and she didn't blame her, but it still sent pain through her heart. "Yeah, I guess." She hissed out a breath as her forearm rubbed over another jagged stone. "Apparently, Blair ran interference a lot to keep me out of Gage's path…"

Rayne snorted. "Oh, I don't think the pretty Blair minded one bit, having to spend so much time with you."

Kelsey grinned, hearing Rayne call him pretty, Blair would pout if he'd heard it. "No, I guess he didn't" She scowled at the rocks. "I just found *that* out too in this last week."

Rayne made an aggravated sound. "I'm going to be one big scab tomorrow."

Kelsey looked down to see her shake it off and reach up, following closely. "Only one? You're doing better than me."

"You didn't know, about Blair? He never tried anything in all those years?"

Kelsey sighed and looked up for the ledge. It was going to be dark soon. "No. I saw him as a brother, but I guess its taboo or something."

Rayne chuckled. "To mess with someone's mate? Yes, taboo would be the mild way of putting it."

Kelsey didn't reply. There really wasn't anything more to say. Her options were to pick Gage or pine for Gage. Rayne was quiet too, for the last part of the climb.

When they were both lying on the ledge, all Kelsey wanted to do was close her eyes and sleep. Turning her head, she looked over at Rayne. She had her eyes closed as she fought to catch her breath. Sitting up, Kelsey moved back until she was leaning against a smooth area on the wall. She'd spent a lot of time here before she went away to school, pondering her future. She grinned. It hadn't exactly worked out the way she'd pictured. There hadn't been any shifters, mates or furry tails, in any of the scenarios she'd imagined.

Biting her lip, she looked over to where she'd scratched her initials into the pale stone. Underneath those were Gage's. The plus sign wasn't very visible, but she knew it was there.

"I'm so tired," Rayne whispered.

Kelsey looked back over at her. "Me too."

Rayne turned on her side and opened her eyes to look over at her. "We wouldn't have made it this far if we hadn't…"

Wincing, Kelsey covered her ears. "Don't talk about that. Ever." She dropped her hands and held them over her stomach. "My stomach is still churning."

Smiling, Rayne studied her for a moment. "We could talk about boys." She wiggled her eyebrows at her.

Snorting, Kelsey rested her head back against the wall. "I've had enough talk about men to last a lifetime." She rubbed her hands over her face. "It's been all mate this, mate that, and then that heat…" she stopped and sat up. "It hasn't come back."

Rayne pushed up until she was sitting facing her. "Maybe your body decided you'd been through enough for the first time around."

Kelsey hissed out a breath. "That's for sure." Looking down at her palms, she cringed when she saw how dirty she was. "I'm not going to mourn it going away."

"I don't think I'd miss it either." She grinned. "My sex life with Devin is quite full enough, I don't know how we'd fit in anymore…"

Kelsey waved her hands, feeling her cheeks heat. "Don't talk about it."

Rayne laughed. "Afraid I'll jinx it?"

That, and hearing about sex was something Kelsey didn't think she'd ever be completely comfortable with. "Something like that."

"It's a good thing." Rayne said as she examined her scraped legs.

"What is?" Kelsey straightened a leg and tried to see how badly cut it was.

"That the heat's gone." Rayne tried to run her fingers through her tangled hair, then shook her head and gave up. "Now when you're horny for Gage you'll know it isn't driven by your cycle to breed."

Kelsey bit her lip, she hadn't thought of it that way. "So, the draw to your mate isn't as intense?"

Rayne leaned back on her hands and studied her. "The sex is intense, and there is a draw to be with your mate, or when they're near, but it's not uncontrollable." She grinned. "Well, unless you don't want to control it."

Kelsey nodded, like she understood when she really didn't. She'd always wanted Gage, but she'd never wanted to devour him like she had with the heat burning through her. "I guess it will get easier for me to figure things out."

Rayne moved over to the edge of the shelf and sat back down. "You're still not sure what you want to do?"

Kelsey followed her over and looked out, hoping she'd see signs of life somewhere. "Honestly, I have no idea." She ran her finger over the rough stone they sat on. "I won't lie and say I don't enjoy being with Gage, but I still don't know if…"

"He hasn't said a word about love, has he?"

Kelsey gave her a shrug. "No."

"Men are so stupid sometimes," Rayne mumbled.

"Sometimes?"

"Kelsey, I've seen the way the man looks at you and watches you. He loves you." She snorted. "Blair has the same look on his face, but it's not as intense."

"I've never noticed any looks from either of them." She blew out a quiet breath. "Well, I've noticed the way Gage looks at me the last few days..."

Shaking her head, Rayne moved over closer. "Like he wants to take a bite, that would just mean he's horny. I'm talking about the way he looks at you when he doesn't think anyone is watching."

Kelsey bit her lip and shook her head. "I don't know."

"And, I think you love him too."

Shrugging, she looked over the darkening forest. "I've been totally obsessed with the man since I grew boobs, or thereabouts."

"It may have started as a teen crush, but it's more now." Rayne nudged her with her shoulder. "Do you trust him?"

Kelsey nodded. "Of course."

"Does he make you laugh when you really want to cry?"

"Sure."

Rayne bobbed her head. "Okay, so does he piss you off like no one ever has?"

Grinning, Kelsey looked at her. "Well, all the guys do, but Gage excels at it."

"I think my mate has the golden award myself." Rayne sobered and looked at her, searching her face. "Can you see your life without him in it?"

Just the thought of no Gage made her chest ache. She remembered what he'd said if she didn't want to mate with him, that he'd go away. It had bothered her then, but now, after they'd shared so much, she couldn't see not having Gage there. "I..." She stiffened and sat forward, there was something moving not far from where they were. "Shhh." She motioned in the direction the noise had come from.

Rayne turned and looked, then sat still and quiet, neither dared to breathe. "Is it them?" Rayne whispered and inhaled deeply. "I can't tell."

Leaning out over the edge, Kelsey took a deep breath and closed her eyes. There were so many scents to sort through. Opening her eyes, she bit her lip. "I'm not sure…" Branches snapping and leaves rustling had them both leaning away from the edge as a large orange tiger came crashing through the trees. It ran at full stride until it was at the base of the rocks, right where they'd started climbing. Prowling from side to side it sniffed the ground and then stopped and looked up.

"Is it Gage?" Rayne looked over the ledge.

Kelsey grinned. "It's Noah." Getting onto her knees, she leaned out and looked down at the animal looking up at her. Noah chirruped at her and then turned around and emitted a louder yowl in the direction of the trees. Heavy footfalls could be heard, with branches cracking as they moved rapidly in their direction.

"Kelsey." Gage came running out of the trees; Devin was right on his heels. They both came to a quick stop beside Noah. Noah turned around and looked up at them. "Honey, how the hell did you get up there?"

"You okay, Rayne?" Devin stared up at them.

"We're both fine." Rayne said relief clear in her voice.

"I didn't know how long it would take you guys to find us, so I wanted to stay put somewhere safe." She called down to Gage. Her heart was pounding at the sight of him.

"And how were you planning on getting down when we found you, honey?"

She could hear the exhaustion in his voice. Biting her lip, she looked at Rayne, who had the same blank look on her face as she couldn't think of an answer. "I didn't think that far ahead."

Blair, Cooper and Gary came through the trees. They all stopped and looked up at them. Cooper shook his head and then walked over to Devin. Blair said something to Gary, who nodded and then turned around. "Gary's going to grab the rope out of the truck." He sauntered over to stand with the other men and then looked up at them. "You ladies all right up there for a few more minutes?"

Rayne hugged Kelsey with one arm and let out a slow breath. Kelsey grinned at her and looked back down at him. "I think we'll be okay for a few more."

"Kelsey, where are they?" Gage's tone was hard.

Kelsey didn't need to ask who, she knew what would be on Gage's mind now that he'd found them. "We don't know where one went, but we left the other hanging in a water drain at an abandoned quarry." She shook her head. "I don't know where though."

Cooper said something to Gage, who nodded. "We have a good idea."

A large, dark tiger came running out of the trees with a rope hanging from his mouth. It was Jake.

Blair took the rope and handed it to Gage. She strained to hear what was being said, but they kept their voices quiet, neither she nor Rayne was able to hear them. Blair looked back up at them, even in the dark she could see his whole posture change. His stance told her that the easy-going man had just become a lethal predator. He stood there for a few more seconds and then headed back the way they'd come. Noah and Jake turned to follow him. Kelsey glanced at Rayne, and they both knew where they were going.

"Just hang on, honey, I'll be up in a few minutes." Gage pulled the rope over one arm and his head and moved toward the rock. Devin was right beside him.

Chapter Twenty-Seven

Ignoring the twinges as he strained his exhausted muscles, Gage pulled as hard as he could trying to cover the last few feet to the shelf's edge. He'd rest later. Recover after he could assure himself, with his own eyes, that his mate was okay. With the grunts coming from Devin a few feet below him, it was obvious he was thinking the the same thing.

Pulling his body up over the edge, he didn't even pause to catch his breath, just reached out and closed his arms around Kelsey's cold shaking body, pulling her in until she was pressed tight against him. Curling his body around hers, he pushed his face into her hair and inhaled her scent.

His cat calmed, assured that she was safe. Her arms were shaking, but she still wrapped them around his waist and squeezed. Inhaling again, he paused. "I smell blood." Leaning back, he gripped her shoulders and pushed her back, his eyes searching over her.

"I got a few scrapes climbing up here," she whispered with an unsteady voice.

"And our feet," Rayne added, "don't forget about our poor feet."

"Let's get them down so we can go back to your place." Devin began moving toward the back of the ledge. "Where is that ring Blair was talking about?"

228

Kelsey pulled out of Gage's hold. "I'll show you."

Gage pulled the rope over his head and followed her.

"Blair used to make me use a guide line," she reached up and patted the large metal ring embedded in the layers of rock. "Until I knew what I was doing."

"I can't believe you got up here." Devin said quietly, looking at his mate.

Rayne looked at Kelsey and rolled her eyes, grinning. "You'd be surprised what we're capable of."

Securing the rope, Gage gave it a few hard tugs to make sure it wasn't going anywhere. "Let's get you down and then we'll talk about how you got free and came here."

Kelsey gave Rayne a look she couldn't identify and then nodded. "We'll have to space out our descent with only one rope."

Gage moved over to the ledge and dropped the rope.

"Got it." Cooper hollered up at them.

"After you." Rayne motioned to Kelsey.

Kelsey nodded and moved closer to the edge. "Just watch how I do this, Rayne." She smiled. "After everything else today, this will be a piece of cake."

Rayne nodded. "A piece of cake would be great right now."

Gage pulled the rope up so Kelsey could get in place.

She took a deep breath and slowly stepped over the edge to the small lip below it. Following her, Gage grabbed a handhold and leaned around her.

"Make sure the end of the rope falls between your legs," she said to Rayne. "Then you won't climb right out of it." Leaning back carefully, she checked the position. "Go slow." She warned, "Without a guide clip and gloves, it's going to be hard to control your speed.

"Can't be any worse than running around without shoes all day," Rayne said in a flat tone.

Gage gave Kelsey the space to start down and then free climbed until he was level with her legs. If she slipped, he wasn't taking any chances.

The descent was slow, he had to clamp down on his impatience and let her go at a pace she was comfortable with. "You're doing great, honey. A few more minutes and you'll be on the ground."

"Okay," she answered him, distracted.

Glancing over his shoulder, he gauged how far they were from the ground. Still too far to jump. Under his skin, his cat was prowling, waiting, trying to hold out long enough to make sure his mate was as fine as she said. Gage knew it was going to take restraint, like he'd never used before, to keep his animal side in check. After thinking he'd lost her, his animal wanted nothing more than to claim and mark her as his.

Kelsey made a quiet distressed noise, bringing Gage back to focus. She stopped and hugged her body in close to the stone. "Just need a minute," she whispered, breathless.

Climbing back up a few feet, his jaw clenched, he leaned over and sheltered her body with his own. "She's too tired to finish this," he called down to Cooper. Crowding her body with his, he leaned down and rubbed his jaw along her cheek. "Think you can hang onto me?" She had her eyes closed but nodded. "Okay, let go of the rope and turn slowly." He his hand on the rocks, making sure he had a good grip. "Wrap yourself around me and hang on tight."

Bracing himself to take on her weight, he clenched his jaw and focused on giving her space to turn without leaning back. Rock climbing in heavy work boots was not ideal, but she was exhausted and wouldn't make it to the bottom on her own. She wrapped her arms around his neck. "That's it."

"How are you going to do this?" she breathed against his neck as she spoke.

"Don't worry about me. Get your legs wrapped around me as tight as you can." He could feel the fatigue in her limbs as she carefully positioned herself. He bit back the rage that was filling him, knowing that his mate had been taken and scared. Unable to stop himself, he growled. Someone was going to pay for this.

"I'm okay," she whispered close to his face, her hand moving to the back of his head to stroke over his hair.

It angered him further that she'd sensed his emotions and was trying to comfort him. The fury burning through is veins gave him the strength he needed to carry them both down the face of the rock.

Once they reached the ground, he wrapped his arms around her and moved to sit on a rock. Her grip on him relaxed, but she didn't move to let go and he didn't think he could either yet. Nuzzling his face into her throat, he inhaled her unique scent, filling his body with her signature. His cat calmed for now, not pushing for anything rash, but Gage knew it was only a matter of time before he had to deal with that.

Neither of them moved as Devin and Rayne climbed down. It took longer than it had them, and as long as Kelsey was in his arms, he was content to wait it out. He kissed the soft skin of her throat for the hundredth time, taking her taste into his system. It didn't please him that he could taste the dirt and sweat on her, or feel her stress and exhaustion. She hadn't moved, just kept her face buried against his neck, breathing slowly. He didn't know if she realized that she was curled up against him because her animal side needed the reassurance of her mate, but it wasn't the time to go into those details to make her understand.

As Devin and Rayne reached the ground, she finally turned her head and looked over at them. Rayne glanced her way briefly, a look passing between them before she turned into the waiting arms of her mate.

Cooper exhaled loudly and sat on the ground. "Once everyone has caught their breath, we'll start the trek back to the truck." He looked from Rayne to Kelsey. "You did good, kitty kat." He shook his head and pulled off his cap, rubbing a hand over his head vigorously. "How did you get from the quarry to here?"

Kelsey tensed and looked over at Rayne, who had turned and was watching her. "Once we got away, we hit the trees, trying to stay off the roads, but all we ended up doing was wandering around not knowing where we were." She took a shaky breath. "I shifted and climbed a tree to see if I could figure out where we were."

Gage stiffened but didn't say a word.

"I saw the rock face so we headed this way." She finished in a quiet tone.

He knew she could feel the tension in his muscles. Not wanting to upset her, he ran his hand down her back in soothing circles. "You did good, honey."

She nodded and pushed her face into his chest, taking a deep unsteady breath.

"How did you get away?" Devin asked, his tone hard, one that Gage understood completely.

Rayne blew out a breath. "I faked being sick so they'd come in the room they had us in…"

Kelsey turned and looked at her. "Then she shifted and held him down with her teeth clamped around his neck."

Gage watched Devin raise an eyebrow, but he made no comment as his eyes searched his mate's face.

Rayne shrugged. "It was the only thing I could think to do. Kelsey wasn't sure if she could shift that quickly." She looked over at him and then to the woman he held. "The second time she shifted though, it was a lot faster."

Kelsey started shaking in his arms, he wondered if she was cold, so her pulled her closer to his body and then realized she was sobbing silently. "Hey," he kissed the top of her head, "it's okay. You're safe now." She just shook harder. He looked at Cooper and then Devin, neither man was helpful. Leaning back, he lifted her chin so he could see her face. "Kelsey…"

"I ate a b-bunny." She sobbed, tears streaking down her face.

Relief flooded him as he tried not to smile but didn't quite pull it off. That only caused her to cry harder. Pulling her back into his arms, he made soothing noises against her ear. "It's okay, honey. You did what you had to do." She continued to shake in his arms. He looked over at Devin who was also biting back a smile. Cooper cleared his throat and pulled his hat back on as he stood up.

"Let's get them home." He turned and started walking toward the trees.

"Can you walk, baby?" He asked her quietly. She nodded, but made no move to release the death grip she had on his neck, so he wrapped his arms around her and stood up with her clinging to him like a child.

Chapter Twenty-Eight

Kelsey rested back in the chair and looked out into the darkness surrounding the porch. At one end of the yard stood Gary, his back to the house, turning her head she saw Jake at the other side of the yard, also standing guard. Sighing, she glanced over at Rayne. She gave her a feeble smile and mouthed 'told you so'.

Gage and Devin were over at the path to the shop with Blair, their voices low as they stood talking quietly. They had been waiting here before Cooper had driven like a madman to get them home. Kelsey didn't know what had happened to the man they'd left at the quarry, but as the men seemed to be taking turns going over to the shop and coming back, she thought the man still lived.

Gage hadn't gone to the shop, he hadn't left her sight since they'd returned. While she'd showered, he'd stood outside the door asking her every thirty seconds if she was alright. Any other time she would have been annoyed by his constant concern, but in this case, she was just happy to be home and that he was here.

Rayne hadn't been given much more freedom, she noticed. Devin had only left for a few short minutes and gone over to the shop, then he'd returned in a worse mood.

Kelsey sat back and observed them together, it caused an ache in her chest to see the love they had for each other.

Her legs felt achy again, so she got up and moved around on the porch to stretch them. She hadn't gotten more than three steps when Gage's head snapped around as he zeroed in on her. He continued to listen to what Blair was saying, but his eyes stalked her every movement.

"He's going to be like that for a while." Rayne told her softly. "The only reason Devin hasn't dragged me off somewhere is because we're already mated."

Leaning back against the rail, she crossed her arms and looked at Rayne. "I don't think Gage would try that with me."

Rayne smiled at her. A tingle under her skin sent a shiver down her spine.

"Don't be so sure about that, honey," Gage's voice rumbled behind her.

Startled, she turned to see him standing on the other side of the railing, looking at her, his eyes darting all over her body before coming back to her face.

"Are you all right?" The concern in his eyes was so genuine; all she could manage was a brief nod.

She leaned over the railing and looked down at him. "You guys have that man over at the shop." It wasn't a question, because she already knew the answer. "Why did he take us?"

His eyes left hers briefly as he glanced down at the ground, sighing, they met hers again. "I didn't ask." Reaching out her caressed her cheek with his knuckles. "I didn't even get in to see him."

Inhaling, she felt peace with the contact. "Why?"

Dropping his hand, he crossed his arms. "Coop and Jake stopped me."

She gave him a puzzled look.

"We need him alive to get information. They wouldn't let Devin in either." He spoke in a tone she had never heard before and it sent a shiver down her spine.

Rayne made a startled noise from behind her, Kelsey looked to see where she was looking. There were headlights coming up the driveway. Someone was here. Gage leapt over the railing and stood in front of her and Rayne. Devin appeared, placing himself between Rayne and the driveway.

A low rumble emitted from Gage and Kelsey's whole body responded. Moving closer, she touched his back tentatively and leaned into his warmth. Reaching around, he wrapped an arm around her while he stood rigid and waiting.

Kelsey looked around him to see a truck and a van pulling up beside Blair at the edge of the gravel. Gage's posture relaxed, but he was in a ready stance as someone got out of the truck. She breathed and audible sigh of relief as Ed stepped into view.

When he tensed again, the van door opened and a large man got out, followed by three other hulking males, she tucked against his back not sure what was going on. Who were they? She didn't have to ask if they were shifters, she'd already scented that answer. Frowning, she looked them over for a second. Did all the male shifters only come in extra-large size?

Beside her Rayne closed her eyes and her shoulders slumped forward, clearly, she knew who they were and that they didn't pose any threat. Slowly she stepped out from behind Gage and held onto his arm with shaking hands.

Ed was up the porch steps and in front of them before she could ask Gage who the others were.

"Kelsey." Ed said in an anguished tone. "Are you okay?" He glanced at Gage briefly, but didn't make a move to touch her. She could feel the tension in the arm she was holding.

Not knowing what was going on, she nodded. "I'm fine. A little scraped here and there, but we're okay." She looked at the truck. "Where's Beth?"

"She stayed with Bruce's wife." He glanced at his son. "We weren't sure what we were driving in to."

"He's over at the shop." Gage said in a low tone. "He doesn't know where his partner is, last he saw him was when he left to arrange a plane to get them out of the area."

Kelsey looked up at him, her heart pounding in her chest. Pulling his arm free from her grip, he wrapped it around her and hauled her tight against his side. The expression on his face reflected what she was feeling. If they'd gotten them on a plane, she probably would never have seen him again.

"Gage."

Kelsey shrank into his hold as one of the large men came over to them.

"I owe your mate a debt of gratitude for keeping my son's mate safe." He bowed his head slightly at her.

It dawned on her that this was Devin's father, the king of all the clans. She looked up at him for a second; he stood so stiff but didn't have the regal air that she'd figured he'd have. She offered him a small smile. "I think it was a joint effort, sir." She gave Gage a hesitant look, not sure if there was some protocol she'd just blundered. His eyes reflected nothing but pride, making her cheeks heat slightly. "What happens now?"

Ed chuckled softly from where he stood beside Gage. "Straight to the point, as always," he said, his voice filled with humor and pride.

Devin's father smiled and nodded in his direction. "Nothing wrong with that." Reaching beside him, he touched Rayne's shoulder briefly and then looked back to her. "We'll be taking him back with us." His face sobered. "He won't be abducting any more of our women, I can assure you of that." She noticed his eyes kept straying to her neck and then he inhaled slowly. Raising an eyebrow, he sent Gage a look and then nodded to her. "I just need to borrow Gage for a few minutes and then we'll leave you in peace."

Gage hesitated before he released her. "Blair."

Blair straightened from where he was leaning against the truck and came quickly toward them. When he reached the porch, Gage stepped away from her. "I'll be right back, honey. Blair will stay with you."

Kelsey nodded and wrapped her arms around her waist. "I'm going in to make some tea."

Gage's expression softened when he looked back at her. "I won't be long."

Rayne stayed out on the porch with one of the men that had arrived with her father-in-law. Blair followed Kelsey into the house but stood silently on the other side of the kitchen while she put the kettle on and tidied up the counter.

"I'm sorry," he said quietly from the other side of the room.

Confused, she turned to look at him. "For what?"

He lowered his lashes to hide his pale eyes from her. "For letting them get to you."

Kelsey blinked in surprise that he'd said that. "It wasn't your..."

Blair's eyes connected with hers. "It was my responsibility to stay with you while Gage was away."

Waving her hands around, she looked around the room. "You didn't know they were coming here. None of us did."

"It's still my fault." His voice was almost sulky.

Kelsey wanted to throw something at him. "That's bull and you know it." She huffed out a breath. "You knew where to find me, that's all that matters."

His eyes moved over her slowly. "I didn't until Rayne sent Devin the image of the cliff."

"She can do that?"

He shrugged. "Part of the mating bond."

Shaking her head, she'd file that for later when her mind had the energy to focus. "Still, I knew you'd look there eventually." She tilted her head and looked at him. "You always knew me better than I knew myself."

Snorting, he shoved his hands into the pockets of his jeans. "Glad you think so. I never had a clue what in the hell was going on in your head." Leaning against the wall, he gave her a hard look. "I can't believe you bounced up to the tops of the trees in your cat form."

Biting her lip, she gave him an exasperated look. "Don't change the subject, Blair." He grinned. "Thank you." She gave him a serious look. "Even though you're denying it, you've always known me better than Gage. So, I knew you'd find me."

"Something I plan on rectifying." Gage said in a low vibrating tone from where he stood in the doorway.

Blair straightened up, gave her an apologetic look, and then turned to Gage. "I'll be outside." Shoulders back, he went toward the door.

Gage moved to let him go past and then turned back to her. "I'm regretting shoving you at him more and more every day."

She watched him clench his jaw a few times. "I wouldn't have admitted it then, but I think he did us both a favor by keeping us apart."

Shrugging, he moved slowly in her direction. "You would have hated me if I'd gone with my instincts and claimed you then."

Nodding, she leaned back against the counter. "Yes, I would have."

He kept moving closer, almost cautiously. She'd never seen him be so hesitant before. "Devin and Rayne are going to head out shortly and go back with his dad." He stopped a few feet from her and rested a hand on the counter, putting the other in his pocket.

"I'm sure Rayne has had enough of our scenic land for now."

He smirked. "I think it was Dev's idea. He wants her back where he knows the land."

Kelsey watched him as he took slow careful breaths, his eyes constantly darting from her neck to her eyes.

"I'm so proud of you." He said barely above a whisper.

"For not freaking out?" *Like I want to right now with you acting so weird?* His hand kept flexing on the counter and she couldn't figure out why he seemed so out of character.

"That too." Humor flashed through his eyes but was quickly replaced with a look she couldn't decipher.

"Well, I may yet, so don't get too attached to that idea." She tried for a carefree tone, but he clenched his jaw and studied her. "Gage, what's going on?"

He shook his head. "Nothing."

Raising an eyebrow, she glared at him. "You're standing there, practically climbing out of your own skin. What's wrong?"

Taking a deep breath, his eyes moved to her throat again. He shrugged, probably hoping he looked nonchalant, but it didn't work for her. "I'm just at odds with my cat right now. I'll be fine after I go for a run later."

Wishing she knew enough to understand, she stepped in front of him and placed a hand on his chest, hoping to offer some reassurance. "About what?"

Pulling the hand out of his pocket, almost in slow motion, he gently grasped hers and held it against his chest. "I almost lost you today." His voice cracked as he said it.

She knew it was true, if she dwelled on it too long, she was going to turn into a blubbering mess which neither of them needed that right now. "You didn't." A lump in her throat made it hard to breathe. "Why are you at odds with your cat? We're not separate from them, we're one. Aren't we?"

He closed his eyes for a moment, squeezing her hand. "For the most part, yeah, we are." Opening his eyes, she stared up into them watching them darken to a midnight blue. "When it comes to you, it's a constant fight for supremacy."

"What do you mean?"

She watched him let go of the counter, and raise his hand. It shook slightly. Running his knuckles lightly over her cheek, he offered her a tentative smile. "My cat only wants one thing where you're concerned," he tipped her chin up and leaned down closer to her face, "to claim you, and to mark you so no other will go near you." His breath tickled over her lips. "It wasn't my cat side that kept his distance from you so you could grow up."

Being this close to him made her whole-body tingle with awareness.

"I fought with myself every day you were away." He grinned shyly. "I picked up the phone almost every day to call you."

"You never called. Not once." She felt like she was being drawn into his eyes the way they held hers.

"I know." Tracing over her bottom lip with the pad of his thumb he exhaled slowly. "If I'd heard your voice, I wouldn't have been able to stay away." He did it again and leaned close enough she could taste his words. "After almost losing you today, I'm ready to give into my cat and make you mine, honey, even though I'll lose you if I do."

It was getting harder to focus on what he was saying and not just his mouth. She wanted to stretch up the last few inches and kiss him. The tingling in her body was her own cat rubbing up against her, because her mate was so close. Searching his eyes, she knew that now, Gage was her mate. There would be no other for her, and her cat was more than content with that knowledge. "What if I still need time?" She asked him and then held her breath.

His expression softened as his eyes came back to hers. "I'm doing all I can to give you that time, Kelsey, but my willpower is only so strong." He brushed his lips over hers briefly. "And I'm afraid I can't cope with shoving you toward Blair to keep my distance." He kissed her again. "Not after having you." Lifting his head, he made eye contact with her. "The idea of another male even looking at you right now, makes me want blood." A low growl rumbled through his chest as he said it.

She caught her breath and closed her eyes as need streaked through her. Inhaling, she took in his scent and opened her eyes to look up at him. "I don't want anyone else, Gage. I just don't know…"

He placed his lips over hers, not moving them, just stopping her from speaking. After a moment, he raised his head and looked down at her. Something flashed through his eyes and then the hand that had been holding hers grasped the back of her head and pulled her close. With a growl of frustration, he crushed her mouth beneath his and kissed her with a passion that made her dizzy. Lifting his head, he inhaled and then released her and backed away. "We should go out and say goodbye to Devin and Rayne."

Kelsey's legs wobbled, gripping the counter, she steadied herself and nodded. "Okay." With shaky steps, she followed him outside.

Chapter Twenty-Nine

It was past midnight, everyone had been gone for a few hours and Kelsey paced around inside the house. The air was damp, a storm was coming in. Gage had stood impatiently while everyone said good bye and then after a long look at her had taken off in the direction of the shop.

Outside in the dark Blair and Jake were taking their turn on watch. She didn't know how long that would be the case, but wasn't going to balk about it after what had happened. The walls were starting to close in on her as her mind raced in a hundred different directions.

Everything that had happened since she came home was stuck on a loop inside her head, and she was going to explode soon if she didn't find some sort of resolution with all of it. It wasn't fair, not one bit of it, yet this was her new reality. Her new life was leaps and bounds away from what she had always pictured.

She could only fool herself for so long, but had to at least give it a try or be disappointed. Her choices in life were limited no matter how she looked at it. The options she thought she had really were limited.

It wasn't the fact that she was a species other than human she had always believed she was. That, in a weird way, felt right to her. Being a tiger shifter was okay with her.

Sure, she wanted to know more, because at this point she was a toddler and that wasn't going to do at all, but it was easy enough to resolve that.

The lies that had been told to her for years were almost acceptable, now that she understood the reasons. Of course, she'd always be a little miffed about the way it had all gone down, but there was no sense in burning energy being pissy about the situation. She would always regret that her parents hadn't told her, that they'd withheld an important part of her heritage from her, but there was no sense in freaking out about something she couldn't change.

Then there was this whole thing with Gage. The man that she'd pined for as a teen, that she'd had fantasies about all the years she'd been away. He was the reason no other male had ever stirred any interest from her. She only wanted one man, and if she wanted him she could now have him forever, and she'd never have to worry about him straying or breaking her heart. There was that marvelous concept as far as the whole shifter world went. Fate found your match and you stayed with them.

So, what was she doing wearing a hole in the floor while he was out romping around the bush trying to stay away from her? She wasn't sure. There was just something that kept her from taking that last step. She loved him, she knew that. *I love him.* He had to love her, she knew this now. Why else would he work so hard to make sure she was happy, make sure she had the time to come to terms with everything? Pausing she looked out the window and watched lightning strike in the distance.

Get it together, Kelsey, you can't make the man wait forever until you figure out what the hell you're doing. He's shown you the patience of a saint and let you have every opportunity to find someone else. I don't deserve you, Gage. Closing her eyes, she inhaled and then blew it out nosily. *And even after you did that I still came back here.* Opening her eyes wide, she looked up at the ceiling and then down to the floor. *I'm an idiot. The answer is right there, and you've been carrying on like a schizoid for the past week whining about options and choices.*

Turning on her heel, she darted for the door and ran out onto the porch. A loud crack of thunder boomed and echoed into the night. It was like the exclamation point on her thoughts. Blair and Jake ran toward the porch as the sky opened and sheets of rain pelted down.

"*That* came out of nowhere," Jake mumbled as he wiped the water off his face.

She looked from one to the other. "Do you think Gage will be back soon?"

Blair held up both hands and then dropped them to shake the rain off. "Who knows, the crazy bastard always loved running in a storm."

Leaning on the railing, she looked out into the trees, hoping he'd be back soon.

"Everything all right, Kels?" Jake asked, moving to stand beside her.

Nodding, she kept her eyes moving along the tree line.

"He'll be fine." Blair added as he went to the other end of the porch and leaned against the corner post to watch the other side of the yard.

A breeze blew the rain onto the porch making Jake back up, she stood where she was, not caring if she got soaked, as she continued to look for him. Inhaling the rain scent, she smiled when she recognized another scent. Turning she went down the steps and started for the path to the shop.

"Kelsey?" Jake called out.

Before she could reach the path, a large white tiger came out of the trees. He was huge she realized, the closer he got to her. Turning his big head, he glanced at the porch to the men that were supposed to be watching over her and then looked back at her. His easy stride brought him to her in very little time.

When he nudged her toward the porch with his shoulder, she turned and ran her hand down over his wet fur. He paused and let her before nudging her again; she refused to move, just kept pushing her fingers through his coat. Gage made a soft yowling noise and she knew, without interpretation, that he was giving her hell for standing out in the storm.

Leaning down, she rubbed her cheek along his large jaw, "Change back," she whispered.

Pale blue feline eyes studied her for a moment before he turned to the porch and chirruped at the men.

She didn't look, but could hear their boots on the wooden steps as they stepped off.

"Have a good night." Jake called out as he headed into the trees. Blair stopped at the tree line and looked back for a brief moment, then straightening his shoulders he turned and followed Jake.

When she turned back to look at Gage, he stood a few feet in front of her, naked, the water streaming over his body. As she looked at him, she realized he was completely at ease standing there without any clothes on. If it didn't bother him, she certainly wasn't going to complain. The water moved over his shoulders to follow the rippled trail of muscle down to his hips.

"You should go inside, honey."

His voice was still deep, something she'd noticed happened just after shifting back. Forcing her eyes back to his face, she shook her head. "I needed to talk to you."

"We can talk inside, you'll get…"

"I've been out in the rain before, Gage; it's not going to hurt me." She watched him clench his jaw as she placed her hands on her hips. "I'm not going to be one of those complacent mates, so you might as well get used to *that* right now." Stepping closer to him, she watched his eyes as they went darker. A flash of lightening lit up the darkness and highlighted his masculine features; he was a beautiful man, something she'd just have to keep to herself. Another flash of light showed the uncertainty in his eyes as he stood there watching her carefully.

His blue eyes didn't stray from her face once; he just stood there tall and proud, even though he wasn't sure what was going on. "Did you hear me?" she asked softly knowing he'd be able to hear her.

"I'd never expect you to be complacent at any time." His tone was controlled, but she could still hear that he meant it.

Moving over until she stood right in front of him, she reached out and ran her hand down over his chest lightly. He hissed out a breath and held himself rigid, his eyes searching hers. "Good." She ran her hand back up to touch his jaw as he clenched it. "Because if I want to stand out in the rain, then I will stand out in the rain," biting her lip, she placed her other hand against his chest and leaned into him. "And I expect my mate to stand out here with me in the rain."

Gage's eyes kept flicking from her lips to her eyes, confusion plain to see as he tried not to look at her mouth.

"Aren't you going to kiss me, Gage?" She was almost vibrating as she watched him just look at her mouth.

He grasped her shoulders lightly and she was afraid he was going to push her away. "If I do, Kelsey, I..."

She stretched up until their mouths were only an inch apart, her body brushed against his aroused one. "Won't stop until you make me yours, I know."

His hands flexed on her shoulders as he leaned back to see her clearly. He blinked several times, knocking the water from his lashes and then inhaled slowly. "Honey..."

"Kiss me, Gage." She felt her cat still, waiting silently within her.

His hand moved slowly up to the back of her neck, grasping her hair lightly. "Be sure." He said with a warning tone in his voice.

"I'm sure." She watched his eyes change when it was clear what she was agreeing to. Before she could brace herself, he picked her up by the waist, his mouth on hers.

"You have too many clothes on," he said against her mouth. She tried to reach for her shirt, but his arms held her too close. "Not here. We wouldn't make it to the porch and the guys are going to be out scouting the property." He kissed her again started toward the porch. "You'll never regret this, honey." Leaning down he nipped the side of her neck.

Feeling like a ragdoll with her feet dangling in the air, she wrapped her legs around his waist. Groaning, he stopped and placed a hand against the railing at the bottom of the stairs, his other hand moving around to grasp her ass and pull her tighter against him. Tugging gently on his hair, she pulled his mouth back to hers and bit his bottom lip hard enough to make him groan. "Do it, Gage, mark me as yours."

He stumbled up the stairs and made it to the door before he crushed her mouth beneath his and pressed her against the wall. Tearing his mouth away, he sucked in a breath. "Baby, I haven't waited this long to fuck it up." Leaning down he licked slowly up her throat.

Kelsey lifted her chin and turned her head to give him better access, her whole body was vibrating, her cat at well. "What do you mean?"

Lifting his head, he bit her chin lightly, licking along her mouth afterward. "You have to accept me..." He kissed her again like he was starving for her. "Claim me as yours."

Her head was filled with wanting him. "I do accept you..." she pulled his head back down and nipped his bottom lip.

Growling, he lifted his head away and shifted her weight so he could open the door; pausing he pressed her back against the frame and kissed her again. "Fuck," he reached down and pulled her shirt up.

She lifted her arms and made fast work of removing it, tossing it aside and holding his head as he attacked her bare shoulder, scraping his teeth across to the base of her neck. Her whole body felt like it was on fire, gripping his shoulders, she lifted her body up and rubbed against him. If he waited much longer, she was going to go crazy. "Gage," she moaned breathlessly. He stopped and bit the skin where her shoulder and neck met, her center clenched as and she moaned again and arched into him, her sensitive nipples brushing against his chest.

Lifting his head, he panted and looked down at her. "Baby, mark my neck." He tilted his head to the side. "I can't claim you until you accept me."

Kelsey blinked, trying to clear the fog of lust from her brain. "You want me to bite you?"

"Yes," he growled and then snapped his teeth together, "now. I can't hold off much longer." Grasping her waist, he turned and stepped into the house, letting the screen door slam behind them.

Taking a handful of his hair, she pulled his mouth back to hers needing to taste him again. He kissed her with bruising strength and it was just what she needed. He stopped at the bottom of the stairs and her shoulders hit the wall. He growled and tore his mouth from hers, lifting his chin and exposing his throat to her.

Kelsey gasped as her cat came to life inside her, exhilarated, she felt her teeth lengthen slightly and paused to run her tongue over them. Looking up she saw Gage was watching her with heavy-lidded eyes, his chest rising and falling as he fought to breathe. Leaning into him, she ran her tongue over his chest and felt his muscles vibrate with the restraint he was using to control his cat. She moved her mouth slowly up to his neck, dragging her lips across his hot skin. "I accept you," she whispered and then ran her tongue along the base of his neck. His hands clutched her hips as he pushed into her, rubbing his erection between her legs.

Closing her teeth over his skin, she felt them sink in deep enough she could taste blood. She wasn't sure which surprised her more, the fact that she wasn't freaking out over liking it, or the deep guttural moan that came from the shaking man that clearly liked it too. Her cat went crazy and she suddenly felt like she was going to combust if he wasn't inside her soon. Lifting her mouth away, she pulled his head down and kissed him feverishly.

She felt him walking again and heard clothes hitting the floor as his mouth devoured hers. She felt a cool surface against her back, knew she was lying on something, but didn't care what. Gage lifted his mouth from hers and reached down, tearing the zipper down on her shorts, leaning over her, he bit around her nipple as he pulled the material down her legs.

He bit her again and she hissed out a breath, grabbing the back of his head so he wouldn't stop. Lifting his mouth away, he gripped her knees and pulled her toward him as he leaned over to kiss his way up her chest. She turned her head, exposing her neck to him when he reached it. Her core was clenching as his teeth nipped over her skin as at the same time she felt his engorged head slide along her wet folds.

With a deep growl, he thrust into her as his teeth sunk into her skin. She cried out, overwhelmed with bliss from the sensations that hit her all at once. He didn't release his grip on her flesh as he began to plunge into her hard enough to send her sliding along the surface she lay on. Gripping one of her knees, he held her in place and continued. Her muscles began clenching around him and she was helpless to do anything but hold on as he drove her quickly to the edge. Gage growled against her skin, without warning she crashed over the edge as the orgasm swept through her.

Removing his teeth from her shoulder, he kept pumping into her and licking over the new mark. "Mine," he growled against her slick skin. Leaning up on his elbow, he looked down at her and increased the motion of his hips. Reaching his other hand under her, he lifted her hips and looked down to watch his body disappear inside her.

He looked at her and she felt her muscles clench in response to the possessive look in his eyes. With a grunt, he changed the angle of his thrusts and began to slam his body against hers. Without warning another orgasm hit, and she cried out biting her lip until she tasted blood.

Gage's whole body tensed and she felt him pulse inside her, and then it felt like he lengthened inside her filling her to the point where he rubbed against her cervix. He called out and pinned her beneath him so she couldn't move. Another wave went through her, she bit into his shoulder to muffle her scream. He groaned against her throat and then licked over his mark on her skin. After shocks went through her causing him to rub against her cervix again and start them all over again.

"Just be still, baby," he panted against her damp skin, "The barbs won't retract until you relax."

Kelsey's inside clenched around him again and she gasped. "Can't."

He chuckled and caressed her leg lightly from her knee to her hip. His breath blew over his mark and it sent shivers through her again.

"Gage," she moaned softly, "You have to stop," her body spasmed around him again.

Lifting his head, he grinned down at her. "Don't count on it." He brushed the wet hair away from her face. "I waited long enough, I'm never stopping."

She let out a breath as she felt the pressure from inside lessen. "Barbs?"

Smiling, his gave her another light kiss. "I'll explain it later, when you can focus."

She nodded and closed her eyes only to open them again and looked around. "Gage, we're on the desk."

Grinning, he reached under her shoulders and pulled up until she was sitting up, his body still inside hers. "It was either this or the stairs, because I wasn't going to make it to the bed." He dropped a kiss onto her lips and pulled her into his chest. "Just let me find my balance and I'll get us up the stairs."

"I could walk."

Looking down at her, he shook his head. "You could, but then I'd have to let you go and I don't see that happening tonight," he kissed her tenderly, "or tomorrow."

She looked up at him, feeling like she was floating on a cloud. "I bit you."

He grinned. "Yes, you did."

Shaking her head, she touched his shoulder. "No, I mean I bit you again."

He glanced at where she touched and nodded. "Yes, you did."

"So, it's not a bad thing if I marked you twice?"

His grin grew wider. "No, baby. You could mark every inch of me and I would never complain. Each mark carries your scent, letting everyone know I belong to you."

Resting her head against his chest, she closed her eyes and concentrated on breathing normally again. "I have so much to learn."

"What do you mean?" He ran his hand up and down her damp back, causing tingles over her skin.

"I don't know anything about our clan, or even about being a shifter." She rubbed her cheek against him, smiling that his muscles bunched in reaction any where she touched him. "I don't even know much about sex."

His chest rumbled as he laughed. Grasping her waist, he lifted her weight into his arms, drawing another moan out of her as she wrapped her legs tight around him and buried him deep inside her again. "I'll teach you everything you want to know."

Kelsey inhaled his scent into her body and then lifted her chin and looked up at him. "You don't smell the same."

"Neither do you, honey, our scents are combined now."

She smiled. "I like that." He walked out of the office. "Gage?

Cuddling her into his body, he kissed the top of her head. "Yeah?"

"How do you have sex in the shower?"

He stopped and looked down at her. "Would you like me to show you?"

She felt his body stir inside her. Leaning forward she nipped lightly at his chest. "I think you should. I think you should teach me something new each day until you run out of things to teach me."

Turning, he headed back down the hall toward the bathroom. "If I run out, I'll make more up."

"When I've learned everything, I need to know about sex, and being what I am, I want to learn how to fight." He paused in his step but didn't stop completely. "I don't want to ever feel helpless again."

"You're a tiger, I think that's lethal enough without knowing how to fight." He nipped at her shoulder, distracting her for a moment.

"What if I'm abducted again and innocents are around? Am I supposed to just shift into a tiger in front of them?"

Stopping, he tipped her back in his arms and looked down at her, his dark eyes moving over her face. "I'll do everything I can to keep you safe, Kels, but if you want to learn to fight, I don't have a problem if that's what it takes for you to feel secure."

She could see the love in his eyes, feel it in the way he held her and couldn't believe she'd ever doubted the way he felt about her. "I want to help the Alliance take down the people that killed my parents."

Gage closed his eyes, exhaling he opened them. "*That*, we're going to have to negotiate."

Stretching up, she squeezed her legs tighter around him and nibble at the mark she'd left on his neck. "Okay, we'll negotiate." She felt him harden inside her.

"I'm serious, Kelsey."

"Mhhm hmm," she bit harder and then licked it making him shudder.

"Baby, I mean it." His grip tightened as he moved into the bathroom.

"Okay." Clenching her muscles around him, made him drop his head down onto her, she hid her smile to his reaction by kissing his neck again. "We're negotiating."

Growling, he backed up and leaned against the wall, so he could grip her hips tightly. "We'll talk about it later." He lifted her up slowly and closed his eyes as she slid up him. "Much later," he whispered.

Moaning softly into his ear, she squeezed her legs so she stopped moving back down on him. "I think we should talk about it now..." She sucked on the mark on his neck.

Gage groaned, "Baby, that's not fair."

Using her teeth, she nipped her way up his neck to his ear. "What was it you said about fair? This isn't school..."

He emitted a low pulsing growl, causing her body to react wantonly. Turning, she found her back up against the wall. "We'll talk to Devin and see what he thinks you could do to help." With a determined look, he thrust up into her and held her pinned there.

Smiling, she watched the look on his face. He was definitely a beautiful man. Her man. "Agreed." Licking her lips, she watched his eyes track the movement for a second before her mouth was crushed by his.

KEEP READING FOR AN EXCERPT OF

PASSION

Animal Senses Book 3

Jacqueline Paige

Prologue

Calum paused when the voicemail came on. Devin was probably busy with his mate, again. He grinned, "Guess your busy with... royal mating... *stuff.*" He chuckled, "I'm at the bottom of some mountain, in the middle of the back-country nowhere—even more than your camp *nowhere* kind of deal. I've tracked my missing clan members to here." He glanced up the incline to the dense, foliage-covered mountain. "I'll let you know when I find out more." He hung up and sighed. Maybe being away right now was a good thing. With Devin newly mated and Kelsey coming home to Gage... it was going to be messy with a whole lot of *true-mate* issues that Calum didn't have, couldn't relate to, and hoped he'd never have to go through himself. His responsibilities with the alliance didn't leave him time for those distractions.

Turning off his phone, he stuffed it into the waterproof bag and sealed it, then jammed it into his pack. Normally he didn't take his phone with him, but this was an unknown area and knowing he'd have it, just in case, made him feel better. The challenge would be not to lose his pack, as he'd been known to do occasionally.

The small village he'd stopped at had warned him away from coming here, despite confirming they'd seen the men from his clan in the photos he'd shown. They'd said there was bad *juju* on this mountain, and few ever came down off it. Calum wasn't sure about the juju garbage, but if there was even a small chance of the males from his clan being on this mountain, he was going up to find them.

That little village was on the strange side. The way the people watched him gave him the creeps. He wondered if they could smell an outside shifter in their territory, but he picked up no scents that led him to believe there were any shifters among them. He may be paranoid, and they could only be watchful of strangers. With the missing males from his clan, and Tomas' association taking females from other clans, he was allowed to suspect everyone of nefarious intentions. If anyone had a problem with his suspicious nature, they could eat dirt as far as he was concerned.

It had taken him over an hour to get this far up with his car. He was definitely considering getting a truck when he got back. His car hadn't been much good for off-roading. He looked around the area he'd parked. It may have, at one time, been a parking area or rest stop, but it was long deserted, overgrown and ignored. If anyone managed to get up here on the not-really-a-road trail he'd taken, they were more than welcome to break into his car. Locking it, he tucked the keys behind the front tire's rim. He'd learned a long time ago to never take keys on trips into the great wilderness. Losing your clothes or pack was almost always a certainty, losing your keys left you trapped.

He looked back down the way he'd come again before turning toward the incline. "This should be fun." He sighed and started climbing.

His senses were on overload, so many scents, all familiar, but not, at the same time. He took his time moving through the thick vegetation, checking for anything that might set off his animal instincts. His cat was already on full alert, which wasn't necessarily unusual, but it made him more aware of what was around him, and a little jittery as well. As soon as he found something to follow, he'd shift and let his animal side take over the tracking.

He walked along a flat area, happy for the break from the upward climb, watching for somewhere he could stow his pack so it wouldn't be found, not that he anticipated this being a high traffic area, he just couldn't take it with him. Nothing said 'not a normal wild animal' like a big black cat carrying a pack around his neck. He chuckled at that thought.

A few times his cat moved against his skin, telling him to hurry up. He wasn't sure if it was the new area to explore, or if he sensed something, but it wasn't like he was drawing this out like a holiday or anything.

When he finally found a spot he'd be able to locate again, he stripped down and stuffed his clothes in the pack. For half a heartbeat, he thought about pinging his location to Devin, just in case, but doubted there would be any signal here.

Shifting, he stretched to his full length and then wasted no time getting moving. This was more like it, four paws meant for this terrain carried him faster than inflexible boots and man-length strides ever would.

When he cleared the dense growth, he paused and scented the area around him. There was a faint smell that tasted familiar, but it was too difficult to tell where it was coming from. He crept through the plush leaves along the ground, trying to see if he could pick it up again. At least one of the missing men had been this way, but not recently enough to be able to pinpoint their every step. The growth here was like it was at Devin's camp, but on steroids. The leaves a deeper green, the trees were twice as thick and taller. All this made staying out of sight easy, but seeing what was around him more difficult.

As soon as he located the members of his clan, he was going to find out what had led them here. They had enough area to run and roam, that was a hell of a lot closer to home. There was no reason to come this far and trek up this stunning chunk of dirt. If it turned out to be for some stupid hormone-enticed reason... he was going to smack them in the head. With a large paw. A few times, at least. He had enough going on right now with Devin learning the ropes to lead the Alliance, he didn't need to be traipsing around some damn mountain looking for stray cats.

Stopping, he sniffed the air. There was... Crouching low, he tried to identify the scents. A nervous twitch moved over his coat, something was off. He inhaled and took more time trying to analyze what he was smelling. Slowing his breathing, he listened. Ears flat, alarms going off in his head, he looked around him. With years of carefully honed animal intuition, he knew he needed to get the hell out of here. Now. Spinning back in the direction he'd just come from, he paused for a heartbeat and realized he was too late.

KEEP READING FOR AN EXCERPT OF

The Huntress

Alterealm Series

Book 1

By J. Risk

Chapter One

I didn't even get both eyes opened and focused before I knew something was wrong. Where was the color? I was only seeing sepia? Everything was brown. Blinking rapidly, I tried to readjust my eyes to see if there was any other hue. It didn't change a thing and for the life of me I couldn't figure out why.

Sitting there, I tried to decipher what was going on and why I was sitting on the ground. Looking down I ran my hand over the dried dusty surface. Why was I on the ground? Craning my neck as far as I could in all directions, I looked around. Okay, where was the pavement and cement? The buildings and streets I called my natural turf?

The why's flying around in my brain suddenly decided the top question, was what the *hell* was going on?

Squeezing my eyes shut, I struggled to recall the last thing I remembered doing. I was hunting down a bounty—a nice one with a large dollar sign attached to her. I had tracked her ass down and…

I confronted her? Yes, I was minutes away from calling Frank and telling him to get out his shiny pen and sign my check.

So what happened between then and now? Not to sound repetitive, which is something that drives me nuts, but *what* the hell was going on?

Startled, I started to check for bullet holes or the deep crevices that knives leave behind in flesh. That had to be it, I'd taken a beating and this was that in between place you sit when your near death's door, but not quite ready to see what lies on the other side.

Finding no critical injury, I slumped forward and rubbed my head. There was some rational explanation for this, there had to be. Had I been drugged? It could be some crazy hallucination. Any minute now I was going to either wake up in my bed at home or some hospital with a cheery nurse leaning over me, reassuring me we are going to be *just* fine. I only had to wait it out a little longer and all would be normal.

To kill time until I woke up, I looked around some more. Wherever this was it looked like a burnt-out world. Not the charred kind of burn, but depleted and completely used up sort.

Vacant.

Sitting still wasn't really a strong trait of mine, so I figured I'd get up and take a look around, there had to be something to see around here. If my body was actually somewhere else for safekeeping, what harm could come to me, right?

I staggered like I'd never stood before, struggling to get my balance. Whatever was going on with me, my equilibrium was totally shot. Standing there swaying like grass in the breeze, I turned carefully trying to see if there was anything around me except rust tinted dirt and nothingness.

My heart stumbled around in my chest when I spotted someone coming in my direction. Yes! I wasn't the only one in this soulless place.

The closer it got to me made me the more I questioned my original conclusion. I didn't know, exactly, but it was not some*one* it was a some*thing*. No one label could describe it. Standing over six feet, it had the shape of a man dressed in jeans and a large, very out of fashion gingham snap up shirt. When I reached the face, I can only describe it as part wrinkle puppy dog with floppy skin crossed with Freddy and Jason after the slash scenes.

It stopped in front of me and instinct had me reach around behind me under my jean jacket for my raptor claw knife, which I put on as regular as underwear when dressing; and that would be everyday, by the way. Relief washed over me when I felt the small circular handle. At least while waiting to survive I got to bring my toys with me.

Big brown eyes assessed me slowly and I wanted to make the call that it was harmless, but yeah, having tracked down anything from a sicko killer to a card shark in the last three years, I knew better than to fall for sappy looks.

"Are you a magishian? You juisht appeared."

A male voice, even though he spoke with a heavy lisp that randomly inserted *ish* into his words. Then again if I had saggy lips like he did, I'd be happy to talk at all. I sized him up for a few more seconds, trying to gauge whether he was really in front of me, or if I was having some sort of psychotic episode. Was a magician good or bad? I decided the play dumb, being blonde did have *some* advantages. "A magician?"

Those brown eyes developed a nervous quiver. Magician equaled bad. "No…"

He looked relieved. "Oh good. I didn't want to have to bash you over the head."

I grasped my raptor tightly and shrugged. "Yeah, me either."

The sky brightened and began to glow a rust orange color. When I asked for some color, I'd hoped for something out of the orange family.

"We better go, they'll be coming soon."

"They?" I glanced around quickly, not wanting to take my eyes off him for long.

He nodded and pranced on the spot, the nervous movement had me on high alert. "The daywalkers." He whispered.

Daywalkers? Did I even want to know? I didn't think so, but this bizarre nightmare wasn't going to be complete if I didn't ask.

Looking me over a few times, his eyes widened under the pressure of his drooping forehead; *that* was quite the expression. "You're not one of them, are you?"

I walked in the day, night and even at dusk, but I wasn't going to tell him that. I decided honesty might work, if not violence was always a good backup. Judging by his expression daywalker ranked on the bad list with magician. "I—I don't know what you'd call me."

Those sappy eyes looked me up and down a few times trying to figure me out. "You better come with me. It's not safe to leave you wandering around." He looked behind him and then motioned behind me and started walking.

I knew in my gut it was a mistake, but as I had no other real options... I didn't know where I was or what was going on and so far he knew more than I did. "Where are we going?"

Pausing he glanced over his shoulder and then lumbered along again. "I'll take you to Troy, he'll know what to do."

My eyes were starting to strain as the sky brightened. "This Troy, he's in charge?"

He stopped so suddenly I almost ploughed right into his back. When he turned and looked at me, his eyes weren't a sad brown any more but were leaning more towards red. It had to be from the strange color of the sunrise. "You're not from Alterealm are you?"

"Is that where we are?"

He nodded.

"Nope."

That nervous jitter of his seemed to return all at one. "How did you get here?"

A reasonable question that I had nothing to offer that resembled an answer. "I don't know that either."

His red eyes darted to the sky. "We have to go."

Turning, he began jogging toward, well, nothing that I could see. Not wanting to find out what he was afraid of, I ran along behind him. All I could think was this Troy person, if he was a person, better have some answers.

He stopped again and dropped down onto his knees. Was he hurt? Surely that short jaunt hadn't winded him that much. He began tapping his hand on the ground. What was he doing? Looking all around us, I kept watch for anything really, not wanting to meet these daywalkers in the slightest. Just when I'd had about enough of his short break, he grasped something in the sand and pulled a door in the ground open.

"We're going to have to use the shortcut. We don't have time to get to the main gates."

Looking down into a hole with a ladder, I glanced around again and despite every muscle in my body telling me to run and get the hell out of here, I started down the metal rungs into a deep hole that would take me, hopefully back to friggin' reality.

About the Author

Jacqueline Paige lives in Ontario in a small town that's part of the popular Georgian Triangle area.

She began her writing career in 2006 and since her first published works in 2009 she hasn't stopped. Jacqueline describes her writing as *all things paranormal*, which she has proven is her niche with stories of witches, ghosts, psychics and shifters now on the shelves.

When Jacqueline isn't lost in her writing she spends time with her five children, most of whom are finally able to look after her instead of the other way around. Together they do random road trips, that usually end up with them lost, shopping trips where they push every button in the toy aisle, hiking when there's enough time to escape and bizarre things like creating new daring recipes in the kitchen. She's a grandmother to eight (so far) and looks forward to corrupting many more in the years to come.

Jacqueline also writes under the pseudonym of J. Risk

Jacqueline loves to hear from her readers, you can find her at

http://jacquelinepaige.com

Author note:

Did you enjoy reading one of my books?
If so, PLEASE help spread the word on social media. You can help by sharing on Facebook, tweet about it, post something on Instagram, Pinterest. Posting a review on your favorite book sites go a long way to help authors. With your help in keeping my books "out there", I can continue writing to keep those stories coming.

Writing and promoting can be very time consuming. I love talking to readers, but the hours spent on keeping so many social media outlets current can become overwhelming and time for writing pays the price. If you can take a few minutes to help, that would be awesome. Thank you!